Never forget
your worth!

HELLO QUARTERBACK

KELSIE HOSS

kh

Editing by Tricia Harden of Emerald Eyes Editing.

Proofreading by Jordan Truex.

Cover design by Najla Qamber of Najla Qamber Designs.

Have questions? Email kelsie@kelsiehoss.com.

**Readers can visit kelsiehoss.com/pages/sensitive-
content to learn about potentially triggering content.**

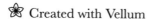 Created with Vellum

For my bad ass readers.
Never play small so they can feel big.

CONTENTS

FORD MADIGAN

CONFETTI FELL AROUND ME, *landing on my shoulders, my hair, sticking to the sweat on the back of my neck.*

My entire body was spent, tired, aching.

But none of it compared to the pain in my chest.

Because while everyone celebrated around me, cheering the other team's win at the biggest game in the world, I'd lost.

We'd lost.

My team had gotten close enough to taste the trophy.

To see the end zone.

To feel the win.

The win that my team worked our entire careers to get. That I dreamed of, my whole life, playing high school ball in secondhand cleats.

But we didn't go all the way.

Because I threw an interception when we needed my best.

So I sat here, on the empty bench, a loser on football's biggest stage.

And I promised myself: I would never feel this way again.

1

MIA

I STOOD in the box suite after the first Dallas Diamonds game of the season, although my attention wasn't on the game.

No, the Griffen Industries suite was purely another networking spot with a football field in the background. It was a place to get ahead while drinking and offering potential clients the experience of a lifetime. Today was all about solidifying my relationship with the Andersen sisters, two women who'd grown an incredible company from the ground up.

I loved their mission of building microhomes for those in need. And better yet? They were underdogs, which I could relate to. Leticia and Andrina spent their childhood in and out of homeless shelters before becoming the first in their family to graduate from college and founding a successful philanthropic business. Although I didn't have as much adversity to overcome as they did, I was a plus-sized, female CEO after years spent working as an executive assistant.

Together, we could make history.

That is if they would first agree to the acquisition.

My plan was to acquire their company, Andersen Avenue and expand into the travel space, using the profits to continue their charitable efforts. There were so many people—those fresh out of college, starting new jobs, working in temporary travel positions and more—who just needed a no-frills place to lay their heads at night.

And on top of the Andersen sisters, I had to convince the board to invest in something we'd never done before with the remaining budget for the year.

Leticia approached me, a smile in her charcoal eyes. "This was great." She flipped long locks over her shoulder, glancing toward the football field. "Do you think Ford will stop by?"

She might have been trying to hide it, but I could tell she was eager to meet the team's star quarterback —and the man voted football's hottest player for the last three years. Couldn't blame her one bit.

"I believe he should be here any minute now." I grinned and checked my watch. There were perks to the company's founder, Gage Griffen, being from Ford's hometown of Cottonwood Falls.

Andrina approached, handing her sister a drink. "Is Ford coming?" She was far less coy about her excitement.

I chuckled. It reminded me of a conversation I might have with my best friend, Farrah. She was here in the suite too with her husband, Gage, but I didn't have much of a chance to chat with her with everything going on.

All the color drained from Leticia's face as she stared at the door, and I followed her gaze just in time to see a player in full uniform and slides walking into the room. All he was missing was shoulder pads, but his shoulders were still broad and strong under the purple and white jersey. His dark brown hair was damp with sweat, contrasting his lightly tanned skin. He caught my gaze with dimensional blue eyes, and I nodded subtly.

His lips spread into an easy grin, the confusing kind that set you at ease while somehow making your heart beat faster. But I stifled those thoughts because this was business—and it rarely left time for pleasure.

"Ford, great game," I said once he got close enough. "This is Leticia and Andrina Andersen." I gestured at the sisters standing next to me, different versions of the same font. They both had dark skin, narrow faces, and almond-shaped dark brown eyes that caught the light in the room.

Andrina, just slightly taller than her sister at six feet tall, nearly stood eye to eye with Ford. "It is *amazing* to meet you, Mr. Madigan. You had a great game today. We're so excited for the season. I really think we have a chance at winning the whole thing this year. Came really close last year. But that's okay. I think the new kicker is really—"

"I'm Leticia," her sister cut in, stopping Andrina's nervous babble. "Can you tell my sister and I are big fans?"

Ford chuckled. "Nice to meet you." He had on all the charm, offering an easy smile, just a hint of a southern drawl in his tone. "But I'm the fan of y'all. Mia's told me all about Andersen Avenue. It's amazing what you've done for the unhoused community in Texas metros."

I thought Andrina might faint, while Leticia grinned ear to ear. "You've heard of us?" Leticia asked, almost like she was in a happy trance.

I smiled and rubbed her arm. "You deserve all the attention you get. What you two have built is truly incredible."

Ford nodded in agreement. "I'd love to hear more about it—possibly once I've showered and am smelling better. Are you two free for dinner sometime this week?"

Andrina swayed, nearly dropping her drink, and Leticia wordlessly put her arm around her sister for support. "We would love that. Mia, would you be able to connect us?"

I nodded. "Absolutely. I'll have Vanover handle the details." I made a mental note to make sure that was the top priority on my assistant's ever-growing list. I didn't know what I'd do without him.

Ford dipped his head and smiled. "I'll be looking forward to it."

The two sisters walked away, whispering to each other, and I looked up at Ford, focusing more on business than his impeccable jawline. "Thank you for that."

His eyes trailed after them for a moment before meeting mine again. Even when he wasn't on the field, there was an intensity behind his gaze that I recognized. I felt it in myself—whether I was on the clock or not, I was still a CEO. "I'm excited to see what you can do with their company," he said. "How close are you to closing them?"

"I think they're warm to the idea. They've been operating on a shoestring budget, and an influx of cash is just what they need—if I can get the board to agree." I glanced around to make sure no one could hear me. "My CFO has been a real pain in my ass."

Ford's upper lip tugged in disgust. "Gage told me about Thomas."

"I know," I muttered.

"He should have let him go."

"He didn't give Gage as much trouble as he does me," I said, "and he's generally good at his job. Plus, he has a lot of sway now with our board. Letting him go would cause a riot."

"As if those old fogies could riot. I'd pay to see it," Ford retorted.

I let out a surprised laugh, and he smiled back at me. I couldn't help but think about Ford and where he came from. Everyone I knew from Cottonwood Falls was so kind, and those who rose to stardom rarely let it get to their heads.

"Is there anything else I can help with?" he asked.

I shook my head. "Thank you, Ford."

"Any time."

He turned to walk away, and I gave myself a second to watch. I might not have been a football fan, but I was certainly a fan of Ford Madigan.

2

FORD

NOW THAT THE press conference and a visit to the Griffen Industries' suite was over, I went down to the locker room to shower up. I knew my family would be waiting for me. They'd come to watch the game today and would be leaving soon. But just as I was about to walk in through the heavy metal door, an older man with dyed black hair and a three-piece suit said, "Madigan, got a minute?"

I dipped my head to Trent Reynolds, the owner of the Dallas Diamonds. "Yes, sir."

He nodded, satisfied at my greeting, and said, "Come here, son."

I followed him down the hallway toward the office he kept on this level. It was full of Diamond gear, from a leather helmet signed by the first ever

Diamonds team to a few jerseys of Hall of Famers who played for the Diamonds. He even had a diamond the size of my fist in a glass display case. It probably could have bought my childhood home and half the neighbors' places.

"Good game today," Trent said, sitting behind his desk and pulling out a cigar box from the top drawer.

"Thank you, sir."

His fingers, just as thick as the smoke, worked methodically to get out the cigar and light it before pulling it to his lips and taking a puff. Thick gray smoke rolled from his nose and lips around the cigar. "Want one?" he asked.

"No, thank you," I replied, watching him, wondering what this meeting was about. I'd played for the team several years now and had met with him personally only a handful of times.

"You've done a lot for this team," Trent said around the smoke.

I dipped my head in acknowledgement. "This team is as much my family as the people I grew up with in Cottonwood Falls."

He pulled the cigar from between his lips, holding it with his pointer and middle finger. "I'm glad you see it that way, because I have a favor I'd like you to do for me."

I nodded slowly. You couldn't exactly turn down

a request from the team's owner, even if he posed it as a "favor."

"My daughter has taken a shine to you, and it would mean a lot if you'd take her out on a date without letting her know we had this particular conversation."

An image of his daughter, Felicity, came to mind. I slammed a mask over my face so my initial reaction wouldn't show.

Felicity was an up-and-coming model with a vocal fry, and every positive thing she said was followed by a "but." I'd spent all of five minutes around her at team functions and that was more than enough.

A date with her sounded like torture, and that was saying something considering I subjected myself to ice baths on a daily basis. "Just one?" I asked.

"A handful. Why not see where it goes? Hell, you might hit it off and be my new son-in-law." He chuckled heartily, then choked on his smoke and coughed for a minute.

I scratched the back of my neck. "Mr. Reynolds, I..."

Trent's eyes narrowed. "You're not seeing someone, are you?" he said.

I felt like I was on the field, judging the defense, eyeing the open players, trying to find a way out of the heavy defensive line coming in to take me out. Not sitting here in this cushy office on a hard chair after the time had run from the clock.

I opened my mouth to say something, anything to back me out of this corner, when he said, "Because if you aren't seeing someone, then you're rejecting my daughter for no good reason. She's a beautiful girl, comes from a good family, a family that's given quite a lot to you and your charities. I would hate to see that relationship sour."

My stomach clenched. The Diamonds contributed generously to my charity, and the thought of them yanking funding just because I wouldn't go on a date with his daughter put things into perspective.

"So unless you're taken," he continued, "I expect you to take my daughter out and behave like the gentleman the world thinks you are and continue to do so until she tires of your company."

There was no arguing. So I nodded, stood to leave. Then he tapped his cigar against a crystal ashtray and said, "I believe your contract comes up for negotiations at the end of this season. Would hate for you to lose your spot so close to home."

My jaw tightened. I didn't take well to bullies. But typically, bullies were scared shitless and had no power once someone stood up to them. This bully held my life and all I'd worked for in his hands.

So I had a decision: I could either come up with a relationship that didn't exist or let him win.

As my sandals swished over the concrete floor, echoed off the cinder block hallways, I had to wonder... Was dating his daughter worth it? I made sacrifices all the time—eating to a specific diet, waking early when it would be easier to sleep in, working my body until it protested with each step. Was this all that different?

I rounded the corner to the locker room, and my family started cheering.

They were already waiting for me. Usually I had time to shower before they met me here, but now I felt a mess. Especially as my dad stepped forward and wrapped me in a hug. His weatherworn face crinkled into a smile as he stepped back and said, "I'm so proud of you, son. For what you do on and off the field."

His kind words hit my heart like a vice clamping shut. What if I couldn't play football here anymore? What if my charity had to close down because I refused to have a relationship with the owner's daughter?

The question had barely passed my mind before my four brothers, two of their wives, and their kids took turns telling me good job. Well, all except my seven-year-old niece, Emily, who had been my biggest constructive critic since I met her and her mom a couple years back.

I picked up her three-year-old brother, Jackson, holding him between me and Emily like a shield. "Can't be too rough on me, Em. I'm holding a baby."

"I'm a todd-ah-yer," Jackson protested.

Everyone laughed while Emily launched into her usual post-game recap. "Coach Hinkle needs to have you throwing more," she said, wise beyond her years. "Why's he having you run this early in the season? We don't want you getting injured. That would be a catastrophe! *Especially* before playoffs." She gesticulated wildly, making the purple bow in her hair wobble.

Jackson squirmed, and I set him down on the ground. His shoes lit up as he went back to his mom. As she picked him up, she gave me an apologetic look. But I shook my head at her. "I'm one of the biggest QBs in the league," I said. "I can take it."

Emily tilted her head. "You're two inches taller than average and twenty pounds heavier. Not that big of a difference."

I held my hand over my chest, pretended to be

wounded while all four of my brothers guffawed at her comment.

For the first time, Emily looked a little abashed. "What? It's true."

"You're right about the throwing, Em. I said the same thing to Coach after the game."

She smiled proudly in response.

Then I said to everyone, "Thanks for coming, guys. Means a lot you could be here."

My oldest brother gave me a quick hug. "Wouldn't miss it for the world."

My other brothers nodded in agreement.

A tight spot formed in my throat, and I swallowed it down. "See you all next weekend for the game?"

Everyone said they'd be back, except for my youngest brother, who had to prep for a college exam early the next day.

We said a quick goodbye and I went to the locker room, my chest feeling heavy as I shed my clothes, grabbed a towel, and went to shower. I walked past my teammates, stepped under the stream of hot water, and closed my eyes just before the water covered my skin, soothing my bruised and tired body.

But I couldn't relax. Not with this problem standing before me.

I didn't want to date Felicity. Didn't want to let the bully win. There had to be a solution...

And then in my mind's eye, I saw *her*. Not Felicity.

Mia, smiling up at me with big blue eyes, soft blond hair framing her pale face, and the way her lips curled around her words as she thanked me just for showing up.

Could she be the answer?

I shook my head. She was the CEO of a billion-dollar corporation. She had better things to do than fake date a football player.

3

MIA

I STOOD in front of the board for our quarterly meeting, just having presented my plan for acquiring Andersen Avenue. I knew I'd crushed the presentation, even though it wasn't a project Griffen Industries typically invested in.

All I needed was a majority vote in favor of the acquisition, and I could extend an official offer to them before another investment banker realized what a good move the Andersen sisters were and took our chance.

"This will use the rest of our allotment for acquisitions for the year," I said. "Unless there's anything else, we can move forward with the vote."

Several people were nodding their heads, shifting

like they were getting ready, but then Thomas stood from his chair. "Actually, I have something else..."

As the CFO, Thomas had missed his calling as a model or a high-powered politician. With a head full of thick brown hair, a winning smile surely assisted by veneers that were flawless, an impeccable wardrobe, and a wife who talked him up at all company functions, he was well-liked within the company. By pretty much everyone except me. I felt like he'd been trying to undermine me since I started in my role as CEO.

Everyone turned to watch him, and I used the distraction to veil the frustration on my face. I sat back down at the long white table, settling into the sleek office chair with chrome finishings.

Now that he had the floor, he said, "Griffen Industries has a long track record of successful invest-ments. None of them in this space. I'd like to find an alternate to propose to the board, more in line with our typical acquisitions and present it at the next meeting."

My gaze narrowed at him. Thomas hadn't even mentioned this in any of our meetings.

The CTO said, "Can't be a bad idea to have more options, right, Mia?"

I ground my teeth together. "I wasn't aware we needed more options."

"Investing based on emotions and goodwill isn't what got Griffen Industries to this point. But it sure as hell will drive us into the ground."

It took all I had not to slug him. "Ignoring data and stalling for another quarter, there's a chance another firm will extend an offer they can't turn down."

Thomas leveled his gaze at me. "Have they had other offers?"

Damn it. "Not at this time. Which puts us at an advantage so we don't have to compete with other offers."

Thomas said, "It seems like the fair thing to do is vote. All in favor of waiting for an additional, potentially more proven investment option?"

I clenched my fists under the table as, one by one, a majority of the people at the meeting raised their hands.

⚘

I GOT BACK to my office and slammed my notebook on my desk, chest heaving with frustration. Those fucking assholes.

I didn't even have to close my eyes to remember Thomas standing pompously at the front of the boardroom, saying, "Investing based on emotions and goodwill isn't what got Griffen Industries to this point. But it sure as hell will drive us into the ground."

My jaw tensed as I shucked my heels and paced in front of the floor-to-ceiling windows of my high-rise office, giving me an unmatched view of Dallas that I couldn't even appreciate right now.

I'd done everything in the board meeting to show them how this could be beneficial for Griffen Industries, including a detailed presentation showing them we could be profitable within the first three years while building goodwill with the public. Something priceless for a company like ours.

I thought some of them were going for it, but Thomas was quick to turn the tables. I had no doubt he'd come back next quarter with some bland company to acquire, just like ones we'd done before. But deep down, I knew he wasn't opposing this acquisition because it could be big for the company —only because it would be good for me.

A knock sounded on my glass door, and I turned to see my assistant, Vanover, with the door cracked. He looked stylish and professional as usual, his wavy brown hair gelled back and his suit perfectly tailored. "Tallie is here," he said. "I can tell her to fuck off."

I managed a smile, grateful for him. For some

levity amidst my frustration. "It's okay, Van. Send her in."

He shrugged like he wouldn't mind the chance to annoy my head of PR. "Can I get you something? Perhaps some ice water to dump on that hot head of yours?"

I rolled my eyes. "An ashwagandha green tea would be nice." My wellness specialist had given me several tips to help with the stress that came with this job. And since I didn't want to have a heart attack at fifty thanks to stupid Thomas, I followed most of her advice.

Vanover nodded and left for a moment before returning with Tallie Hyde. She had a sharp nose and an equally pointed gaze with hazel eyes, pale skin, and a caramel-colored bob.

She glanced from my head to my bare feet. "Grounding only works if you're not six hundred feet in the air," she deadpanned.

I gave her a wry smile. "Is something happening? We don't have a meeting scheduled." The last thing I needed right now was a crisis.

"We do now," she said, approaching my glass meeting table with an armful of manila folders. Her short hair fell over her face as she leaned over, stacking them neatly on the table.

"What is this?" I asked.

"You know not all PR happens in the outside world, right? Internal PR is an essential part of my position."

I nodded slowly, standing across the table from her. It was important to keep the employees in the organization satisfied and help them feel like a part of the team. One of the reasons I'd been looking for just the right CPO for a while now and why I wrote a "Letter from the CEO" once a month.

Tallie tucked her bob behind one ear. "Well, Thomas is running a campaign of his own to undermine you as CEO. If you don't watch out, not only will he tank this acquisition when it comes to a vote next quarter, but he'll also get you booted from this position at the earliest opportunity."

As if on cue, Vanover returned with my tea. If it wasn't steaming hot, I would have chugged it. He handed it to me, then passed Tallie a cappuccino with a swan swirl on top.

"Thank you," she said, taking a sip. I swore her eyes lingered on him a moment longer than usual as he dipped his head and walked away.

We both sat at the table. I blew on the tea and then took a scalding drink before setting it down. "Tell me you have a plan. Because right now, the only idea I can come up with is decking him in the nose."

"Good thing that scenario is included in our emergency procedures."

I couldn't tell if she was joking.

She took another drink, and for a moment, it struck me how different it was to be sitting at this table with Tallie, when I used to be at the secretary's desk, watching her work with Gage.

Life had changed so much in the last few years.

Immune to my nostalgia, she said, "There are several ways to change your employees' perception of you. However, most of these are tactics you're already doing well. Fair pay, generous benefits, time off, a culture of accountability and integrity, volunteering..."

"But..." I said, eyeing the folders.

"You can become more relatable, more sympathetic," she said.

I raised my eyebrows. *Relatable?* I'd done everything I could *not* to be relatable, rising above what society expected of a chubby blond secretary. I'd worked my way up, obtained a master's degree, worked with the best mentors money could buy. I wanted to be an outlier, not another predictable statistic.

"How would you suggest I become more relatable?" I asked. "I don't have time for a puppy."

Tallie's lips quirked in half a smile, and she

tugged a folder away from the stack, dropping it on the floor. "What do you think most of our employees do when they go home?"

I shrugged. "Work out, hang out with family, go on dates, have a life?"

Tallie nodded. "What if you picked up a sport?"

"Hot yoga doesn't count?"

She shook her head. "Too individual. Maybe softball? We have a company league."

I laughed. Genuinely. "*Next.*"

She shuffled aside another folder. "You could be seen publicly with your parents. Having aging parents is something so many people can rela—"

"Next," I said.

She opened her mouth to argue, but I shook my head. "My family is off-limits. They are not pawns in this company's game."

Nodding solemnly, she picked up the last folder. "You could have a relationship."

I pushed back my chair to stand and started pacing again. "What is this? The eighteenth century? I need a man to gain approval in this company? No. Dating someone just to get ahead is against everything I stand for! I made damn sure nothing ever happened with Gage because when I earned a promotion, I didn't want anyone to think I'd slept my way to the top."

Tallie eyed me evenly, unphased. "Are you done?"

I pressed my lips together, continuing to pace.

"What does Thomas's wife do at every company event? Every day when she brings his lunch to the office?"

My shoulders sagged as I stared out over the city, the skyline hazy with smog. "She campaigns for him." We both knew it. Every word out of her mouth was strategic. And charming. And earning Thomas's favor amongst the board.

"Can't we ask an employee to talk me up?" I asked.

She folded her arms across her chest, making her blazer's shoulders bunch. "You could. But it won't be as effective since you're paying them."

"Thomas pays his wife to stay home!" I rebutted. Their kids were all grown, they didn't have a pet—or really anything their team of housekeepers didn't care for.

"We both know plenty of rich housewives who hate their husbands," she replied. "Thomas's relationship is refreshing. Gives people hope. That's something you could have too, with the right partner."

My phone speaker buzzed, and Vanover said, "Look sharp." Our code that someone important was walking through.

I stalled by my desk and slipped my heels back on. "You have to be kidding me, Tallie. This was your idea? Throw a ball around? Exploit my parents? Date someone? I'm not in middle school. I'm perfectly capable of running a company without a man." Then I remembered Vanover listened to almost all my meetings so he could take notes. "A man other than Vanover," I corrected.

I glanced through the window to see him stifling a smile at the reception desk.

Tallie stayed seated, keeping her calm far better than me. I practiced a breathing technique, taking two quick breaths and then releasing them slowly.

"I want you to listen with an open mind," she said.

I paused for a long moment. "Okay."

She eyed me skeptically.

"Okay!" I shook out my shoulders and leaned back against my desk.

"Picture this—you have a high-powered 'boyfriend,' someone who is well-liked amongst the company. He comes to charities, galas, and the company picnic with you. In the moments you're separated, he talks you up to the people who respect him—the ones you're trying to win over. When the vote comes next quarter, you won't only have the data and vision on your side—you'll have the swing vote."

I blinked slowly, absorbing her idea.

Tallie said, "It only takes one person being your hype man, to have confidence in you, to show everyone else that they should too."

I looked up at her. "You really think this will work?"

She squared her shoulders, nodded. "If it doesn't, I'll resign."

Studying her, I could tell she meant it. "Why would you do this, Tallie?"

She lowered her gaze and looked back up at me. "My mom and I lived in a homeless shelter after she left my dad. For me, this isn't just business. This is personal."

I nodded. "Okay then, let's get started."

4

FORD

I WALKED into an invite-only café in downtown Dallas with my agent, Brock Hudson. Local celebrities were given a golden card to show at the door to ensure we had a semi-private place to spend time together without anyone listening in. Of course the paparazzi had figured this out and were always stationed along the sidewalk with their constantly flashing cameras.

After getting inside, we picked a couple seats in the corner and ordered drinks. Brock was massive, a former lineman turned agent. He seemed out of place with the café's stiff, modern chairs and tiny drinking glasses.

While we waited for our drinks, Brock said, "Why the extra meeting, son?"

I glanced around just to doublecheck no one was listening. "Things aren't good, Brock."

Brock tensed, leaning forward and resting his elbows on his knees, making his dress shirt stretch dangerously around his shoulders. "What is it? If it's that private, we can take it to my office."

I shook my head. I knew better than to trust his office, where a team of agents worked. Here, there was music playing loudly that made it impossible to overhear the intimate conversations taking place, and I didn't bring business to my house. That was my place to relax and be with family. So I explained, "After the game yesterday, Trent suggested my contract may not be up for renewal."

"*What?*" Brock's eyes widened so far they would have popped out of his head if he'd been a cartoon.

I glanced up, seeing a server returning with our drinks. She passed me a frosted glass of green tea and gave Brock his espresso in a comically tiny cup. We both thanked her, and I took a sip, just to wet my lips. After she left, I explained, "Trent wants me to date his daughter or risk my spot on the team."

"Felicity?" Brock said, looking even more confused. "What's the problem? She's a good-looking girl."

I raised my eyebrows. "The problem? She's daddy's little girl, Brock. She gets what she wants, and apparently that's a relationship with me. It's all a distraction from what I should be focusing on. Winning the championship this year instead of sitting on the sidelines watching everyone else celebrate."

He twisted his lips to the side, mulling it over. "So it's date her or get fired?"

"Unless I have a relationship with someone else..."

"Do you?" Brock asked, just as the café door opened.

Camera flashes followed the pair walking inside. Hayden French, a famous singer my nieces adored and... My eyebrows drew together. *Mia.*

She looked gorgeous in a dark blue dress that cinched in at her waist and showed off her curves. Her smile came easily as she said something to the singer and they sat down in a pair of chairs near a window. As if he was putting on a fashion show, he withdrew his sunglasses and posed subtly in the reflective window, mussing his hair. Did Mia notice it?

Brock said, "Are you seeing someone, Ford?"

My mind snapped back to the conversation, "No. I have shit to do that's bigger than a relationship." It came out rougher than I meant it, but Brock didn't seem to mind.

"The charity," he said knowingly.

I nodded. Even a gulp of tea couldn't help the tightness in my throat. "But I have about five seconds to start dating someone and make it look real. If Trent's this serious about me going out with his daughter, imagine how it will go when it's time to break up."

Brock drained the rest of his espresso and then set it down. He took a long moment to wipe his lips with a napkin while he mulled over all the information. "A decision to let you go would *not* go over well with the fans. Maybe he's bluffing."

I'd considered the possibility but doubted it. If I understood one thing, it was the lengths a person would go to for their family. "Trent can spin my release in any way he likes, and I couldn't even defend myself because of my NDA," I returned. "And you weren't there in his office. He wasn't bluffing. He meant it."

Brock swore and pressed his thick fingertips to his temples. "Give me a second to think."

I nodded, sitting back and glancing across the café again, toward Mia. The pop star was making her switch places with him... What the hell?

She sat down with her back to the window, and sunshine passed through the glass, glancing off her blond hair. She looked like a cherub.

Now Hayden was looking past her, still mussing

his hair. Did he make her change seats so he could *see his reflection better*?

Was this a business meeting? *Please let it be a business meeting and not a date.*

But then I saw him reach across the table and hold her hand.

Fuck.

That wasn't business meeting behavior, even for vapid pop stars.

I tried to read Mia, but her friendly smile gave nothing away. Didn't she know that he didn't deserve her? That she deserved better than someone so self-obsessed he had hardly given her a second glance despite sitting across from her? How could a person like him ever be faithful with women throwing themselves at him?

I knew it wasn't my place to intervene. I was nothing more to her than the friend of her former boss. An acquaintance. And no matter how hot she was, I promised myself a long time ago to stay single until I had accomplished everything I wanted in life. No distractions.

Brock shifting in his seat caught my eye, and I looked back at him. He steepled his fingers, saying, "Why don't you take Felicity out, go out with her once a week for dinner? You have to eat sometime."

I raised my eyebrows at him. "Brock, women like

that hear it's once a week and are determined to prove you wrong."

He sat forward, leaning his elbows on his knees. "So you need help finding a girlfriend then, because that's the only alternative I'm seeing to going out with Felicity or calling Trent on his bluff."

I lowered my gaze. I didn't want to date at all. I just wanted to focus on the game, on my goals.

"Your family is here. Your friends are here," Brock reminded me. "You've built up these players and this program. Imagine the hours you've put into getting to know your teammates, finding out what makes them tick and getting the best of them... Tell me this, Ford, are you willing to lose your place on the team over this?"

His hard gray eyes met mine, and I slowly shook my head.

"You and I both know games aren't just played on the field. Find a way to win this one. Or call me, and I'm sure I can find you a new team." Brock got up to leave, tossed a few bills on the table, and walked away.

I sat back in my chair, frustrated. One of the reasons I signed with Brock was because I liked how straightforward he was with me. But now, the truth was hard to handle. Maybe I was making Felicity worse in my mind because I was rebelling... Maybe she wasn't so bad?

Tugging my phone from my pocket, I typed "Felicity Reynolds" into the search bar. Within seconds, several headlines popped up.

Model-actress continues feud with co-star

Model reveals sordid details post-breakup

This model's Instagram post is causing an uproar, here's why

It took all I had not to groan. I didn't want to be just another headline in her dating history. I didn't want any part of this.

I glanced up, seeing Hayden put the charm on Mia. And out of curiosity, I typed her name into the search bar.

From secretary to CEO

How this CEO motivates her employees

CEO sighted volunteering with unhoused for local nonprofit

I glanced up Mia, knowing if the media could find dirt, they would. Mia didn't have any. It made me respect her that much more, and frankly, pissed me off that Hayden took for granted the woman who was sitting in front of him. She could do better.

5

MIA

HAYDEN FRENCH SAT across from me at the posh café in downtown with drink prices so obscene they weren't listed on the menu and an exclusive guest list more upscale than the one-of-a-kind designer rings Hayden wore on all his fingers.

He paired the jewelry with skin-tight jeans, distressed sneakers, and a smug smirk on what magazines called "America's most kissable lips." And he was perfectly positioned in front of the café's mirrored windows to have his image reflected back at him.

Every so often his gaze tracked from my chest to his reflection, and a sparkle lit his eyes.

I had to give it to him—Hayden French was

handsome, and all of America loved him, but not as much as he loved himself.

I swirled the glass stir stick through my vanilla latte, wondering when this date would finally be over. Hopefully Tallie had a backup plan ready to go.

"Tell me, Mia, has anyone ever written you into a song?"

My eyebrows drew together, almost surprised he asked me a question about myself. "My mom used to sing 'Mama Mia' to me," I deadpanned.

I could have sworn I heard someone snort behind me, but Hayden didn't crack a smile. Instead, he leaned forward, scrubbing a hand over the short stubble on his chin that made him look perfectly messy. I wasn't sure what he was about to say, but it wasn't words he spoke.

He sang.

The opening lines to his most popular song, "Hello Beautiful." But instead, it was "Hello Mia."

My cheeks instantly flushed with embarrassment, and I darted my gaze around the café to see if anyone was watching. This was so not on brand for Mia Baird, CEO of Griffin Industries, a multi-billion-dollar corporation making waves in the world like no company had ever done before. It was *humiliating* to be treated like some kind of groupie.

"Hayden." I reached for his hand, only to get

him to stop as a rally of applause went through the café.

I made a mental note to tell Tallie never to set me up on a date with another singer.

Hayden nodded graciously to his nearest admirers and turned smoldering brown eyes back on me. His gaze flicked to my lips and then back to my breasts before returning to my eyes. "I need to excuse myself for a moment. Be right back, Mia ore."

Oh, he did not.

I forced a smile, and as soon as his back was to me, I got out my phone. There were several texts, one from the mayor, another from my best friend, Farrah, asking me how the date was going, another from Gage responding to a question I had, and then one from Tallie. I tapped out my response.

Mia: He's a 10 but he keeps checking himself out in the windows. He's a 2.
Tallie: He's a 2, but in an office poll, he ranked in the top three favorite celebrities. He's a 10.

She sent me a screenshot from a social media account that was already showing images of us going into the café together. The caption called us a "future power couple." They also said I was too old for him.

Mia: Pass.

Out of the corner of my eyes, I saw Hayden sitting across from me again and tucked my phone back in my purse. Just fifteen more minutes of this date before I could excuse myself to my next meeting. But when I looked up, it wasn't Hayden filling the chair after all.

My lips parted as I took in the wall of muscle opposite me. Even dressed casually in jeans—that actually fit—a nondescript navy-blue shirt, and a Madigan Ranch ballcap, he breathed influence, *power*. From the broad shoulders, the pull of the shirt against his biceps, the outline of his quads through his jeans... Damn.

But with all of that to look at, the part that distracted me most was the green-blue of his eyes, like they couldn't pick a color so decided to be both.

"Ford Madigan," I said with a smirk.

He grinned. "Mia Baird."

I picked up my cup and casually sipped the lukewarm latte. "I'm surprised to see you here. Gage always thought this place was over the top."

"I was meeting my agent."

"Ah, I see."

He had the kind of eyes that smiled even when his lips didn't, and I had to wonder what he was smiling about this time. "Your family doing well? They must be proud of such a famous son."

Ford batted his hand. "My other brothers are giving Dad grandchildren, and all I got was second place at the Super Bowl."

That had me laughing, genuinely. And that was rare for me at work when I had to put on the front of determination, power, grace, and do it twice as well as any man had before me.

A ringed hand dropped onto Ford's shoulder, and Ford looked up to see Hayden towering over him territorially. The sight was almost laughable, a pop star trying to intimidate the best quarterback in the NFL.

But Ford handled the tension with ease, standing up and shooting a crooked smile Hayden's way. "Had to catch up with an old friend." He stepped away from the chair, adding, "My niece is a *huge* fan of yours."

Hayden's expression eased, and Ford reached out to shake my hand to say goodbye. As if on instinct, I returned the gesture, feeling more than his large, warm palm. There was a slip of paper in his grip. And something in his eyes told me to keep it a secret.

I casually held it in my lap as Ford walked away. I watched him return to his seat and take a sip of what looked like green tea.

Hayden studied me for a moment. "You know him?" His stare was solidly on me now. I tilted my head. Was he... jealous?

"I do know him." An awkward silence hung between us, so I continued. "Hayden, I'm sorry, but my phone was blowing up while you were in the restroom. I need to get back to the office and put out a few fires."

His expression settled back into the smooth, unbothered façade he put on the cover of every magazine. "Let me walk you to your car."

"That's... nice of you," I said. Unexpectedly nice.

We got up, and I swore I could feel Ford's eyes on me just as surely as I felt Hayden's hand settle on my back. At least he had the sense not to let it drop too low as we walked out of the café, a million camera flashes sounding around us as paparazzi clamored to ask if we were together.

"No comment," I said smoothly as my driver opened the door for me.

Hayden leaned in, and I realized it was for a kiss. I quickly turned my cheek, feeling the pressure of his lips for half a second, and then ducked into the car. "Goodbye," I said to him, and my driver, Zeke, an older Filipino man in a sharp black suit, shut the door. As soon as he got in, I said, "Drive. Please."

"That bad?" he said, looking at me with amused dark eyes in the rearview mirror.

"No comment," I replied with a smile.

Then I reached to the paper in my hand, unfolding it to see neat handwriting inside.

You can do better.

6

FORD

I SAT BACK DOWN in my chair and watched out the mirrored window as Mia's driver sped away from the curb and Hayden turned to the paparazzi, waving like a pageant contestant. What a dweeb.

The valet pulled up with a bright red convertible, the top down. He flicked on his sunglasses, slipped in the driver's seat, and sped away, tires peeling on the asphalt. I wondered what Mia saw in him. She didn't seem like the kind of person to get blinded by fame.

My phone vibrated in my pocket, and I tugged it out, seeing a text from her. I knew she had my number, but this was the first time she'd used it outside of business.

Mia: I can take care of myself, you know.

My lips quirked into half a smile.

Ford: Is that why you let him waste an hour of your time looking at himself in the window?

A text bubble came up and then disappeared, and I scrubbed my hand over my mouth, far too eager to see what she'd come back with.

Mia: What are you trying to say?

My fingers tapped across the screen, letting her know.

Ford: If I was sitting across from you, I wouldn't be looking away.

I bit my bottom lip, thinking of Mia and her straight blond hair falling just past her shoulders. Her light blue eyes that saw more than most people's. Her curvy figure that would be so soft under my hands.

Mia: Is that so?

Now I couldn't fight the smile. I knew flirting was a bad idea, especially since I'd sworn off a relationship. And since she was going out with another guy.

So instead of responding, I asked a question of my own.

Ford: Why are you going out with pop stars?
Mia: It's a long story.
Ford: Come back and tell me.

My stomach squirmed, caught between the desire to see her and the need to focus on my goals, but also out of desperation for this situation. Brock was right. I didn't want to lose this game with Trent. And I may not have been looking for a relationship, but I could surely treat Mia better than Hayden French while we were "together."

Mia: That might get the gossip rags going... What about dinner tonight?
Ford: My place?
Ford: To avoid the gossip rags.
Mia: Send me the address.

I bit my bottom lip and did as she asked, then finished my tea and left the café. I had to prep my chef for dinner before going to afternoon yoga class with the team.

IF YOU'VE NEVER SEEN a three-hundred-pound lineman do downward dog, I highly recommend it. For men who were usually so strong and powerful, they possessed an odd amount of grace. It was like seeing a bear tap dancing or a bull synchronized swimming. But every lineman on the team, as well as the rest of the players, were lined up in a gym for a yoga class led by one of the city's top instructors.

Coach Hinkle had us do one class a week to help with mobility on the field, and he swore it helped prevent injuries. Something that could cost us a season.

I followed the instructor from the back corner of the group. My best friends, Krew and Milo, were on either side of me. Somewhere between downward dog and cobra, a memory came to mind.

I chuckled under my breath, remembering my brother Knox telling me about one of his first dates with his now wife. They hadn't been together long when he had the idea to do goat yoga followed by dinner at a fancy farm/bed and breakfast.

The date had been going well... until a goat climbed on his back and peed all over him.

Milo, our team's center, looked over at me from between his arms, his pale freckled face bright red. "Don't laugh at me," he grunted.

Krew grinned wide, his locks shifting as he turned

his head to look at Milo. "Why not? You look funny as hell."

Milo shook his head, stepping his right foot forward into warrior one. "I saw you wobbling on tree pose," he said.

"It's not about you," I said, to stop their bickering. Then I whispered to them the story about goat yoga, making both of them stifle laughter.

The instructor at the front of the gym gave us a pointed look. "When your mind wanders, come back to your breath," she said.

Not wanting to be a bad influence for the rest of the team, I focused on the flow for the rest of the class, and when we were done, the guys and I got up from our mats. I put a sweat towel around my neck and took a long drink from my Stanley—yoga was always harder than I thought it would be.

Krew chugged his water and then said, "Any plans tonight? I was thinking about catching that new movie that's coming out."

Milo started walking to the locker room, Krew and I on either side. Over the low hum of conversation around us, Milo said, "Mom's making chicken and dumplings. I told her I'd be there. You know you're both invited though."

Krew nodded. "Yeah, I'll come. Always up for some home cooking."

Milo looked at me. "You in?"

I shook my head. "I'm busy tonight."

They both stared at me, knowing I hardly had a life outside of football and my charity, especially since my family was a couple hours away. Krew finally said, "Something with the charity?"

I could feel heat blooming on my cheeks. How would I explain this?

Milo said, "If your family's coming to town, I'm sure Mom can put a leaf in the table."

"That's not it," I replied.

Now they were both really staring at me, even as we reached the locker room and went inside. Our lockers were all next to each other. I took off my shirt, tossing it in the back of the locker.

Krew hit my arm, saying, "Is there a girl?"

"There is." I bit my bottom lip, bracing myself for their reactions. "I have a date with Mia."

7

MIA

I ASKED Vanover to arrange for my personal stylist to come to the office and bring me an outfit for my whatever-it-was with Ford that evening. On one hand, it was like the perfect opportunity had dropped into my lap—a date with a well-respected man who could help me gain favor with the board.

On the other hand, the less pragmatic side of me was *giddy* that Ford Madigan, the star quarterback of the entire NFL, had been flirting with me.

Deep down, I knew I was a catch. I was determined, kind, loyal, fun to be around, had an amazing job, parents I loved to pieces. Nevertheless, it was hard to ignore what the tabloids and people online said about my weight. Especially when they conflated my size with my looks. They acted like beauty and fatness were mutually exclusive. You couldn't be beautiful *and* fat, at least in the court of public opinion.

Of course they were wrong. And apparently Ford Madigan agreed.

When my stylist left my office, Tallie came in, eyeing me appreciatively. "Hayden French gets business attire and Ford gets Miss America? No need to ask who you're more excited to see."

I tried not to blush as I batted off her comment and reached for my purse on my desk. "Hayden's so self-absorbed. I don't even know why he took a date with me."

Tallie smiled slyly. "Maybe there's a rumor going around about Griffen Industries acquiring his record label."

"Tallie!" I scolded. So that's why he'd come on so strong. He was trying to score points for his career... just like me.

"Sorry." She raised her hands. "He would have been major help with the board. That's what this is all about, after all," she reminded me.

I needed to remind myself of the same thing. Even if there was a little niggling hope in my chest that this thing with Ford could be the start of something real.

He was handsome, yes, but he was also kind. And

modest, unlike so many men of his stature. Most guys who reached his level of success were so full of themselves and never wanted to talk about anything outside of their favorite topic—number one. All the times I'd been around Ford, we'd had real conversations. Ones where he wasn't dominating or staring at my chest.

"Was Ford on your list of options?" I asked her.

She shook her head. "He's never dated before." After a beat, she added, "Do you need anything before you go?"

I shook my head and pressed the button on my desk phone that would call Vanover. "Can you have the car ready?"

"Yes, ma'am," he replied.

I lifted my finger from the button and looked to Tallie. "Wish me luck?"

She smiled. "As your publicist, good luck, and as a fellow female with functioning eyeballs, I can't wait to hear all about it. Ford is a *catch*."

I cracked a genuine smile, one I rarely showed to the men in this company. "Thanks, girl."

"Any time."

Tallie and I left my office, both of us stopping by Vanover's desk. "You can go home, you know," I told him, adjusting my purse to my other arm. It was always heavy, with a notebook for ideas, a tablet in

case I had to work on the go, a book to learn something new, and of course little toiletries I might need
throughout the day.

Van looked up at me from behind his computer.
"Just a few things to prep for tomorrow. I'm sure
Tallie will take enough rest for both of us," he teased.
"Perhaps on a bed of manila folders?"

She clutched her stack of folders to her chest.
"Don't you insult my office supplies."

"You act like they're your lovers," Vanover
replied, eyebrow arched.

She winked. "Jealous?"

"Okay, children," I said with a chuckle. "I'm
leaving. Don't burn the house down while I'm
gone."

Vanover smirked. "Bye, Mom."

"I'm in charge, right?" Tallie said.

Laughing, I gave them a wave and went to the
elevator. But when I got in and the big metal doors
closed me into the space on my own, my heart
started to pound.

Was I really about to go to Ford Madigan's *home*?

According to the address displayed on Zeke's
navigation screen, I was.

I sat in the back seat and dialed my best friend's
number while Zeke drove me toward the outskirts of
Dallas. Farrah and I had grown up next door to each

other, and as only children, we were the sisters neither of us had.

She'd married my former boss, Gage Griffen, and now the two of them raised four children together in the most adorable home in Denton. The man had billions in the bank, but they both thought it was better to raise their kids in a more modest setting.

After a few rings, she picked up, and I could hear their baby chattering in the background. "Hey, girl, hey," Farrah said.

I smiled at the familiar greeting and found it easier to settle back into the beige leather seats. "I miss you."

"Same. I need to have Vanover pencil me into that busy schedule of yours. You know, in between all your dates with pop stars."

Letting out a chuckle, I said, "You know, I have access to my calendar as well. Text me any time and I'll set it up."

"I will," she said. "What's up?"

"Well... I'm on my way to Ford Madigan's house for a date!"

"WHAT?" she cried. I heard her mutter something, probably to Gage, and then I heard a door open and close, and then it got quiet. She must have locked herself in her bedroom. "Tell me *everything*."

Fiddling with the hem of my dress, I filled her in on all the drama with stupid Thomas and then the awkward date with Hayden and how Ford had passed me that note at the café.

"Oh my gosh, he totally likes you," she said, excitement in her voice. "Especially since he was telling everyone at the Cottonwood Falls Fourth of July barbecue that he wasn't interested in dating. Must have just been waiting for the right woman."

My lips curled to a smile despite myself. "I haven't felt this excited about a guy since Ryan Pendleton asked me to prom."

Farrah laughed. "Ford has way more hair than Ryan Pendleton."

"Yeah, now. But back then, Ryan had the *best* hair." I giggled at the walk down memory lane. I almost hadn't recognized Ryan at our fifteen-year high school reunion when he came in with his wife of ten years, saying they already had four children and a fifth on the way. We were leading completely different lives now.

"What are you wearing?" Farrah asked.

"Let me send you a pic." I held the phone in front of me to text her a picture the stylist had taken for me before bringing the phone back to my ear. Out the window, I could see the suburbs giving way to more impressive houses spread out against the countryside.

"Gorgeous," Farrah said. "He won't be able to keep his hands off you."

"No sex on the first date," I replied. I was raised by older-than-average parents who told me all the old-fashioned rules of life—this was one of the few that had stuck.

"Even if the first date's at his house?" Farrah said, skeptical.

I bit my lip. Would I really be able to resist Ford if he wanted to hook up? I wasn't so sure. "It has been a while..."

"Maybe the dry spell ends tonight," she said.

From the front seat, Zeke said, "This is his drive-way." I looked in the mirror, almost blushing. He heard probably more than he wanted to, driving me around all the time.

"Thanks," I told him, then I said to Farrah, "I'm almost there. Wish me luck."

"You don't need luck with tits like those."

I cackled. "Love you, bye."

"Bye," she said, a smile in her voice.

The car slowed in front of Ford's place, and Zeke got out to hold the door open for me. "Need me to wait?" I could see a hint of concern in his eyes.

I bit my lip, looking to the front door of Ford's modern house set in the private countryside outside of Dallas. "I'll be okay," I said to both of us. "You can go."

8

FORD

I FINISHED ROLLING my shirt sleeves as I walked toward the front door. The security system had alerted me to a car coming down the driveway, and I wanted to be there for Mia when she arrived.

I looked through the mirrored front window, and my jaw nearly hit the floor. The path to the house was her runway as she walked to the door in a flowy dress the color of a pale Texas sky. It wrapped around her like the wind, her hair brushing over her shoulders, drawing more attention to her cleavage on display.

She was nearly at the door when I remembered to swing it open. Her looks may have caught me off kilter, but damn, her perfume had my mind spinning circles like the blades of a windmill. Soft, sweet, expensive, classy—like the woman in front of me, looking up at me with the prettiest blue eyes.

Fuck, maybe this really was a bad idea.

"Hi, Ford," she said sweetly, not looking away. She wasn't shy—I liked that about her.

"Mia." I stepped back, swallowing hard, and let her walk through. My eyes drifted, admiring the way her hips swayed under the light blue fabric. Fuck. That image would be running through my mind all night.

I gave myself a quick shake of the head and closed the door after her. "I'll hang up your bag," I offered.

She passed it to me and uttered a soft "Thank you," before stepping farther in and looking around at the massive framed art hanging on my entryway walls.

"I like this," she said, admiring one of horses grazing the countryside. "Did you pick it?"

I nodded. "A friend of mine from back home is an artist. I asked him to paint some custom pieces for me." Putting my hand gently on her shoulder, I shifted her attention to one across the hall. "This one's inspired by the creek near my home." Her skin was warm through the dress, and I had to make myself withdraw my hand while she examined the image.

The painting showed flowing prairie grass leading up to a stand of trees. Amongst the branches, so small you couldn't tell much detail, were five horses tied to the trees and waiting for their riders. My brothers and me. "We used to spend summer afternoons cooling off in the stream."

"It looks idyllic," she said, eyes darting back and forth across the canvas.

My throat felt tight as I saw it through her eyes. So much of my childhood was idyllic, and then other parts, not so much. "Cottonwood Falls was a great place to grow up."

She turned to me. "I've never been in a professional football player's home before. Do I get a tour?"

I grinned. "Nothing much to show. My bedroom's that way, the guest wing is there for when family comes to visit. This is the living room." I stepped into the open space with comfortable furniture and a giant TV I used to watch game film more than any movies or shows. "There's a pool out back." I gestured toward the sparkling water out the tall patio doors. "And this way is the dining area and kitchen."

I could only imagine what my mom would think of my kitchen with its double ovens, a massive refrigerator that would have actually kept up with five boys, and plenty of counter space with granite instead of laminate posing as butcher block.

"The design is gorgeous," Mia said. "Very modern compared to the surroundings."

My lips lifted as I gazed through the big patio door showing my pool and the massive grounds covered in green grass and dotted with mature oak trees. "Had to have the best of both worlds." After a pause, I walked toward the fridge. "How do you feel about steak?"

Her heels clacked against the stone floors as she followed me. "Love it," she said. "As long as it's not cooked like a shoe."

"I'm not sure how you cook shoes," I teased.

She chuckled, the sound warming my heart.

"My chef prepared the meal for us," I admitted. "Which means it will be done perfectly." I opened the fridge. "Do you like wine?" I asked her. "I also have beer, seltzer, tea, lemonade..."

Her smile was warm as she said, "Wine is great. Whatever you have is fine."

I pulled out a red wine my chef said paired well with the dinner, then I poured her a glass and got myself an ice water. I handed her the drink, and our fingers brushed as she took the stem.

The heat sent a shock through me stronger than any hit I got on the field. I missed the touch of a woman, the soft brush of fingertips over my body, the sharp grip of nails dug into my back.

"You aren't drinking?" she asked, seemingly unphased as she stood by the counter with me.

My unexpectedly strong reaction to her touch left me struggling to find words. After a moment, I said, "I only drink water, sometimes an electrolyte drink or tea. But let me live vicariously through you."

She smiled slightly as she swirled the wine to get its aroma. Seeming satisfied, she looked down and took a sip. "So good."

"I'll have my chef send the label to Vanover," I told her, going to the table. I pulled out a chair for her, and she easily slipped into it like she was used to people taking care of her.

Good. She deserved to be treated like a queen. And my heart sank because she'd never agree to this —something fake when we both knew she was more than worthy of something real.

"Let me get our food," I said, giving myself a chance to turn my back and hide my emotions.

After putting on my oven mitts, I pulled out the pans of steaks and roasted vegetables, then plated them for both of us, careful to make it look good for her. With her job, she must have been used to fine dining for every meal, and I didn't want to let her down.

I looked at her hopefully, bringing the plate to the table, and she smiled down at it. "Looks delicious."

"Glad to hear it," I replied, sitting across from her. "Dig in."

"You don't need to ask me twice." She cut into it and brought a bite to her mouth, letting out a soft moan that sent blood to all the wrong places in my body. "It's great."

I shifted in my seat. "I'll let my chef know," I replied, taking a bite myself. Logically, I knew it was good, but I could hardly taste it through my nerves. This was harder than stepping on the field for any game, even with fifty thousand people watching.

Maybe I shouldn't ask her to be my fake girl-friend after all. It was embarrassing, for both of us really. But then I thought of all I'd be giving up just because I couldn't swallow my pride.

Good thing she liked the wine; otherwise, I'm sure she'd splash it in my face.

"You seem distracted," she said. Was that a hint of disappointment in her voice?

I shook my head. "Not at all. I've been looking forward to this all day." Even if I was nervous too.

She glanced down for a moment, then tucked a blond lock behind her ear. "Is that so?"

I nodded. "Tell me, what were you doing with Hayden French?"

9

MIA

FORD WASN'T one to dance around the topic. No, he'd gone straight to the question that had a more-than-slightly embarrassing answer.

Years in boardrooms had taught me to school my expression, even when my heart was beating out of control and my stomach was lurching.

"It was a PR opportunity," I answered simply.

He raised his eyebrows, the dark brown lines arching over turquoise eyes. "And here you said it was a long story."

The response was so unexpected, I had to laugh. "You're right, I did."

He smiled a crooked smile that did nothing to slow the rampant pace of my heart. It was one thing to see him in a room full of people, another all together to watch him in his home. Relaxed, yet confident. Inviting, but still mysterious.

All alone with me.

I swirled a strand of floppy asparagus around my fork. "Promise you won't judge me?"

He dipped his head in promise. "You have no idea the stories about my teammates that have been covered up. I'm sure yours is nothing in comparison."

I tilted my head in question.

He leaned a little closer over the table. And I was so mesmerized by his perfect bone structure, the changing color of his eyes, I almost didn't hear what he said next. "Let's just say that the rhino didn't get out of the zoo on its own last year."

My jaw dropped. "No way."

He nodded. "Pretty sure I'm still sore from the sprints Coach had us do as a punishment."

That made me laugh. "I've only ever heard of high school teams running when they got in trouble."

I shook my head. "Where do you think those coaches got the idea?"

Silence hung between us, his question heavy in the air. I bit my bottom lip, gauging how much I should reveal.

But I liked Ford. He was the one guy I actually wanted to have a chance with, and I wasn't building a relationship full of potential around a half-truth.

"Do you remember me complaining about Thomas?"

He grimaced, then nodded.

"He blocked the acquisition of the Andersen sisters' company so he can propose one of his own to challenge me next quarter. And between him and his wife, they're campaigning internally to win the board's vote."

"Mia..." he breathed. "Does Gage know about this?"

"He's on the board," I said, "but he didn't make it to the last meeting. Tara had a dance recital." I smiled on the last sentence, amazed that the man who used to work nonstop would miss a quarterly board meeting to watch toddlers in tutus.

Ford shook his head, and I continued. "My publicist had the idea that a relationship would level the playing field. Thomas has his wife, and I'd have someone to 'campaign' on my behalf. So she set me up with Hayden because, apparently, he's a hot commodity at Griffen Industries."

Ford smirked. "Do you work with a bunch of twelve-year-old girls?"

"It seems so." I chuckled and set down my fork. "But I definitely cannot spend enough time with Hayden to pull off a fake relationship. You're right— I deserve better, even if it's make-believe."

So there it was. All my embarrassing truth out in the open. All except for the fact that I was excited to be here with Ford, to try something real. If I still had a chance after sharing all that.

But Ford didn't look disappointed or put off at all. He looked... relieved.

"So you don't think I'm crazy?" I finally asked. "Or pathetic?" I added.

He leaned forward, a genuine smile on his face. It lit up his eyes, making them almost sparkle like the sun catching the ocean. "Actually, the opposite," he said.

My eyebrows drew together. "What's the opposite of pathetic?" I asked.

"Admirable," he said without pause. "Even more so than you were before."

There was my heart picking up pace again, and I didn't even bother hiding the way those words made me smile. He admired me?

He flattened his palms on the table like he was steadying himself. "You might not play football, but you know your game. You're committed to it, to doing whatever it takes to win."

I nodded, feeling more understood than I had in a long time. "Most people don't get the sacrifices it takes to get to our level, much less respect them."

He took a sip of his water, and the way his throat

moved as he swallowed was tantalizing. "You're right. I've been with women before who wanted me to take my foot off the pedal when I needed to be pushing it to the floor. It's a big reason why I've been against dating."

So Tallie and Farrah were right about Ford being against dating? My heart soared even further because he'd chosen me as a potential match. Me. He recognized me in a way that few men did. As an equal. It wasn't poetry or a box of chocolates or even a boombox on his shoulder, but to me, it was even better.

"I would never ask you to play small," I said. "Especially when I'm chasing goals of my own."

He dipped his head in the most adorable way, clasping his hands on the table. "This couldn't be more perfect," he said.

I almost couldn't believe those words had come out of his mouth. "You mean it?"

He nodded. "The owner of the Diamonds wants me to date his daughter... unless I'm already in a relationship. And you wanted a fake relationship as well. If it's okay with you, we could date for the season. It would get Trent off my back and help you gain favor at your company. I know I'd be great at talking you up, and I'd be spending time with someone who doesn't make me feel like I'm listening to nails on a chalkboard. What do you say?"

I blinked, taking in his words.

Any height my heart had soared to instantly vanished as it smashed on the ground and then got ran over by a garbage truck—a few times for good measure.

Ford wanted a fake relationship to get him out of a bad date.

That's why he'd brought me over here.

Not because he liked me.

But because he needed me.

I thought I might be sick.

"Mia, are you okay?" he asked. "You look a little pale."

I shook my head. "Where's the restroom?"

"Let me show you." He stood, taking my arm like he knew I needed steadying, and walked me to the powder room around the corner from the kitchen. His touch was like fire on my icy cold skin. Could he sense through our touch how pathetic I felt? Because right now it seemed like each of my cells was screaming the word.

How was I in my late thirties and feeling like the girl picked last in gym class all over again?

I got inside and shut the door, locking myself safely inside.

Ford called, "Can I get you anything? Medicine?"

"No, I'm fine," I managed. "I'll just be a second."

When his footsteps faded away, I got out my phone and texted Zeke, rockets of shame launching down my spine.

Mia: Can you come back to pick me up?

I set my phone down and leaned against the bathroom counter, looking at myself in the mirror. Really looking.

I was in my late thirties, no real relationship to show for it. No engagements. No major breakups, not even a divorce under my belt. And for a long time, I'd been okay with it because like Ford said, I was willing make sacrifices to win what really mattered to me: my career.

I wanted to be a success no matter how many people thought I couldn't be one. I'd done what it took, learning this company inside and out, getting my master's degree online while working sixty-plus-hour weeks. I'd given up dates, shut down relationships in the early stages, even broke off an engagement, and truly committed to my work.

And now I had another choice.

The opportunity to "date" someone extremely well-liked within the company was here.

Could I sacrifice my pride enough to take it?

10

FORD

I CAME BACK to the bathroom and knocked softly on the door. "Mia?"

The doorknob jiggled in response, and I stepped back, seeing her come out of the bathroom. Thankfully, some of the color returned to her face. She glanced at the cup and plate in my hands. "You got me ginger ale and crackers?" She seemed surprised. And a little touched too, judging by the tender note in her voice.

At least it seemed like she was doing better than before, when her color quickly shifted from pale to green. "Of course. You looked like you really weren't feeling well."

"I'm okay now," she said softly, looking up at me.

Her blue eyes were clear, and this close to her, I could smell her perfume again.

"If the food didn't set well, I can order something else," I offered, stepping back. She brushed past me, her shoulder grazing my chest.

I felt like I'd been seared. Maybe this was a bad idea, asking someone my body reacted so strongly to for a fake relationship.

She reached the table, picking up the wine and downing the glass. My eyebrows rose, and I set the crackers and ginger ale on the table. She clearly didn't need it anymore.

I opened my mouth to take back my offer just as she said, "I'll do it." If I wasn't standing across the table from her, I'd try and get a closer look, see if she wasn't joking. Or already feeling the effects of the wine.

But Mia was deadly serious as she leveled her gaze at me. "I'll be your fake girlfriend."

"Wow, Mia, that's um..."

She was all business as she cut through the fluff. "In an arrangement like this, we'll need some clear boundaries and a plan of action. Can you bring me my purse? I'll get out a notebook to write it all down."

Now I understood completely how this woman

controlled boardrooms and ran a billion-dollar company. She was intimidating, powerful... and incredibly sexy when she took charge like this. I turned on my heel, no longer Ford, but a player in her game.

I went to the hall closet, retrieving her surprisingly heavy purse, and brought it back to her. She opened the cream-colored leather and retrieved a simple notebook and pen.

"We need to create SMART goals." She wrote SMART alongside the paper. "Specific, measurable, achievable, relevant, and—"

"Timebound," I finished.

She looked at me, surprised.

"I know I'm a jock, but I paid attention in my college business class," I teased.

She gave me an apologetic smile that made my stomach all soft. So I focused on the paper. "Specific would be start a fake relationship that appears real to everyone else."

She nodded. "Measurable. For me, it would mean acquiring the Andersen sisters. For you, getting out of dating..."

"Felicity," I finished for her.

Her face pinched. "Felicity Reynolds."

"Know of her?"

She nodded. "I've heard of her. Now I know why

you're so desperate." The teasing lilt to her voice made me laugh.

After a beat, she said, "Achievable? Can we make everyone believe this is real?"

The real question was if I could keep myself from believing it is. But I didn't say that out loud. Instead, I said, "What do you think it will take to make people buy in?"

She blinked slowly, long dark eyelashes fanning over pale cheeks. I swore her chest hitched with her breath. "Public appearances," she began. "Going to your games. Some posts online."

I leaned in close, because she hadn't mentioned the most important part. I wanted Mia to know just how much this mattered to me. "Trent will be watching me to make sure I'm not pretending solely so I can avoid his daughter. My career, my life here in Dallas close to Cottonwood Falls, is on the line. It won't be enough to stand in the same room and say we're together." We were inches apart. I could tell I was making her uncomfortable, but I needed to press, to see if she could really act interested in me. If I could pretend without letting myself fall over the edge.

Leaving no space between us, I flicked my gaze to her lips. "Could you kiss me, knowing it means nothing?"

She blinked, then forced her gaze to meet mine. Her voice was strong, belying the worry in her eyes. "For my company, I could do anything."

I stayed close, searching her eyes for the truth. When I found it, I used all of my strength to step back. "Good."

She nodded, seeming far less affected than me. "Relevant..." She added a check mark by the word in her notebook. "Timebound?"

"It has to be until the end of the season or until Felicity gets a boyfriend," I said.

"That will be a couple months past our board meeting—which will help with the believability on my end."

I nodded. "Should we shake on it?"

She arched an eyebrow and closed her notebook. "I'll have legal send you a contract detailing our respective obligations along with an NDA."

Wow, she really was taking this seriously. "You can trust my word," I insisted.

"Sorry, Ford, but someone willing to put on an act to fool the entire world isn't going to fool me too."

Her words left an uncomfortable feeling in the pit of my stomach—even if they were true. "Okay."

She stood up, tucking her notebook in her purse. "Call Vanover once you've signed the documents to set an appointment with me. We can discuss the game plan."

"We can't do it now?" I asked. I had the evening free.

She shook her head, a smile in her eyes like she was in on a joke I didn't yet know. "This is my personal time, Ford. Our arrangement is one hundred percent business."

I tilted my head. "I thought we were friends."

"We're business partners," she corrected. Then she walked out of the house.

I watched her walk to the car waiting in the driveway and slip into the back seat. The driver glanced toward me for half a second before closing the door behind her and driving her away.

At the end of the driveway, the car turned and disappeared from sight. I waited for a moment before turning and looking back at my empty home.

I'd gotten exactly what I wanted... so why didn't I feel like celebrating?

11

MIA

VANOVER SWEPT INTO MY OFFICE, a scheming smile on his lips and a ceramic mug in his hand.

"What are you so happy about?" I asked, taking my afternoon green tea from him.

"Maybe because I just signed for a floral delivery from *the* Hayden French. Don't tell anyone, but I love him. I swear 'Hello Beautiful' was stuck in my head for a full month when it came out and—"

The door to my office opened, and a man wearing a black polo and khakis came in carrying an obnoxiously large bouquet of flowers in every shade of red, orange, and yellow that existed. My lips parted as I took them in.

Vanover directed the delivery man, saying, "On the table there would be great."

The man set it on the table where I typically held small meetings, his muscles straining as he did. Once the arrangement was put in place, he stood up, took off his cap, and wiped his brow. "Enjoy, Ms. Baird."

"Thank you," I said. The man left, walking toward the elevators, and then Vanover said, "There may be another reason I'm a little chipper today."

I eyed him suspiciously. "You're typically not this coy."

He smirked. "Then I'll get right to it. You have a meeting with Ford Madigan in half an hour."

My stomach dropped. "What? That wasn't on my calendar this morning!"

"The mayor rescheduled, so you had an opening." He smirked and examined his fingernails. "Unless you wanted me to schedule your stylist first."

I set down my tea, then rolled up a business magazine with a picture of me on the cover. "Out, out, out." I playfully hit him on the shoulder.

He chuckled, scooting through my door and letting it close behind him.

Shaking my head, I walked to the table with the arrangement, peeking through it for a note. I found a small envelope tucked amidst a lily and a rose and opened it. There was a typed note saying, *A bouquet as beautiful as you. May we see each other again? -H*

"Well then," I muttered as I tossed the note in the

trash. Then I went to my desk and pressed the call button on my office phone. "Vanover, bring me Tallie, please."

Within a few minutes, she'd arrived. "Ford Madigan is my fake boyfriend," I announced. "He's signed the legal paperwork and will be here in half an hour." Might as well get to the point, right?

Several emotions crossed her eyes, the worst of them pity. "But I thought—"

I shook my head, not wanting to go there. To hear my hope echoed in her words. "When Ford arrives, we'll be drawing up a plan with further details and deliverables. I'm assuming you had a detailed strategy laid out in that manila folder of yours when you suggested Hayden French?"

She nodded slowly, short brown hair bobbing with the motion. "I did. I'll bring you the list so you can discuss it with him. I can also get with Vanover and Ford's PA to schedule events for both of you once we know what he'll agree to."

"Great," I said. "That's all."

"Mia, I..." Tallie began.

I lifted a corner of my lips. "C'est la vie." I shrugged. "Now go get me that file."

"Gotcha covered," she said.

AFTER TALKING with Ford last night, I did my research on him. Or rather, dug into his history, trying to find a reason not to do this. It was one thing to fake a relationship with a pop star who only cared for himself. Another to pretend something was real with a crush who had zero feelings for you.

But everything I learned about Ford made me like him more.

He was six feet, four inches tall.

Two hundred and fifty pounds, which was slightly larger than the average league quarterback. There were a lot of stats where he excelled compared to other QBs in the league, and even those throughout history, but he'd yet to win a Super Bowl. He was younger than me too, but so accomplished.

But more than that, he had an incredible charity that offered free counseling services to children who lost their parents. I was trying to find out more when Vanover came over the speaker, saying, "Look sharp."

That six-foot-four-inch man I was researching just seconds prior came walking out of the elevators wearing distressed jeans and a T-shirt with a ballcap and sunglasses, like he really didn't want any attention. The modesty was far too endearing. I could see him through my glass wall as he approached with my assistant.

I gave a slight wave, and Vanover walked him to my office.

"This is for you," Vanover said, passing me a printout of Tallie's notes. After a pause, he said, "It's already smelling lovely in here from those flowers Hayden sent you."

I barely abstained from rolling my eyes. Besides, he was right. The garish mix of roses and lilies blended, filling my office space with a pretty floral scent.

With the door closed, Ford's eyes were on the arrangement. "Hayden sent you flowers?"

"And asked me for a second date." I shook my head. "Maybe he wanted some more window time."

I thought it would get a laugh out of him, but Ford's lips were tugged down at the corners. Not wanting to read too much into it, I said, "Let's go over this packet. I'm sure you're busy."

"I have a cupping appointment in two hours," he said. "I'm free 'til then."

"Cupping?" I asked. "Are you shopping for drinkware or something?"

That brought a smile to his face. "It helps with muscle recovery," he said shortly.

"Ah." That didn't help me understand at all. I made a mental note to research it as I brought the packet, along with my notebook, to the table with the flowers sitting between us.

Ford shifted them to the side so he could see me while I opened up Tallie's packet.

I already knew she was the best, but this report was next level. There were paragraphs upon paragraphs of fake relationships throughout history, how they ended, ways they went wrong, and methods she suggested to avoid those downfalls. She also had an estimated relationship timeline, along with already scheduled events where I could potentially bring my fake boyfriend. There were footnotes and sources cited. I was so dang impressed.

"This is intense," Ford said, moving his chair closer. The movement wafted the heady rush of his cologne my way. Damn, he smelled good. My mouth was practically salivating, and I reached for my green tea, taking a sip.

With my senses cooled, I read, "It says here that we should go out in public, be seen together before we officially announce that we're dating."

Ford nodded slowly. "I'm busy with practice sessions during the day, but dinner is usually good for me. Sometimes I can make a lunch work."

We were dangerously close to starting this fake relationship, nailing down details that couldn't be undone. I closed the folder and leveled with him.

"Ford, you know when we start this, it's not something we can go back on, right?" Not to mention, it was risky to pull a move like this.

He stared at me like he knew there was more to my speech.

I took a breath. "I know these outings and events together may seem frivolous, but this going badly could reflect worse on me than me just being single and sticking it out. I need to know that you're committed to this."

He covered my hands with his. I couldn't tell if the gesture was comforting or electrifying as he said, "I'd do anything to stay close to my family," he said. "Even if it's a little uncomfortable."

There it was, another jab to the stomach. A reminder that he really didn't want to be spending time with me, despite the crush I'd developed for him. But I'd gotten the answer I wanted. He was committed. And he'd already signed the paperwork.

I pushed the button on the receiver on the table and said, "Vanover, can you schedule Ford and me for lunch tomorrow?"

Vanover replied, happily, "At the café?"

I shook my head. "The most public place you can find."

12

FORD

I DIDN'T BOTHER with the hat and sunglasses that were always in my truck for when I went out in public. No, this time I was in a nice button-up with the sleeves rolled, a pair of jeans, and still somehow felt completely naked as I waited for Mia outside like Tallie instructed. I was to open the door for her when her driver arrived.

A nondescript vehicle pulled up along the sidewalk, and I could hear people pointing and talking about me. But then my phone went off in my pocket. I pulled it up and saw a new text.

Mia: Last chance to back out.

In response, I opened the car door. Her eyes held

mine as I took her hand and helped her out. There was no going back now.

The instruction packet that Tallie sent me bordered on neurotic, covering everything that I should do on this first date, including placing my hand low on her waist as we walked into the building. What she hadn't covered was the way my body would react to touching Mia's shapely curves, feeling the swell of her ass right below my fingertips.

It also didn't help that Mia was wearing a silk top that was incredibly soft to the touch. Had she done that on purpose?

We reached the front door, and a host held it open for us, shooing away a few people who were following us and taking pictures on smartphones. Once we got inside, a server led us to a table that was marked as reserved. It had a white tablecloth with a votive candle sitting on top, and it was clearly in the window so people could see us from the street as they passed by. A crowd of people was already forming in the window.

Mia asked, "Is it like this for you everywhere you go?"

"Unfortunately," I said, shifting my gaze away from the window and trying hard to pretend the people weren't there.

She chuckled softly like it had been a joke, and I

supposed it was. Milo preferred to lay low like I did, but Krew enjoyed the attention. He got a thrill from signing autographs, living out his childhood fantasies.

A server came by, and I ordered a water while Mia purchased a coffee. She glanced at the gold watch around her wrist, saying, "I have eleven minutes until noon. I'm getting my caffeine in."

I chuckled at the comment. "No coffee after noon?"

She nodded. "My nutritionist is giving me ideas on how to handle the stress of being a CEO. Who knew that drinking caffeine late at night would keep you awake and spike your cortisol?"

I chuckled at the sarcasm in her tone. Then I got distracted by the way she fluttered out her napkin and put it over her lap.

She said, "Does the team have a nutritionist?"

I nodded. "Actually, I have them work with my chef so I'm only eating things that are on my plan. I learned a lot about nutrition in college though. That's what I majored in."

She quirked an eyebrow. "Because your favorite subject in high school was lunch?"

I had to laugh at the way she teased me. She didn't pull any punches or try to be cutesy like a lot of girls did, nor did she try to talk about football like she knew the sport. I found it refreshing.

"I was probably interested in nutrition because I grew up on a ranch," I confessed. "We spent a lot of time talking about the best foods for the animals we raised, and I guess it made sense to me that I should learn that for humans too."

She nodded. "Do you ever miss living in the country?"

"All the time. I bought a house as close to it as I could."

She smiled. "I am a city girl through and through. I love my condo. And my coffee shops. And having anything delivered at a moment's notice."

A server returned with our drinks, and she took a cautious sip from her black coffee. As soon as it hit her lips, her eyes fluttered closed and her shoulders relaxed.

It was cute, endearing. I smiled as I said, "I can see liking the amenities of the city. But don't you ever long for the peace and quiet?"

She shook her head. "The city is its own kind of white noise machine. Somehow it all fades into the background and helps me focus on what really matters."

I leaned closer. The smell of her perfume blended with aromatic coffee was more than intoxicating. "And what really matters to you now?"

She bit her lip, glancing toward the window and

then back to me, and I realized that this was a show for her. For us. She was pretending to be interested in me because of our agreement—it made my chest feel heavy in a way I couldn't quite explain.

When you got to my level, a lot of people wanted to know you because of who you were in the world, not because of who you were as a person. And Mia was one of them—to be fair, I was one of them to her as well. We were both benefiting from our arrangement.

"Acquiring the Andersen sisters matters to me," she answered. "I know it's a long shot, but I really believe Griffen Industries can make a difference this way... What matters to you?"

Before I could answer, the server appeared again to take our orders. I ordered something that my nutritionist would approve of, and Mia got something that sounded delicious. When the server left, we were sitting across from each other quietly, and I realized I didn't know how to act, what to say when I wasn't being my real self. So I decided even if this relationship was fake, I didn't need to be fake too.

I took a sip of my water and set the glass down. "You asked me what mattered to me," I said.

She nodded.

"My charity. The team donates a lot of money to

it, and that's part of the reason why I want to keep working with the Diamonds."

"I read about it," she admitted. "The headlines at least." Then she asked the obvious question. "Did you lose a parent?"

My throat was unexpectedly stiff as I swallowed down a lump that formed there. Something about her looking at me with those blue eyes, talking about my mom, it hit me in my feelings. So I nodded and said, "I was so young when she passed. Cancer."

Mia tilted her head, her blue eyes so full of compassion it almost threatened to drown me. "I'm so sorry," she said.

"I can't go back and help myself, but I can help other kids who are going through the same thing. That's why I want to keep fundraising, to create an endowment so we can bring on more counselors and end the waitlist."

"That's amazing, Ford," she said. "It really is."

I smiled at her praise. "Thank you." For some reason, the way she was looking at me, like she admired me, made my chest feel lighter. The reaction confused me. I had thousands of fans, and she'd declared us merely business partners, so why did her approval affect me this way?

The food arrived, and we ate the rest of our meal while talking about nothing important. I walked her back to her car, and just like Tallie asked, I leaned in, kissing Mia on the cheek. Her skin was soft and warm under my lips, and I didn't want to pull away. So I lingered a moment longer, humming, "Do you think it's working?"

She pulled away, an emotion in her eyes that I couldn't quite read. "I hope so. Goodbye, Ford."

13

MIA

THE MORNING after my date with Ford, I had a meeting with Tallie to brief me on the public's reaction. At this point, I knew better than to go rogue and read headlines about myself. Tallie reviewed them daily and passed on the info, withholding some of the harsher, more personal critiques.

I sipped on my coffee, answering a few emails nested in a never-ending inbox, until a knock sounded on my glass office door. Tallie and Vanover waited for me, side by side. Both of them had worn charcoal pantsuits with green button-down tops.

I had to grin as I waved them in. "Didn't know we instituted a dress code."

Tallie and Vanover glared at each other, and Vanover said, "Unhappy accident."

"You didn't call each other last night to prep?" I teased.

Tallie glared.

Chuckling, I said, "Van, can I please get a refill on my coffee and whatever Tallie wants?"

Vanover nodded. "I'm drinking a matcha latte, so I'm assuming you'd like to copy that too."

"Latte," she huffed, and when Vanover didn't move, she added a "please."

Seemingly satisfied, he left us in my office, where we met at the big glass desk overlooking all of Dallas. It was a beautiful view, and I tried not to get lost in it too often. Especially not when I was dying to hear Tallie's take on the news.

"Well?" I prompted.

Tallie opened her folder, tugging out a glossy photograph of Ford and me. My lips parted at the image—how Ford and I looked together, him pressing his lips to my cheek, my eyes closed softly, dark lashes fanning over my pale cheeks. His hand rested comfortably on my arm, like he'd done so a dozen times before.

We looked like... a couple.

When I glanced back up at Tallie, her eyes were alight with excitement. "This image—or some version of it—has circulated every major newspaper and gossip column in the country, several major sports outlets, as well as most local papers in the state."

I looked down at the image again. "The headlines?" I had to brace myself for her answer. Even though I knew I was a strong, successful woman, there was a part of me that also knew I would forever be judged harshly for my weight, my looks, far more than I would ever be praised for any of my accomplishments. Especially when dating a man known for his physical abilities.

Tallie waved her hand. "Doesn't much matter. People are talking, speculating, which was the goal at this stage any—"

The door to my office opened, and we looked up. I'd expected to see Vanover entering with our coffee. Instead, Thomas opened the door without knocking and oozed in like an oil slick in his black Armani suit and gelled-back hair.

"I'm in a meeting," I said pointedly.

He glanced at the photo on the table, and I hurriedly swept it away.

"Seems very important," he drawled.

"Yes?" I asked, letting impatience color my voice. I knew he never would have barged in on a meeting when Gage was in charge. "Something better be on fire."

"It's this damn company that's on fire," he said.

"While you two are gossiping over a picture, I met with a potential acquisition in the retail sector earlier and we could hardly talk business around all the questions they had about your new fling with this quarterback."

I got up from the table and stepped closer to him, slowly, letting his impatient ass fume while I approached. When we were nose to nose, I narrowed my gaze and said, "Are you having trouble steering a meeting? Sounds like a personnel issue."

He sneered. "Is that a threat?"

"It's an observation. Much like I'm also observing you, in my office, interrupting a meeting and throwing a tantrum like a toddler." I enunciated each word, letting them hit him one after another. "Toddlers have no place in this office or this company, Thomas. Do you understand me?"

He stared me down until my office door opened again. This time, it was Vanover—with a troop of flower deliveries behind him. There were at least a dozen people carrying two arrangements a piece of all different styles. From small and rustic to lavish and gaudy, they had them all.

"What is..." I began while Thomas grumbled something indiscernible.

One of the delivery people stopped, passing me a

note. Before opening it, I gave Thomas another glare.

He clenched his fists like he was about to stomp his foot, then turned on his heel, muttering something about, "God damn circus..."

Shaking my head, I looked around me at all the people in my office, waiting on me.

Eyebrows drawn together, I flipped open the paper, seeing a handwritten message.

When we're together, I'll be the one buying you flowers. Let them know which one you like best and toss the rest. – Ford

My gaze did a double take between the note and all the people filling my expansive office.

Ford had done this?

Vanover cleared his throat. "Where would you like these, Mia?"

His voice drew me out of my shock long enough for me to look at all the bouquets surrounding me. They really were stunning, all on their own. I walked through the room, seeing them all, until I found an arrangement of sunflowers and lavender. The bunch was so bright and pretty and reminded me of my childhood.

My mom used to grow flowers in our garden and pick wild bouquets to bring to the neighbors. "Ford wants me to pick one," I explained, then gestured to the sunflowers. "I'll keep this one."

Immediately, the room whipped into a frenzy as the sunflowers were set on my desk and then the meeting table. The other delivery people began to leave with their bouquets.

"Wait," I said.

They paused.

"What are you doing with the other arrangements?" I asked.

The one in charge shrugged. "Bring them back to the shop, see if we can sell them?"

"Can you deliver these to a different location? I'll cover the cost, and Vanover will give you the addresses."

The person in charge of the delivery nodded, and then they marched out of my office, going to Vanover's desk. I asked Vanover to send them to the people at the assisted-living center where my parents were and then sat back down, staring at the arrangement on my desk. Hayden's gaudy delivery was gone.

When I finally met Tallie's eyes again, she was grinning. "Does Ford remember that this is fake?" she asked.

My heart stutter-stepped, because I had been asking myself the same question.

"It's all for show," I reminded us both. "We wanted to impress the people here in the office too."

Tallie didn't look convinced but also didn't argue. "Let's plan for the next phase."

"And what is that?" I asked, my eyes drawn again to the flowers.

"Your first real date."

14

FORD

MY MUSCLES FELT rawer than a freezer burnt steak when Coach ended practice. Part of me welcomed the fatigue, knowing this was part of being the best. Success rarely felt like effortlessly flying on clouds; it felt like hard work, sore muscles, and being so tired you fell asleep before your head hit the pillow at night.

After five years playing on a college team and the same amount of time on a professional team, I understood that fact. Pain came with the territory.

I stumbled to the locker room, showered off, then went to one of the facility's small recovery rooms with an ice bath and a television. I left the TV off, instead playing a podcast episode on my phone, an interview with Kobe Bryant about Mamba Mentality.

His mindset made me feel understood in a way, inspired in another. Even though we didn't play the same sport, we played the same game.

I stripped out of my towel, put on swim trunks, and stepped on the platform leading to the pool of circulating ice water. The movement made sure there was no hot spot around my inflamed muscles.

Knowing it was going to sting like a bitch, I sucked in a breath and stepped in before I could second-guess myself. The best way to get through something hard was to face it. Avoiding pain only added to the length of time you'd suffer—once with anticipation and another time when the challenge actually arrived.

The water felt like needles against my skin, and my heart and lungs constricted like the water was so cold the breath had frozen inside me.

I forced myself to take deep, calming breaths while focusing on the podcast.

If I could control my nervous system in frigid water, I could control it on the field when it mattered most.

If I could sit through this pain, my muscles would heal faster, get stronger.

I would master myself, body and mind.

I sank all the way down to my chin, letting the water swirl around me. Surprisingly, being doused in ice water felt awfully similar to seeing Hayden French's bouquet in Mia's office.

I knew we couldn't date for real—I had my goals to focus on and she her company—but the thought of him getting any closer to her... I clenched my fists, trying to think of something else and landing back on Mia.

The delivery people told me she'd chosen the sunflower arrangement... and instead of letting them discard the bouquets, she asked that they be delivered to an assisted-living community.

My heart clenched at the knowledge.

I was already having a hard time not looking forward to our date, even though this was all fake.

The podcast rose in volume with the host's exclamation, and I realized I hadn't heard a word they'd been saying. I swore at myself under my breath.

This was just one of many reasons why I'd instated my no-dating policy. I couldn't even focus on a personal development podcast episode without my fake girlfriend taking over my mind—imagine a relationship that was real.

A knock came on the door, and I looked over, seeing the shoulder of a suit through the window.

"Yeah?" I called out.

The door opened, and Trent Reynolds walked in, black leather boots clacking on the cement floor. He wore the smile of a snake oil salesman about to make bank. "Ford," he said. He tapped on my phone to silence it.

I dipped my head. "Mr. Reynolds. I feel a bit underdressed."

The old man chuckled roughly. "Make sure you always have the upper hand, Madigan. That's something my father taught me."

Trent had clearly taken the lesson to heart. "How can I help you?" My chest already felt like sinking, and I had to remind myself to breathe. To stay calm. This was all a play, whether it happened on the field or not.

"My daughter has a charity event this weekend, and unless you're otherwise occupied—"

"Actually, I have a date with my girlfriend this weekend," I said.

His lips pursed. The silence he left us in was far more uncomfortable than the freezing cold water.

Finally, I realized he was waiting for me to speak. "We've tried to be discreet until now to keep her out of the fans' way—you know how... protective they can be. But it seems I've been sending the wrong message about my availability. I assure you, I'm taken."

He twisted his lips to the side like he was tasting the bitter news. "Who is she?"

Something in his eyes made me want to protect her, shield her from him knowing her name. But this was part of the agreement. So I forced my voice to remain strong, the best defensive line I could offer. "Mia Baird. Griffen Industries CEO."

I saw the lightbulb hit his eyes. "Her?"

Something about the surprised, dismissive way he said it made my fists clench underwater. Even as a father, he had to know his daughter had no chance when it came to a woman like Mia. "She's an accomplished woman who worked her way up to the company's highest position from the ground floor. We have quite a bit in common that way."

"Isn't she a little..." He hesitated, and I could only imagine what he planned to say next.

"Tread carefully, sir," I warned. "We wouldn't want to say something that couldn't be taken back."

His gaze narrowed under carefully groomed gray eyebrows. "You are nothing like the quarterbacks I've known."

I lifted my chin. "I'm better," I said. We both knew it was the truth. And at the end of this season, I'd have the ring to prove it.

He cleared his throat. "I'll expect to see Ms. Baird at our team dinner. Not as a stand-in for my daughter, but as your date. I don't take kindly to lies, young man. Because if time's taught me anything, it's that talent can always be replaced."

I dipped my head in understanding while fighting a shiver.

He turned on his heel and left the room, and finally, the shivers broke out, making the water tremble around me.

This was serious and nothing I could back out of now. Everyone had to believe that what I had with Mia was real. And tonight's date would be the time to prove it.

15

MIA

TONIGHT, my stylist and makeup artist had come to my penthouse to prepare me for our first date. Not because I wanted to impress Ford, but because I knew that photos of us would hit everything from major newspapers to the biggest influencers' TikTok accounts. I had to look *amazing*. Like a successful CEO who scored a quarterback, not a friend he met for dinner.

As the stylist tied the straps at the back of my red silk dress, I wondered if Ford's heart was racing as much as mine.

A million different ways I could mess this up were playing through my mind—each of them ending with me getting humiliated on a national stage and earning a vote of no confidence from a board swayed by a doubting fucking Thomas.

"How's that feel?" my stylist asked.

I rolled my shoulders and then swung my arms side to side to test the fit. "It's perfect." I turned to her, offering a grateful smile. "How do you always find the dresses that make me look like a Kennedy?"

She chuckled. "You look better than a Kennedy."

I raised my eyebrows.

"You look like a Kardashian."

I had to chuckle at the compliment, which was really showing the difference in our ages. But it was nice all the same—I knew she wouldn't compare me to the powerful, beautiful family unless she meant it. "Only because I'm dressed by you."

She squeezed my side, then snapped at the makeup artist. "Add some bronze to that cleavage of hers."

The makeup artist rushed over, dusting some powder over my chest that highlighted the girls without making me look obscene or overly done up.

I stared at myself in the mirror, in the red, ruched dress that gave me an hourglass appearance without being restrictive at all. She paired the dress with matte black heels, a matching black purse with everything I'd need, and diamond stud earrings. With flawless makeup and my hair in an elegant twist at the base of my neck, I felt like royalty. "Thank you, fairy godmothers."

They both smiled at me, and I glanced at the clock on my wall. "Ford should be arriving in the limo any moment." Zeke was driving us both to the event.

My stylist said, "I'll clean up everything here. You go along, Cinderella."

I smiled at her, then walked toward the private elevator. It was already waiting for me, the doors opening instantly when I pushed the button. Without pause, I stepped onto the marble floor, seeing myself in the mirrors reflecting muted light.

I couldn't help wondering what Ford saw when he looked at me. Because even though I knew we were trying to impress everyone else, deep down, I wanted to impress him too.

The elevator dinged open, and like something out of a fairy tale, Ford waited at the back of the limo. Over our years as acquaintances, I'd seen him all types of ways—sweaty after a game, serious after a press conference, in casual jeans and T-shirts. But never had I seen him like this.

He wore a suit that fit his broad, muscled shoulders perfectly and tailored black pants that hugged his strong thighs. He leaned back casually against the limo as if he were just as comfortable there, waiting for me, as he was on the football field.

And whether he meant to or not, I saw his eyes track slowly up and down my body before his lips lifted in a grin. "Beautiful."

With a smile, I did a spin.

He whistled, making me laugh.

Maybe that was the best and worst part of this— enjoying being around him, all the while knowing we would never be more than friends.

He held the door open for me, and I stepped into the back seat, catching a hint of his cologne. The desire that rushed through my body was so foreign, so strong, I nearly toppled over on the way to my seat.

If Ford noticed my stumble, he didn't say a thing. Instead, he slid in after me and closed the door. Within seconds, Zeke was pulling out of the garage.

Here, alone in the back seat with the privacy window separating us from Zeke, I realized yet again how large this man was. He was at least half a foot taller than me, pure muscle and hard angles, and I was practically salivating. If he could hear the thoughts going through my mind, sense the way my body was reacting to his presence, he'd think I was no better than the groupies who lined the stadium after games, hoping for a player to take them home.

Finally, the silence felt so thick between us that I said, "You look nice too, Ford."

His shoulders seemed to relax at that comment. "Thank you." His tone was warm as a towel fresh out of the dryer. My mom always used to give one to me, even if I hadn't showered, and wrap me up in the warmth.

We drove without speaking for another couple minutes, and the silence made me restless. As if sensing my nerves, Ford reached out and caught my hand in his.

I looked at his large hand enveloping mine and then up at him, where a reassuring smile played along his full lips. "Better practice, right?" he said.

My smile faltered. I thought he'd been trying to comfort me, but no, it was all strategic with him. Why did I want to avoid the truth so badly? I was too old, too successful, to be pining after a guy who had no interest in me, who didn't appreciate all I had to offer.

So I reminded myself of that, even while linking my fingers through his. "Are you up for this?" I asked, doubting myself mostly. "Tallie leaked to the press that we'd be at the restaurant tonight. It'll be... chaotic."

He rubbed his thumb over the back of my hand,

almost like it was instinct. "I've dealt with the press before."

"Right."

More silence.

"Ford, I'm going to need some encouragement here. I'm freaking out a little."

He reached up his free hand, holding my cheek in his palm. "No need to worry. Just keep your eyes on me, Sunflower."

My lips quirked. "Sunflower?"

"That's the flower you chose, right?" he said. His voice held a note of emotion to it—I couldn't quite tell why, though.

"That was quite the display you sent to the office," I replied. A little butterfly fluttered in my stomach at the reminder of Tallie's words. *Does he know this is fake?*

Heat intensified his gaze as he said, "I meant it. I'll be the only man sending you flowers."

"Why?" I asked. "Jealous?"

But his response was completely serious. "Because my girl will get what she needs from me. No one else."

Before I could respond, the limo had slowed and then stopped. And then the back door opened, leading us into a hoard of paparazzi with blinding flashing cameras.

16

FORD

I COULD FEEL Mia stiffen as the door opened and the photographers swarmed. Security was doing their best to contain the paparazzi behind the velvet rope, but they couldn't exactly stop the shouting coming our way.

"ARE YOU TWO DATING?"

"ARE YOU JUST FRIENDS?"

"MIA, WHAT WOULD HAYDEN THINK?"

"YOUR FANS ARE DISAPPOINTED, FORD. ANY COMMENT?"

"FORD, WHO IS MIA TO YOU?"

Despite the tension in her shoulders, her voice was calm as she said, "No comment." But I found the reporter holding a mic with the logo of the largest station I recognized. I held Mia to my side, her body soft and warm against mine, as I spoke directly to the reporter.

"Who is Mia to me?" I repeated the question. I looked at her, taking her in unabashedly—luckily, I could get away with indulging myself when we were putting on a show.

My eyes drank in her high cheekbones dusted with a rosy color. Her full lips, lightly glossed. Her soft, pale shoulders, contrasted by bright red fabric plunging into her cleavage. Then her curves, the arc between her chest and hips and thick thighs I wanted to sink my fingers into. God, she was so hot, I'd need a thousand ice baths to cool me down.

When I looked back to the reporter, I said, "Mia is an incredible woman, a hard worker, a selfless leader, but to me? She's everything." I hoped Hayden French, and any other man, would get the message that she was mine. I hoped Thomas would know he picked the wrong woman for a fight. And I hoped the people on the board at Griffen Industries would know Mia had my support, one hundred percent.

Everyone went crazy, snapping more pictures, shouting more questions. But I kept my eyes on her, watched the way her lips parted in surprise. She was so beautiful, it took all I had not to kiss her right then and there.

Using the last bit of my willpower, I applied light

pressure at her lower back and led her into the restaurant. But the night was far from over.

We walked into the building and rode an elevator to the very top floor. The elevator doors opened to a beautiful rooftop dining area overlooking all of Dallas. Bright oranges, reds, and yellows streaked across the sky like they were meant to add to the painting of Mia, her red dress a drop of fire in the sunset.

She was a few steps ahead of me when she realized I wasn't keeping up. Then she turned back and gave me a questioning smile. Her skin glowed golden, each ray of the sun highlighting her features, illuminating her eyes, tinting the wisps of hair that fell around her face.

I knew this moment would be in my mind as long as I lived.

When I thought of beauty, this image would come to mind.

And the force of that realization hit me hard, because "beauty" was something I always reserved for the ranch in Cottonwood Falls. For the rolling hills dotted with cattle or the way a horse trotted across green pastures.

Not a person.

Definitely not a person I wasn't actually dating.

Realizing I was trailing behind again, I caught up

to Mia, who was being greeted by a host. He led us to a table near the corner of the dining area with a panoramic view. Of course, I knew this was Tallie's doing—it was the most visible spot in the restaurant frequented by all of Dallas's elite.

I pulled the chair out for her and helped her in, trying not to be distracted by her perfume. Then I went to my own seat while the host excused himself and said our server would be by soon.

When he left, I said to Mia, "You were great out there, with the press."

She gave me a stunned look. "Me? You were a natural."

I dipped my head in gratitude. I received praise daily, but not from Mia.

"What do you think you'll have?" she asked me.

I scanned the menu in front of me, trying to decide, until Mia said, "Oh my gosh. Hayden's here."

I looked up just in time to see Hayden French approaching our table with a bronze-skinned brunette on his arm. She wore heels as tall as the skyscraper we dined in. And Hayden? He wore a smile that didn't reach his eyes at all.

"Amelia. Forge."

"It's Mia," I corrected. "And Ford."

Mia nodded. "Good to see you, Hayden. And

Bonnie, I recognize you from the *Sports Illustrated* cover. That swimsuit was stunning on you."

That's where I knew her from. She smiled in response and opened her mouth to reply when Hayden interrupted.

"Did you get my flowers?" he asked Mia.

I looked up at him, not needing my height to stare him down. "She won't be needing any more flowers from you," I cut in.

"Is that so?" he asked, the smile falling from his lips, Bonnie long forgotten.

Something carnal rose within me, and I lifted my chin. "It was a bit awkward to see your flowers on the table next to the ones I got her."

Mia spoke up, "Thank you, though, Hayden. They were lovely." Her tone was the perfect blend of sweet and diplomatic with a hint of finality.

His gaze flicked away from me to Mia. As he opened his mouth to argue, she said, "Bonnie, it was lovely to meet you." A clear dismissal.

Bonnie smiled back. "You, als—"

"Come on," Hayden groused. He snapped his fingers, and two security guards came out of the woodwork, following them to the door. I stared at them in shock. Did that really just happen?

Mia let out a giggle, and there was my answer.

The sound was so light, so unexpected, I had to

laugh along. When the server came and poured her a glass of wine and me a seltzer water, I lifted my glass.

"What are we toasting?" she asked.

"Your epic roast of Hayden French," I replied. "A French roast if you will."

She tossed her head back, laughing. "I didn't roast him! I just... maneuvered well."

She might have played it off like it was no big deal, but I was seriously amazed by her. She could have let the awkward situation drag on, but I loved that she held her own, without even batting an eye. She was a strong woman, something I admired. Then a genuine smile formed on my lips. "And let's toast to our first meal as a couple."

I couldn't be certain, but just before she clinked her glass to mine, I thought I saw her features fall.

17

MIA

A DOZEN conflicting feelings tugged at my chest as we pulled up to my building after the date. Enjoying dinner with Ford had been so easy, like sliding into a warm bath. But then he would say something that reminded me it was all for show, and disappointment would seep through me stronger than a shot of whiskey.

Sitting next to him on the limo ride home was like walking a tightrope in my own mind, trying not to fall for him and trying not to be saddened he wasn't falling for me.

By the time Zeke parked the limo in the parking garage, all my nerves were frayed, and I could have easily slid into bed and slept for the next twenty-four hours. But I had some work to do the next day. With the football game Sunday morning, I needed to research in preparation for meeting with some stakeholders and potential partners in Griffen Industries' suite.

Zeke opened the door for me, and I went to get out, but Ford took my hand. "One second, Zeke," he called. Then he said to me, "Hold on, I have something for you."

I turned to look at him, surprised. "You do?" I hadn't seen anything in the car.

But now that he was reaching toward the corner, I realized there was a black box I hadn't noticed against the black leather seats. He held it in his large hands, then pulled it open, showing a purple and white jersey inside. Upon lifting it out, I realized printed on the back was his name and number.

I held it gingerly in my hands, the slick material soft under my fingertips.

"I had it made for you," he said gently. "I thought you could wear it to the game."

"Oh..." I looked from him to the jersey, my features falling.

"What?" he asked, confused. "I thought it would be good for the press?"

Another pang strummed at my heartstrings. "That's not it. I just can't wear this in the suite when

I'm supposed to be working. I need to be in business professional—even at a game."

"Ah," he said, and if I wasn't mistaken, he looked a little disappointed too.

I made to hand the jersey back to him, but he shook his head. "You keep it. Maybe it would make a good nightgown. I remember my brothers and I used to wear my dad's old jerseys to bed."

The peek at his past made my lips curl up. "Thank you. And good luck on Sunday."

His smile was warm as his blue eyes. "Thank you, Mia."

Something about hearing him say my name made my stomach swoop. So before he could see me react, I tucked the jersey back in the box and stepped out of the car. Giving Zeke a quick thanks and good night, I went to my private elevator. Once the doors opened, I got in and turned to watch the slick black car leaving the garage, taking Ford Madigan with it.

Heaving a sigh, I shucked my heels and waited for the elevator to take me upstairs. The marble floor was cold against my tender feet. The lift whooshed as I was carried to the uppermost floor of my building.

When the doors slid open, I set my shoes by the entrance and went farther into my penthouse, the jersey box still tucked snugly under my arm. The entryway light was on and waiting for me, but I had to turn on the light as I went to the living room, with its cushy beige chairs, the coffee table crafted from driftwood and glass.

Everything had its place, from the art on the wall to the bowl of fruit on the kitchen island. There were hints of my success everywhere, including the floor-to-ceiling view of the city, glittering with lights below. But there was no sign of a relationship outside of my close friend, Farrah, and my parents.

Except for the gift tucked under my arm.

I walked to my bedroom, seeing the perfectly made bed done by my housekeeping service. I tossed the black box on the white covers, then slipped out of my dress. Taking off the strapless bra was such a relief.

The tall windows reflected my naked body. My breasts, which hung so much lower now than twenty years ago when I graduated high school. My apron stomach folded over my hips. It seemed like all of me was sagging, except for my head, still held high.

In the reflection, I watched myself open the box and slip the jersey over my head, the material sliding over my body until the hem rested right below my ass.

I was surprised how sexy I felt, and I had to go to my walk-in closet with its floor-length mirror to get a better look.

Surrounded by all my clothes and shoes, I stared at myself in the mirror, in disbelief of how *cute* I looked.

My entire wardrobe was designed to be professional, stylish, powerful. I had the most expensive designer gowns and suits, but I'd never felt as gorgeous as I did with Ford Madigan's name on my back.

It was a shame I couldn't wear this jersey tomorrow. Or better yet, every single day.

In consolation, I kept it on as I went to the bathroom and washed away the day's makeup and released my hair from its twist. My blond locks fell around my shoulders, and for a moment, I allowed myself to wonder what it would feel like to have Ford here with me. To watch him react to me, naked underneath his jersey.

But then reality sank in. An ex-boyfriend's comments about my schedule here, a complaint about my priorities there. Sometimes I wondered if a relationship could hold two successful people or if one person's ambition was destined to suck up all the air.

Wasn't that the case with my former boss, Gage? He'd fallen in love and stepped down as CEO so he could spend more time with Farrah and her children from a former marriage.

I respected his decision to have a family, but it wasn't mine. I loved my job. I wanted to fall in love too—with someone who understood. Was that too much to ask?

With my mind running wild with fantasies and questions, I slipped under my covers, hit the button to put out all the lights, and slowly fell asleep to the quiet hum of the air conditioner.

I DECIDED to stay in my condo the next day, buckling down without any distractions. I hardly turned my head away from the computer screen until I heard the sound of my front bell. A delivery.

Confused and half-dazed from working so intently, I walked to the front door, rubbing my eyes. I only realized I was still in the jersey when my doorman, a sweet older man in a green and gold suit, gave me a sheepish smile. "For you, Ms. Baird."

I straightened my shoulders, mustering all my dignity. "Thank you."

I took the black box from him, wrapped in a black silk ribbon, thinking it looked an awful lot like the gift Ford had given me. But when I walked to my living room and set the box on the coffee table for examination, I realized there was no telling who it was from without opening the package.

A tug of the ribbon was all it took for the material to fall away, and I lifted the lid. Seeing the contents made my lips spread into a smile.

It was a purple blazer, made to look like Ford's jersey, all the way down to his name and number on the back.

I bit my lip, holding it up, and a piece of white card stock tumbled to the ground. When I picked it up, I instantly recognized the handwriting from the flower delivery.

Like I would let my girlfriend show up to the game without my number on her back.

18

FORD

GAME DAYS WERE all about trusting myself and the work I'd put in all week. So instead of watching more game film or squeezing in additional personal development, I made it a point to clear my mind of all the noise.

For home games like today, my personal mindfulness guide, Bernét, came to the house to lead me through a meditation exercise and then breath work. For games where I wasn't at home, we always video called and did our work digitally.

But being in person was better, with a blend of essential oils diffusing throughout my home gym. But when we finished and a driver came to take me to the stadium, my mind kept straying to Mia and the package I was having delivered.

My tailor had agreed to the last-minute project, and I couldn't wait to see what she thought. If she'd wear it. Checking my phone revealed no new messages from her, so I had to wait.

After several hours of prep in the locker room, the team took the field to warm up. And when I looked at the suite I knew Mia used, I saw her watching from the window... in her new purple blazer.

Damn, did she look good.

Her hand lifted in a wave. And even though I couldn't wave back, not with my coach watching, I sent her a smile.

"Okay, lover boy," my friend Krew said, bumping my shoulder and making our shoulder pads crackle.

I shoved him off, saying, "Get down there. Let's get some passes in."

SEVERAL HOURS LATER, the game was over with another win on our record. As the quarterback, I was one of the first players to be interviewed by the press after a game. I expected to be asked about the massive play we made toward the end when Krew ran sixty yards for a touchdown, but the first question out of the reporter's mouth was, "Any comments on the special outfit Mia Baird, CEO of Griffen Industries, is wearing today?"

My lips formed a lopsided grin. "Thought y'all were supposed to be watching the game."

The reporter laughed, tossing back her short brown hair. "There's a reason news teams bring multiple cameras."

I glanced toward the box, then rubbed my thumb over my bottom lip. "Mia sure looks good in purple, doesn't she?"

Several reporters and dozens of questions later, I'd performed my duties. A few guys from the other team stopped me to say hello and shake hands. Guys I'd known for years—and after the game, we were all friendly. But mostly, I wanted to get up to the boxes.

My family had come to the game—and Tallie had informed me I was supposed to walk Mia out to her car for a potential photo op.

Photographers surrounded me, taking countless pictures as I walked off the field. When I first started as the first-string quarterback, all the attention was unsettling. Now, I was better at accepting this part of my job.

Off the field, I found my family waiting for me outside the locker room. My brothers, sisters-in-law, nieces, nephew, and my dad were all there.

Over the years, the Madigans had grown, and

living close by, I'd been lucky enough to see it, getting to know all my new family members just as well as the ones I'd grown up with.

As soon as I came into their view, my niece Emily came running up first. Taking her in my arms, I asked, "What did you think? Was I better at staying in the pocket? Did I throw enough?"

She nodded, making her curly brown hair bounce. "You did great. Tell Coach Hinkle good job."

I grinned at the praise and gave my brother Knox and her mom, Larkin, a surprised smile. "High praise from this one."

Emily smiled back at me. "You're winning the Super Bowl this year. I can feel it."

That made me even happier. "Thanks, Em."

My preteen niece, Maya, came up next, holding her little sister, Leah, on her hip.

"Fud," Leah said, reaching for me.

I chuckled, picking her up and holding her while tucking Maya under one arm. "Thanks for coming," I told them. I didn't really want kids, but having nieces and a nephew, seeing my brothers become parents, was the joy of my life.

Once the kids were bored of talking to me, my dad came over and clapped my back. Then, my brothers got a turn to say hello.

Fletcher was the oldest, then Knox, Hayes, me, and my youngest brother, Bryce, who was just about to start his senior year in college.

Hayes waved us all closer, kind of like a huddle, so we were the only ones who could hear him. "So the girl," Hayes said with a salacious grin. He bit his lip ring like he was eager for all the details.

Knox rolled his eyes at our brother. "Locker room's that way, in case you haven't noticed."

Hayes looked to our oldest brother, Fletcher. "Back me up."

Fletcher held his hands up in surrender.

Now I was rolling my eyes. "Wimp."

So Fletcher asked, "When do we get to meet her?"

I shifted uncomfortably because I didn't like lying to my family. After all we'd been through, you learned just how important these relationships were. But I couldn't risk word getting out either—there were eyes and ears everywhere in this place. "Maybe later," I finally said. "I better get upstairs to see her. See y'all at my place?"

They said they would be there—everyone was going to stay the night, and I couldn't wait to have us all under one roof except for Bryce. It was hard for him to break away with his school schedule.

I went toward the suite, but my dad caught up to me. "Hey, let me tag along."

A pit grew in my stomach. "You don't have to—" I began.

But he shook his head. "She's your first girlfriend since college. I have to give her the official Madigan welcome."

I gritted my teeth into an echo of a smile. "Great."

We walked together down the thinning hallway, and even though Dad wore his Diamonds shirt, he paired it with blue jeans and cowboy boots like he always did. Sometimes, like now, I missed Mom more, feeling her absence just because of his presence.

But I didn't have room to dwell on it because Dad said, "Gage introduced you two?"

I nodded.

Dad's smile crinkled his face. "Seems like yesterday y'all were playing together in the creek. Hard to believe you're all grown with jobs of your own now."

It was true. Time really did fly. Unless you were bringing your dad to meet your fake girlfriend and hoping the person who knew you best in the whole world wouldn't call you out on the charade.

We reached the executive box—the most expensive one the Diamonds offered. And for some strange reason, my heart rate ramped up. Had to be nerves because Dad was here. This was a mistake—introducing him to my fake girlfriend.

I was about to tell him I'd forgotten something in the locker room, backpedal faster than I even did in the game, when Tallie came out and said, "Ford, there you are!"

19

MIA

FORD and an older man just a couple inches shorter than him walked into the suite. Immediately, I spotted the resemblance between them—broad shoulders, high cheekbones, noses like Roman statues, and blue eyes that welcomed you in like the scent of an apple pie wafting out a window in springtime.

Except instead of a football uniform, the older man wore broken-in denim and boots with a purple Diamonds T-shirt.

I smiled at both of the men as Tallie led them into the suite.

My gaze connected with Ford's, and his tense expression spoke volumes. This man mattered to him.

When Tallie brought them close enough, Ford said, "Mia, this is my dad, Grayson Madigan."

I smiled, extending my hand to him. "It's so nice to meet you, Mr. Madigan."

His hand was worn and calloused as it firmly grasped mine. "You too, Mia. You can call me Gray."

I dipped my head in understanding. "What did you think of the game?"

Pride brightened all of Gray's features, making him look at least ten years younger. "Oh, it was great. Don't think I'll ever get used to seeing my little boy as a football star."

Color tinged Ford's cheeks. "Dad."

I had to chuckle at how cute he was when he was embarrassed.

Gray shook his head at his son. "What? It's true."

Ford gave his dad an exasperated smile, but you could still see in his eyes how much he admired the man. Before I could respond, Tallie stepped in, saying, "Mia, the car is ready."

"Great," I replied as Ford said, "We'll walk you down."

The three of us headed toward the elevators as I asked Gray, "What do you do for work?"

Gray removed his Diamonds ballcap, scratching the back of his head. "I run our family ranch. We have a couple hundred head of cattle. And a few horses."

"And one old dog," Ford added.

I smiled. "Bet it's peaceful out there."

Gray nodded. "Most of the time—'til all the grandchildren come around."

Ford chuckled knowingly. I wondered what it must be like, to have a big family like that. I'd never know, growing up as an only child without close family on either side.

The elevator doors slid open, and we all stepped in. "How many grandchildren do you have?" I asked.

Gray lit up, just like when he spoke about Ford. "Four with one on the way."

"How exciting," I replied.

He nodded. "My wife and I had five kids, and I always loved having little ones around. Made life interesting, for sure."

The elevator dinged as we reached the ground floor and began getting out. "So tell me," I said. "Was Ford always so determined to get his way?"

Gray tossed his head back and laughed. "You do know him pretty well, then."

I smiled at that and noticed Ford shaking his head as he suppressed a smile. The conversation was fun and easy, and my heart fell a little at the realization that Gray and I might not get much more time together. He was so down to earth, unlike a lot of the people I spent my time with these days.

Gray drew me out of my thoughts, saying, "What did *you* think of the game, Mia?"

"Oh..." No one really asked me about sports. Maybe it was because I was a woman or maybe because I was so busy networking during the games I didn't get much of a chance to actually watch anymore. I wracked my mind for anything to say other than Ford looked really good in football pants. I settled on, "I'm glad the team got a win. Do you think you'll make the Super Bowl again, Ford?"

Ford answered, "That's the goal." There wasn't a hint of doubt in his voice.

We reached the doors to the gated parking area where the players and famous attendees kept their vehicles. Instead of a limo, a black town car was waiting for me.

Several paparazzi lined the barricade, snapping photos of the three of us. Gray shied back, clearly uncomfortable with the attention.

One reporter extended their microphone at us, hoping to catch a soundbite. "Are you two officially together?"

Ford and I exchanged a look, and then Ford faced the camera with a smile that looked real. "That's right. I got lucky with her."

I smiled up at Ford and then nodded at the paparazzi. Zeke was already waiting with the door open so I could climb in without being hounded even more. I said a quick goodbye to Gray and then to Ford, but he caught my hand before I could leave.

"Hey," he said low enough for only me to hear.

I looked up at him. "Yeah?"

His expression softened as his gaze raked over me. "You look good in that blazer."

My smile came easily, and I replied, "Thank you. It was a gift from my stubborn boyfriend." And then I got into the car and let my driver whisk me away.

A smile was still on my face when I got out my phone to check it. A message from my best friend was waiting for me.

Farrah: Just saw you on the news! Looks like things went well with Ford – although I'm upset I had to learn it this way!!

I cringed at the fact that I hadn't even followed up with Farrah to tell her about this whole mess. Life had gotten away from me since then, and I needed to tip the priority scales back toward friendship.

Mia: Can I come over?
Farrah: Of course.

I leaned forward, asking Zeke to change course. Within half an hour, I was in the subdivision where my best friend lived with my former boss and three of their four children. The oldest, Levi, was already in college, making a splash on the baseball team.

When I got out, I smiled at their home with the bright yellow door and the perfectly manicured grass. The lawn hadn't looked as amazing when Farrah first moved in, but of course, Gage had to spend his billions somewhere if they weren't going to raise their kids in a mega mansion on the beach.

It didn't take too many steps in my purple heels to reach the front door. I pressed the doorbell and heard Andrew's changing voice call, "Come in!"

I shook my head, still amazed at how quickly time flew. I swore he was a little boy just yesterday, and now he was in high school, with a crackling voice, pimples, and the hint of a mustache.

I twisted the knob, letting myself inside. Unlike my minimalistic condo, their home was full—of love, of life, of people.

Andrew was playing some kind of racing video game in the living room while Cora sat at the table, carefully painting her nails a shimmering shade of orange. Gage was cooking something in the kitchen in a T-shirt and shorts. Photos of their life together lined the walls, along with Andrew's artwork, progressing from his younger years to more recent works that could have been on display in any art museum.

Andrew said a quick hello, followed by Cora saying, "Hey, Mia." And then Gage grinned at me from the kitchen. "There's my favorite CEO."

"I'm so glad to see you all!" Then I walked toward the kitchen to chat with Gage. Before he was my best friend's husband, he was my demanding, uptight boss. "It's crazy to see you not in a suit."

"Crazy to see you in a Ford Madigan blazer," he retorted.

My cheeks blushed at the reminder of Ford's gift. I'd almost forgotten I was wearing it with how comfortable it was.

"I still can't believe he's breaking his no dating rule," Gage said. "He hasn't had a girlfriend since college."

Something about that fact made me smile. At least I didn't have to share Ford with anyone else. I went to sit at the kitchen island while he worked on chopping vegetables—it was nice to see this side of him. He had all the money in the world, but he found comfort, happiness in this. Otherwise he wouldn't be doing it.

"Where's your wife?" I asked. "And Tara?"

"Finishing up a bath. Shouldn't be too long," he

said, going to the fridge and getting me a beer, cracking off the top. "How's the company treating you?"

I took a sip of the tangy liquid. "Thomas is a shithead," I said, to which he gave an understanding snort. "I'm worried he's going to force a vote of no confidence the second he gets a chance."

Gage's jaw tightened. "That piece of shit. Do you want me to——"

"You can't do anything," I said. "The last thing we want is the polarization of people picking sides. Nothing brings people together like a common enemy. Right now, all he has is their ears. I don't want him to have their loyalty too."

Gage gave me an approving look.

"What?" I asked.

He shrugged. "Just chose the right person for CEO is all."

I smiled, a sense of relief sweeping over me. Deep down, I knew I was doing a good job, but it sure helped to hear it from someone I trusted and respected. I had my mouth open to thank him when a little ball of energy with wet, brown ringlets rushed up to me. "AUNTIE MIA!"

"Tara," I said happily, picking up the two-year-old and holding her in front of me. "You are so big!"

She smiled at me, big blue eyes squinting. "I took a shower!"

I hugged her to my chest. "You smell like strawberries!"

Farrah huffed as she sat beside me at the island, half her shirt soaked. "So do I."

I gasped playfully at Tara. "Did you splash your mommy?"

Tara laughed so gleefully it made me giggle too. Then she squirmed out of my arms, toddling over to Drew in the living room and sitting on his back. Farrah shook her head at them and said, "Come to the bedroom with me so I can change?"

I nodded, then lifted my beer to Gage and followed her back to the room.

While she changed out of her wet clothes into pajamas, she said, "Spill! I need someone to talk to me about something other than Troll dolls, Sephora, or the difference between oil and acrylic paints."

Laughing, I leaned against the wall by her dresser and said, "Can do." But when I opened my mouth to tell her what was going on... I couldn't make the truth come out.

Because honestly? I was embarrassed.

I made my living off being capable. I was either the smartest person in the room or able to hire people who solved the problems I couldn't. But when it came to Ford, my instincts had been so wrong before that first date.

So, I did something I never did... I lied to my best friend.

"It's still really new with him," I said.

She smiled at me and climbed into her perfectly made bed, patting the place next to her. We sat back on the pillows like we did when we were teenagers listening to the latest CD that came out. "So what's with the jacket?" she asked.

I laughed, taking it off so I could show her. "He gave me a jersey, but I said I couldn't wear it because I had to dress business professional. And then this showed up at my place the next day."

She grinned, taking the stylish Dallas Diamonds blazer from me to study the design. "I love it... So it's going well?"

I bit my bottom lip and nodded.

For the next half hour or so, I told my best friend every moment I'd shared with Ford, how easy it was to talk to him. How he had flowers delivered to my office. How he started calling me *Sunflower*.

And while we talked, I let myself pretend it was real.

20

FORD

AFTER THE GAME, my family came over to spend the night.

I loved having them in my home. In fact, they were a big reason I'd purchased such a large house. I wanted them to feel comfortable at my place so I could see them more often.

Even though my brothers were all so different, we were like the pieces of a puzzle. Interesting on our own, but more complete when we were together.

Fletcher was the smart, serious one in our family, now a successful doctor running a medical practice in Cottonwood Falls. Hayes had his own body shop and was the rebel of the group, with enough ink to fill a printer, piercings all over (even in places I didn't want to think about), and had a revolving door of women

to keep him company. Knox worked as a police officer, but he was also the mischievous one of all of us,
always bringing the fun. And then my baby brother,
Bryce, was the quiet, thoughtful one of the group,
adding only words that really mattered. Together, we
just... worked.

Tonight, the kids, my dad, and the wives were
splashing around in the pool while four of us five
brothers sat around my firepit. They drank beers and
made fun of me for my choice seltzer water. Proof
that no matter how famous I got, they were sure to
keep me humble.

"So," Fletcher said. "What's the deal with Mia,
really? I thought you weren't dating 'til you had a
ring." He chuckled at his own joke. "Get it?"

"Stupid," Knox laughed.

Hayes rolled his eyes, biting back a smile. And I
shook my head at the lot of them. I didn't want to
talk about this. Not with my brothers. "That was my
plan, but plans change." I shrugged and took a drink
of my seltzer.

Fletcher eyed me suspiciously.

Hayes leaned forward, resting his elbows on his
knees. The fire caught his lip ring, making the silver
look gold. "I could see why you broke your rule for
her."

All eyes were on him.

"What?" he said. Then he nudged my leg with his boot. "Come on, you know she's hot."

Jealousy flared up in my chest, so strong and unexpected, I couldn't find the words. "Excuse me?"

"What?" Hayes taunted. "You saw her ass in that pencil skirt. Everyone did on the jumbotron."

My vision was going red when Fletcher gave a pointed look at our brother Knox. "Don't murder him, Ford. There's an off-duty cop around."

"Oh, shut it," I said, flipping off Fletcher.

My brothers all chuckled at that, but my laugh came out as harsh and forced as it felt.

They were all watching me like they knew I was still seething.

"Shit," Hayes said. "Sorry, I didn't realize it was that serious with her yet."

"It's not," I said.

They all gave me dubious looks.

"It's not," I repeated. But they were still disbelieving, so I got up and walked to the pool, shrugging off my shirt. The kids were more fun anyway—even if I could feel my brothers' skeptical gazes on my back.

THE WEEK FLEW by until my next public appearance with Mia. There were practices and meetings and press interviews, and then finally, there was the gala benefiting my charity, Ford's Friends. For the last several years, I had gone by myself, but tonight, Mia was my guest.

I'd never been more nervous.

After my brothers caught on to my feelings the weekend before, I was more determined than ever to stifle whatever attraction I had for her. This was a business deal, plain and simple.

Because even if Mia was sexy, you know what else was sexy?

A championship ring.

A renewed contract close to my family with plenty of money to support my charity.

Achieving my goals before life was ripped away from me, like it had been for my mom.

Whatever infatuation I had with Mia wasn't worth losing all that, even if I did have a chance with her. Which was doubtful. She was a successful older woman. And me? I was on the verge of losing my contract.

With my priorities back in check, I put on my suit and tie, visualizing the evening before me. I was determined to keep my focus on the charity, on what the funds raised could do for grieving kids in Texas. I imagined what it would be like if no one ever had to go without grief counseling, if no widowed parents had to sacrifice financially to support their child's mental health.

That thought drove me as I finished getting ready and then went to the car waiting for me out front. Usually, I didn't mind driving myself places, but with Mia and me set to arrive together, it made sense for me to use her car service.

I got in and chatted with her driver, Zeke, until we arrived at the massive condo building Mia called home. It wasn't too long before she stepped out of the elevator, and my mouth went slack.

She looked more stunning than I'd ever seen her, adorned in a shimmering silver dress that cut across her cleavage with off-the-shoulder sleeves and a slit that showed her luscious thigh as she walked toward me. Her blond hair was pulled back, showing diamond earrings dripping from her ears.

I forced myself to swallow as she approached. "Wow, Mia... You look incredible."

She smiled, doing a spin for me. I loved how she did that. Instead of shying away from my compliments, she embraced them, giving me even more of her to enjoy. When her spin ended, she faced me, a free tendril of hair fallen across her forehead.

I reached out to brush it back, stunned by how soft her skin felt beneath my fingertips. How my heart fell when I had to pull my hand aside.

"Shall we?" she asked, gesturing toward the limo.

I nodded and held the door open for her. I didn't trust myself to speak. Especially not when I watched her get into the car, catching a clear view of her bare shoulders, the baby hairs trailing down her neck. It was unexpectedly alluring.

Championship ring. I reminded myself.

Contract.

Charity.

I followed her into the car and shut the door to see her reaching for the refrigerator toward the front. She pulled out a bottle of champagne and two glasses. "Let's celebrate your charity tonight," she said with a warm smile. My eyes hungrily trailed the path of her dark red lips.

She set the glasses aside and tugged at the cork.

It popped, and her lips formed a surprised O that was incredibly cute and impossibly sexy at the same time.

I was *fucked.*

This was going to be a long night, convincing myself I couldn't have what was right in front of me.

21

MIA

I COULDN'T GET over Ford Madigan in a suit.

Something about broad shoulders, a fit body, and perfect tailoring of the navy-blue fabric had me practically salivating. I needed the chilled champagne just to cool myself down.

But even better than his looks was watching him interact with donors at the gala. He always introduced me first, putting his hand on my lower back and making sure I wasn't an afterthought in the conversation but an active participant.

I'd never been with a man, romantic or otherwise, who was so willing to share the spotlight with me, even when he fully deserved for it to be shining on him.

And not only was Ford kind to me—he treated everyone we spoke to with equal respect, whether it was a caterer passing out hors d'oeuvres or one of his major donors. I'd wondered if he'd been trained by Tallie herself, but I was starting to discover... this was just Ford. The only place he was acting was in our relationship.

"Ford, Mia," someone said behind us. I recognized the voice instantly and turned to greet Ford's dad, Gray, with a genuine smile on my face. There was a pretty, older woman on his arm in a simple black gown matching Gray's black suit.

"Gray," I said, accepting his offer for a quick hug. Then he smiled at the woman next to him. "This is my friend, Aggie."

She smiled at me, her eyes crinkling warmly in the corners. "Nice to meet you, Mia. I'm a big fan of your work."

My lips parted. "Is that so?"

She nodded. "My cousin lives in the town where GI bought the tire plants, and it's been great for their family. She said the raise last year made a big difference for them."

Warmth spread through my chest, and I almost got choked up. *This* was why I did what I did. Not to get approval from board members who never stepped foot outside the city—but to make a difference in the lives of real people. Like the ones the Andersen sisters served.

"Thank you for saying that, Aggie," I finally replied. "You made my whole night."

Ford squeezed my side supportively, and I smiled up at him to see his genuine look of admiration.

"You all must be so proud of Ford too," I commented. "What he's created from scratch is simply amazing."

Gray's eyes shined as he nodded. "I didn't have much money after we lost Maya. I wish..." His voice broke.

Ford let go of me for a moment to hug his dad. "I know," he said gently.

Aggie and I exchanged a knowing look before the pair broke apart. Gray wiped at his eyes and said, "I'm proud of you, son. We'll let you mingle." He held his arm out for Aggie, and she easily slipped her arm through his.

As they walked away, Ford and I watched. "What's the deal with them?" I asked him. They acted more familiar than just friends.

He leaned close to me, like he was sharing a secret. "Dad goes to the same diner every day for lunch, where she works. They've been 'just friends' for years now. I think he's afraid to start over after Mom. And she's so much younger than him..."

"You're younger than me," I commented with a smile. "No one seems to mind."

"How much younger—" He broke off his line of questioning. "Wait, I know better."

I laughed, loving his old-school manners. My parents would definitely approve of him—if this were real. "I looked you up online. I'm just over ten years older than you."

He gave me a devious smile. "Cougar."

I had to toss my head back and laugh at that. "I suppose I am."

He grinned in response before yet another donor came to chat with him.

Although I would have been comfortable to mingle on my own—as I'd done for hundreds of work events over the years—the only time Ford left my side was when he had to address his guests.

I sat at a table with his dad and Aggie, sipping a glass of sweet white wine while he approached the microphone.

There wasn't a hint of shake to his voice as he began speaking. "Everyone, thank you so much for coming to the third annual Ford's Friends gala..." He shared some stats about the charity and who they'd been able to serve so far and then his lofty goals for the future of the organization. It was wild to think he'd have dedicated therapists in every county of Texas within a few years, but deep down I knew he could do it. "Thank you all for coming and for your dedication to helping children," he continued. "Speaking from experience, a good grief counselor can make a world of difference and change the course of someone's life when they need it most."

I pictured Ford as a young child, losing his mom and feeling lost. Gray, who sat on the other side of Aggie, would have been twenty years younger when it all happened—left alone with five young boys to raise on his own. My heart went out to them.

Aggie covered Gray's hand with hers on the table.

I was glad they had each other.

Ford concluded his speech by saying that he was personally matching all donations made that evening and stepped off the stage. The program manager spoke next, sharing more stories of children and families who the charity had helped, followed by one of the grief counselors who shared how much she enjoyed working with Ford and the families in need. More people were crying than had dry eyes by the end of it.

And when the night was over, I saw Ford in an entirely different light. He wasn't just a football player; he was a humanitarian.

And for the first time in a long time, I felt inferior in the company of a man.

I knew Griffen Industries was doing good work in the world of business, but Ford had inspired me. I wanted to do more as Mia Baird, not just as a CEO.

The gala wound down around ten, and Ford took me aside as the caterers began cleaning up. "I know it's getting late—you don't have to stick around if you don't want to. I just want to stay and make sure they don't need anything."

Again, he was surprising me. Most people wouldn't bother—would let their team handle it. I shook my head. "I'm happy to stay here with you."

"In that case..." He went to a tray setting on a table and retrieved a couple extra glasses of champagne, handing one to me.

I raised my eyebrows. "You're drinking."

"Just one—to celebrate the night."

"You raised a lot of money," I commented.

"And spent the evening with a hell of a woman," he added, holding out his glass for a toast.

My cheeks warmed as I clinked my glass to his, then took a sip of the fizzy liquid. "I'm impressed by you, Ford Madigan."

He raised his eyebrows. "Really? That means a lot coming from you. You're so successful, Mia."

I had to smile as I shook my head. "You're too modest, Ford. You saw this problem in the world, and when most people are enjoying their fame and fortune, you're working hard to help other people. Not just tossing money at it and looking the other way."

He took a sip and gazed out over the emptying tables. "What would you do, if you could?"

I studied him. No one had ever asked me what I could do to give back. Sure, people wanted to know what I could do to make them more money or position the company in a better light. Not anything like this. "I'd help other women like me," I answered instantly.

"So, beautiful and successful?" he teased.

I laughed at that, trying not to pay too much attention to the compliment. "There aren't many women at the top of companies like Griffen Industries. Especially not plus-sized women. Even less women of color. I'd coach them—the ones who are really hungry for it—and show them that it is possible to be this size and do a damn good job."

He pinned me under his thoughtful blue gaze and said, "So why don't you?"

I didn't have an answer. "I'm not sure."

We were quiet for a beat before I plucked up the courage to ask him a question that had been bothering me for weeks. "If you don't mind me asking, why are you so against dating?"

His shoulders stiffened a bit as he set down his drink. "I want to win the Super Bowl."

"I don't know much about football," I countered, "but I do know the last quarterback to win the Super Bowl has a wife and two kids. And he's just a year older than you."

Ford lowered his eyes, waiting while the cleanup crew pulled the trays from the table where we sat. Then he looked up at me, his gaze tortured. "My mom wasn't all that much older than me when she passed."

I nodded slowly, taking in his statement. "You're afraid to die."

He pressed his lips together, shook his head. "I'm afraid to die without doing all I could while I lived."

The words were powerful, hanging in the air for a moment. But I still didn't fully understand. Couldn't he have it all? "Wouldn't you be missing out on love, romance? For so many people, that's the meaning of life."

"You've dated before," he said.

I nodded.

"How many times were you asked to play small,

take a back seat so the relationship could be front and center?"

I pressed my lips together. Far too often. He read my answer in my expression.

"Any old fool can fall in love. Not everyone can change the world."

22

FORD

THE NEXT MORNING when I checked my phone, I saw a text message from Mia. It was a logo with the word RISE.

Mia: For my charity.

I grinned at the graphic. It was like her—bold, bright, impactful.

Ford: I love it.
Mia: Thanks for the extra push.
Ford: Any time.

I clicked my phone off and left my room, going

out to the kitchen for breakfast. My chef was already working on it and said, "Just a few minutes, Ford."

"Thanks," I replied, heading to the coffeemaker and grabbing a cup. I always allowed myself one in the morning. Something about the smell of freshly brewed coffee was irreplaceable. I think because it reminded me of quiet mornings on the farm, slowly waking up to hear my parents talking softly over a cup of coffee.

As I sat at the table drinking coffee by myself, I looked at my phone, realizing I wanted to text her more.

Continuing the conversation would be purely indulgent for me. So I set my phone aside and tried —failed—to get her out of my mind.

Over the next week, I felt a sense of restlessness like never before. I was doing everything required of me, going to work, training, going to (and winning) my out-of-town game, but it still felt like something was missing.

I didn't want to admit to myself that it was Mia. Mia was missing.

Although I couldn't deny it when Tallie messaged me and relief immediately washed over me.

Tallie: Mia had a lunch fall through today. It would be a

great chance for you to bring lunch into the office and talk her up. Are you free?

I had to make myself wait thirty seconds before texting her back and saying I was. Wouldn't want it getting back to Mia how desperate I was to see her.

Tallie: Great. I'm going to need you to pick something up, and you're going to accidentally go to the wrong floor. You'll go to floor thirty-five instead of thirty-six and walk until you find the glass office in the corner. That's where Thomas works. Talk with his secretary, see if there's anyone else there you can chat with. They might ask you to sign autographs. If they do—sign them. Be your likable self and slip in positive comments about Mia. Think you can handle that?
Ford: Easily.

Instead of going to a restaurant, I had my chef prepare something so that I could bring a home-cooked meal to Mia. I was sure she dined out all the time with her work schedule, and if she was anything like me, I missed eating at home when I'd been out for a while.

I shouldn't have been as nervous as I was getting dressed and ready to go to meet her in her office. I shouldn't have been nervous as I went to the florist and picked up a bouquet of sunflowers and lavender.

But I was. Even as I got into the elevator and pressed the button for the thirty-fifth floor.

As soon as the elevator doors opened though, I knew my play. I knew my purpose, and I was willing to fulfill the role. Especially after she had done so well for me at the Ford's Friends gala.

The thirty-fifth floor in the Griffin Industries tower looked similar to the thirty-sixth floor. But instead of being taken up by Mia's office and a conference room, there was a lot more going on here.

A receptionist sat in front of a desk right where the elevators opened. As soon as she saw me, she said, "May I help you?"

"I'm bringing a friend lunch," I said like Tallie instructed. "Thomas Weatherford."

"Need me to show you where to go?" she asked.

I shook my head. "I've got it."

I started walking back in the similar direction as Mia's office, like Tallie had told me to, and I realized that this floor had way more people on it. There were offices along the walls, and even a bank of people working at half cubicles.

At first, no one noticed me, but then the murmurs started.

A guy wearing a suit came up to me and said, "Ford Madigan?"

I nodded.

The guy said, "Are you here to see Miss Baird?"

I offered him an easy smile and said, "Yeah, I am. Her office is that way, right?"

The murmurs were going around us, and I could see people looking up from their desks, talking, whispering to each other. Tallie was a genius.

The guy talking to me said, "I can take you up there... for an autograph," he joked.

I laughed, setting my bag of food and the flowers down on a table. "I'm happy to sign an autograph for you." I raised my voice a little bit. "And anyone else who might want something signed."

The guy seemed gobsmacked and eager at the same time. "Really? Are you sure?"

"Of course. Mia tells me all the time how amazing you guys are and how hard you work. It's the least I can do for you giving her such great support."

I could see his chest puff up with pride. People always loved when others said *good* things about them behind their back.

He said, "I actually have a Diamonds football on my desk. I'll go get it."

Someone else was already walking up to me with

a legal pad and a Sharpie. "My son loves you," she said, grinning. "He's not going to believe this."

For the next half hour or so, I took selfies and signed legal pads, a football, a poster, and even a blazer.

That is until a stern voice said, "What's going on here? My receptionist said you wanted to see me?"

I turned to see a guy that I knew of but had never officially met. *Thomas.* I offered him a grin, saying, "Sorry, I must have misspoken. I was actually heading to Mia's office and hit the wrong floor."

He layered a smile on his lips that didn't quite meet his eyes. "Sorry, Mr. Madigan, but we're on a tight deadline here. I'm sure you understand."

A few people in line to get my autograph frowned and sagged. "Of course," I said to Thomas. "I shouldn't have assumed... Mia is always happy to let me interact with her direct staff no matter how busy."

Another dig at Thomas.

He was about to answer when I saw a familiar face walking into the room in leather loafers.

"Ford, there you are," Vanover said. "Mia has been waiting on you."

I gave him an apologetic look and said, "Sorry, I got caught up." I looked to the people who were still waiting to get something signed. "Next time I'm in the office, I'll ask Mia if she can send out an email so we can all chat," I promised.

They seemed to perk up at that, and I swore I saw Thomas's jaw muscles flex angrily.

"Come now," Vanover said, waving his hand at me. His expression was calm and collected, but I suppressed my smile until we got into the elevator to go to the next floor.

Vanover leaned over and whispered, "How did it go?"

"Perfectly," I said. I couldn't wait to tell Mia.

23

MIA

THE NEXT TWO weeks were going to be slammed with work travel out of town, so I asked my best friend and both of our moms to meet me for lunch. The four of us tried to go out at least once every couple of months to catch up.

Today, we were eating at the café with an exclusive membership, and I swore Farrah's mom kept glancing around, shocked at all the stars she recognized. It was fun to see how giddy she got about it.

My mom, on the other hand, could care less about fame and fortune. She said anyone who walked the red carpet had once worn a dirty diaper that needed to be changed. Maybe that was part of where my confidence came from—truly believing that all people were equals.

As we were waiting for our food to be delivered, Farrah said to me, "Are you expecting a call from someone? You keep checking your phone."

Slightly embarrassed, I tucked it back into my purse. "Sorry, this is girl time."

Never mind that I wasn't expecting to hear from anyone—just *hoping* to hear from Ford.

After he dropped by the office yesterday, I'd gotten several emails from my employees thanking me for giving him the time to chat with them when he should have been eating with me.

It had been a really successful drop in. I wanted to message him and tell him thank you and how much it meant to me, but we'd gone by a silent-but-understood rule that we weren't the kind of fake relationship couple who texted each other regularly. In fact, there were only a handful of messages between us.

But I could already feel myself starting to miss him. Especially since I knew I'd be going out of town soon and it would be a couple weeks before we could see each other again.

As if she could read my thoughts, my mom said, "Tell us how things are going with Ford."

Heat found my cheeks because no one close to me knew that the relationship was fake. But I couldn't bear breaking the news to them, especially when I didn't want to believe it myself. "He just brought me lunch to the office yesterday. It was nice."

Farrah smiled. "Any activities on your desk?"

I gasped at my friend. "My mom is here!"

Farrah chuckled, and her mom, who looked just like the older version of Farrah, said, "What? We're all adults here."

"True," my mom said, "and he is such an upgrade from your last boyfriend. I'm so glad you're with someone who makes you smile so big."

My heart stung at the mention of my ex. And how happy I was in my relationship with Ford.

"I saw Christian the other day," Farrah's mom commented.

All of us were staring at her now. "You did?" I said. I was way too interested.

Her mom nodded. "He acted like he didn't recognize me, and I was fine not talking to him. He was with another woman. There was a child with them, but I didn't know if it was his or not."

My chest twinged painfully. He was living the life that he wanted.

But so am I, I reminded myself. In fact, on the outside looking in, I had it all. A great job, a beautiful home, incredible friends, and a killer wardrobe... I just wanted love to be part of the equation too.

Farrah said, "*Please* tell me he's going bald."

My mom and I laughed, but Farrah's mom unfortunately shook her head. "Maybe one day."

Before the conversation could continue down that route, a server brought our food, and we dug in.

A few bites in, Farrah's mom asked me, "Anything new going on at work?"

I set down my BLT, actually feeling a rush of excitement through my chest. "I am starting a mentorship program for plus-sized women in business."

Farrah said, "Seriously? That's great."

My mom tilted her head, asking, "Why plus-sized women specifically?"

I frowned, knowing that this was just one of the areas where we couldn't connect. She had been thin her whole life and wouldn't know all of the struggles plus-sized women went through, even if she raised me. But I knew she supported me deep down, and the question didn't come from a bad place. "I don't know if you know the stats, Mom, but plus-sized people, on average, get paid less than their counterparts, even working in the same job. And that's if they get in the door. They're less likely to get called back for an interview, and imagine running a business with that kind of bias existing. Not a lot of women who look like me make it to the top. Especially in male-dominated fields."

Mom seemed genuinely stunned at that information. "Wouldn't that be discrimination?"

I shook my head. "Size isn't exactly a protected class. And a lot of people misunderstand plus-sized women. They think we're just unmotivated, lazy." I saw Farrah tilting her gaze down. Her ex-husband had done a number on her, calling her fat, lazy, saying that no one would ever want her. "It couldn't be further from the truth," I finished.

My mom nodded thoughtfully. "Well, I'm glad you're making a difference. What do you think mentorship will do?"

I smiled, glad she always had my back. "I think one of the best things we can do for women is to show them what's possible," I said. "And now that I've made it here, I'm ready to give them a hand up."

Farrah set her fork down and said, "I totally agree. I know it might not have been the case every time, but when I was applying for all those jobs right after the divorce and I kept getting rejected, part of me was wondering if some of those employers were judging me because of my size. I was lucky that I had you, Mia, to help talk me up and help me get my foot in the door at Griffin Industries. You changed my life." Her voice broke on the last sentence.

My eyes stung with emotion, and I understood Ford in a whole new way.

He got to experience this feeling all the time with Ford's Friends, to see the impact he was making. That meant prioritizing his work so a relationship didn't detract from moments like this.

But as I ate lunch with my friend and our moms, I had to wonder... couldn't we have both?

24

FORD

FOR THE NEXT COUPLE WEEKS, Mia was too busy with meetings and work travel to talk. I missed her, a feeling I usually didn't have for people outside of close friends and family.

I convinced myself that had to be it—we'd developed more of a friendship in the time we'd spent together. So I let myself be excited to see her when she got back from her trip. The team dinner was tonight, and that meant she was coming with me. Trent would be there, watching our every move so he'd know it was real.

I waited eagerly in front of my house for Mia's driver to collect me. It was one of those fresh fall days that breathed life into the world and made crispening leaves rustle in the trees. My heart beat quickly, knowing I'd be able to see her soon. I wanted to know all about her trip.

I watched leaves rustling until the long black limo cut through the tree-lined driveway toward my house. Dress for team dinners was business casual, so I was in a Diamonds polo and khakis. The breeze caught the athletic material of my shirt as I went down the steps to meet the car. The driver got out on his side, but I reminded him, "Zeke, you don't need to bother for me. Mia, though—"

"Precious cargo," he said with a warm smile.

"Exactly." I reached for the back door of the limo and got inside.

I'd expected to be alone, so I nearly jumped out of my skin seeing Tallie sitting there.

She examined me casually. "I should have warned you I'd be here."

"You think?" I muttered, settling in across from her. I swear she never got rattled. "What's going on?"

"I'm going to prep you during our drive to Mia's. She mentioned this night was very important to you, so a refresher of the talking points is never a bad idea."

"That's... thoughtful," I said. In fact, it was exactly Mia's brand of thoughtfulness to bring in an expert when I needed it most. I was touched.

Until Tallie countered, "It's not thoughtful. It's *smart*. Mia didn't get to where she is without looking ahead." The respect she held for Mia was clear in her tone. But so was the death of any thought that Tallie's presence had been special for me.

"Let's get to it, lover boy," Tallie said. She pulled out a manila folder with talking points and had me read over them by myself. The level of detail that went into this plan was like none other—she even included phrases for me to say to teammates, their plus ones, Trent, and Mia for when people could overhear us.

"Where did you learn to do this?" I asked Tallie, holding up the sheet. Even the team's publicist wasn't this thorough.

"No time to talk about that. Let's practice the lines."

"Sure." I could respect her focus. We got to work, and I found it was easy to say the phrases meant for friends, but when I got to the part directed to Mia, I had a hard time. My hands were sweating on the page, making it flimsy.

Tallie said, "Practice the look. The one that says you think she's beautiful and you aren't noticing anyone else in the room."

I attempted it on Tallie.

She frowned.

"What?" I asked defensively.

"You look like you just took too many laxatives."

I buried my face in the folder, groaning.

"What's going on?" Tallie said. "You were doing great before."

"It's weird doing this part with you instead of Mia," I admitted.

Tallie let out a small sigh and looked at her watch. "Well, we should be at her place soon." She leaned back against the leather, distractedly raking her fingers through her short hair.

Within a few minutes, we were in the parking garage. I hurried out of the limo to hold the door for Mia. My dad had taught me to always hold the door open for a woman.

The elevator doors opened, revealing Mia in a purple blouse with white linen trousers and dark brown loafers. Seeing her in Diamonds colors made me smile. "Gorgeous," I told her.

Her long blond hair flared around her as she did a spin for me. I couldn't help but grin as I took her in.

"Just like that," Tallie said, poking her head out the door. "That's how you look at her at the event."

I turned to her. "What?"

"That look was on the sheet—you got it perfect."

"Right." I cleared my throat. "Uh, thanks." I needed to get my head in the game and stepped aside so Mia could get in. As soon as we were in the car together, I wanted to ask her about the trip—about all she'd done while we were apart, but Mia got right to business.

"So Tallie prepped you?" Mia asked when Zeke had started driving away.

Before I could answer, Tallie said, "Everything except his lines for you. Ford, let's try the first one on the list." Tallie passed Mia a paper while I looked down at my own.

"I'm so lucky to have you." Say it while squeezing her hand and looking into her eyes.

I looked up at Tallie desperately. Was I really supposed to do this? It felt so... intimate.

But she leveled her gaze at me like this was all business. Which embarrassed me, because my heart kept forgetting that was all this was meant to be.

"Okay." I took a breath, scooting closer to Mia. I held out my hand, and she put hers in mine. I looked into her soft blue eyes and said, "I'm so lucky to have you." But my eyes darted away. It felt too intimate, too vulnerable to say to her out loud. Especially with Tallie watching.

Tallie tsked at me. "That was not very convincing, Ford. You look like you were trying to swallow a lemon. Like a whole wedge."

A hurt look flickered over Mia's features, but she quickly schooled it. I realized she was far better trained at her poker face than I was. And I didn't want to let her down. So I nodded, knowing I needed to do better. For her, but also for me.

This night could make or break my contract with the Diamonds.

I reached for Mia's hand again, loving how soft her skin felt against mine. I had callouses from weightlifting and so many reps with a football, but her hands were silky smooth. And warm too. I looked up from her hand, meeting her gaze.

This time, I held it, let myself really see her. The starburst of all shades of blue in her eyes. The fullness of her pink lips. The dainty way her nose lifted at the tip. I thought of all she was doing for me, how easy it was to spend time with her instead of dating daddy's little girl who only wanted me for my status, how much it would mean to be able to stay in town. And I said, "Mia, I'm so thankful I have you."

The words came out earnest, heartfelt, because I meant them, not because I was putting on some kind of act.

She looked down shyly, then smiled back up at me. "Thank you, Ford. I think we both got lucky."

I wondered if she'd practiced her lines. Her words were so much more convincing than my first try.

I almost forgot I was holding her hand until her fingertips slipped from mine. "How was that?" she asked Tallie.

"Good," her employee replied. "Next."

My jaw clenched as I looked down at the paper.

Kiss her softly when it seems like no one's paying attention.

"Oh no," I said. "Is this really necessary?"

Mia shifted in her seat. "Surely holding hands is enough. We can say Ford doesn't like PDA."

Tallie's eyebrows drew together, silently scolding us both. "Look, couples in relationships *kiss* from time to time. You had to know that was part of the arrangement. And besides, you're both *acting*. Actors kiss all the time with it meaning nothing at all. And you both have far more on the line than a paycheck."

Mia nodded slowly. "You're right..."

And maybe she was, but my heart was still racing like I'd just run a mile at full speed. Mia and I had to kiss. We had to make it look real while faking it inside.

Mia looked up at me. "We don't have to do this if you don't want to. I—I understand kissing me isn't every man's idea of a good time."

My eyebrows drew together. "What does that mean?"

Tallie looked really busy examining her fingernails while Mia said, "Ford, look. Most men I've met since becoming CEO are interested in me for what I can do for them, not for who I *am*. I know I'm not everyone's cup of tea, and I'm okay with that. But I would really rather not kiss you when you're having such a hard time forcing yourself to kiss me."

"Mia..." I began.

She looked down, a hint of vulnerability in her features before she covered it up with a determined look.

And fuck if it didn't make me feel like an asshole. How could I tell her that all I'd been doing is forcing my feelings down before they could grow out of control? This would just be one step closer to completely falling for her, and I knew nothing good waited for me at the bottom.

"It's okay," she repeated. "We'll hold hands. It will have to be good enough."

Tallie looked like she wanted to protest, but I held my finger up to her. I wanted Mia to hear me. "Mia, you're beautiful. And you're strong. There are men who want a weak woman—they feel like they can't be strong unless it's by comparison. Real men know better, because a strong woman can thrive without you but thinks her life is better with you in it."

Her lips parted in surprise, letting me see all the emotions crossing her face. And before she could erase her feelings, I leaned in to kiss her. To show her there was nothing wrong with her. That I wanted her, no matter that I shouldn't.

She was beautiful, strong, cunning, and incredibly successful, which made her irresistible.

I let myself give in to her pull, cupping her face in my hand and drawing her closer until our lips touched, hers pillowy soft against mine.

And instead of holding herself strong, distant, like I thought she might, she tilted her head—just slightly—to let me in.

Forgetting Tallie was watching, fuck, forgetting we were riding in the limo at all, I took every ounce of affection she was willing to give me.

That was the problem with gasoline. It only needed a spark to create a blaze that could destroy everything in its path, including my self-control.

Recklessly, I deepened our kiss, touching my tongue to hers, tasting her mouth, letting my racing heart beat for something *good*. Something purely for my enjoyment. Not to reach a goal.

I could have kissed her forever, but she pulled back, making me instantly grieve her touch.

Her eyes blinked open hazily as she looked at me, lips a darker pink than before. It took all I had not to kiss her again.

And then I heard clapping. Tallie grinned at us and said, "*Exactly* like that."

But I couldn't be any less excited because I knew —I had lost control with Mia. There was no coming back from a kiss like that.

25

MIA

FORD DID *NOT* REACT to that kiss like I did. My whole body had come alive and fallen apart in his hands. I had lost myself in his touch, in his lips, and when I realized how strongly I reacted, I had to pull back.

But Ford?

He looked *pissed*.

His features were drawn, jaw muscle ticking like a bomb, seconds from detonating. I wanted to ask him why he looked so upset, but I knew better than to ask questions I couldn't handle the answer to. Even if a million worse possibilities were whirling in my mind.

What if he was upset for how much I enjoyed it? Surely, he could tell. A part of me had thought he had liked it too, but maybe he really was just a great actor. *What if he regretted kissing me?*

My thoughts were in all sorts of tangles as Zeke pulled up to the convention center where we were having the team dinner. But one emotion started to take over all the others.

Indignant rage.

Who was Ford to be upset about kissing me? He might have thousands of groupies, but I was a catch too. Anyone would be lucky to kiss someone like me. And his reaction? It was humiliating. For both of us. It showed his poor taste and my stupidity at entering into this agreement. Not to mention my publicist had seen the whole interaction and was now busy looking at her folders—anything to avoid looking at the train wreck happening in front of her.

But I knew one thing. I wasn't someone to just sit back and take this kind of treatment. So a plan formulated in my mind as we got out of the car and walked inside.

In front of us, the room was laid out with dozens of circular tables with stunning centerpieces inspired by the Diamonds' colors. The team's event planner had done a beautiful job, and the business part of my brain that never turned off thought maybe I should poach them for Griffen Industries.

"Ford, you have to introduce us," someone

said, taking me out of my thoughts. It was a hulking guy even taller than Ford, dressed in boots, khakis, and a purple button-down that had the Diamonds' logo above the breast. He had pale, freckled skin and a shock of rose-gold curly hair.

"Milo," Ford said, shaking his friend's hand and smiling. Finally, something other than that sour look. "Mia, this is the team's center, Milo."

I grinned at Milo and shook his proffered hand, saying, "It's so nice to meet you! Pookie Butt's said so much about you."

Milo's eyebrows scrunched together, an amused smile on his lips. "Pookie Butt?"

He glanced at Ford, who was staring at me in horror. My inner rebel was shouting her victory cry while on the outside, I pretended it was a slip. "Oh, silly me," I said. "That's what I call Ford."

Milo covered his hand, laughing, while Ford said, "You do not call me that." The tips of his ears were turning pink.

I looked up at him, giving him a falsely innocent smile. "It's okay, Pookie, surely Milo's had some pet names in his day. Isn't that right, Milo?"

Milo's face was red from silent laughter. "Right." Milo waved a teammate over. "Krew, you gotta meet *Pookie's* girlfriend. She's a hoot!"

I squeezed Ford's hand, hanging on to his arm like the adoring girlfriend Tallie told me to be.

He gave me a *What the fuck are you doing* look in return.

I held back a laugh as Krew approached with all the swagger of a professional wide receiver. His name was recognizable and often talked about on the news or in local circles. Tonight, he wore some slacks with white sneakers and a gray button-down that had the top few buttons undone. His perfectly white teeth contrasted his dark skin.

"What's this about a Pookie?" Krew asked, rubbing his hands together. I could feel the other people milling around the room starting to take notice.

Milo gestured at Ford and said, "This is Pookie." Then he looked at me. "Thank you, Mia, you've given us years of material."

Take that, Ford, I thought. Out loud, I said, "It's nice to meet you, Krew! And don't worry, if we hang out long enough, you two will have nicknames too."

They chuckled, and we chatted for a few minutes about what their potential nicknames could be. But they both agreed nothing would be as good as *Pookie Butt.*

When they left to get a drink, Ford took my hand and pulled me aside, saying, "Why don't we get a quiet moment alone, *darling?*" I could hear the tension in his voice and almost gulped.

He led me to a corner of the ballroom, away from everyone else, and leaned against the wall, bracketing his arms above my shoulders. "Hold on to my arm," he ordered, stone faced.

"You're bossy," I countered.

"Just do it—it's one of the poses Tallie wrote down."

His dedication to her plan was endearing, which he had no business being right now. But I followed his directions, hanging on to his muscled arm and propping my foot against the wall. In some distant part of my mind, I wondered what we looked like to the others, if they thought us a cute couple or if we looked like we were putting on an act.

When I looked up at him, he lowered his head, putting his face inches from mine. Up this close I could see the scar slashing through the side of his chin, and I wanted to ask where it came from.

"What was that about?" he demanded.

I leveled a gaze at him. "Having a little payback."

"Payback? What the hell for?" He looked genuinely confused, which stunned me more than it should have.

And now that he was asking, I realized I shouldn't have let my pride get away from me. Because now I

either had to lie to him or admit that he hurt my feelings—neither option was appealing.

So finally, I said, "Was it really that bad to kiss me
back there?"

Now his eyebrows drew together, like that was the
last question he expected me to ask. "What?"

"In the car," I replied impatiently. "You looked
pissed after you kissed me." My voice broke,
betraying my hurt. And I hated how quickly he
picked up on it.

His posture shifted instantly, concern in his gaze.
"Mia, that's not it at all."

"Then what is it?" I asked. "Because I'm about
two seconds from calling this and going home. I'll
lose my job before I let a man humiliate me like that
again."

"Mia, I—"

"Trouble in paradise?" came a silky voice.

We both stood straight and jerked our attention
toward a woman in a slinky purple dress. She had
almond-shaped brown eyes, straight brown hair, and
a body like a model. And the way she looked at Ford,
like he was a gazelle and she was a lion on the hunt,
made me want to defend him in a way I'd never
wanted to protect a man before.

What was going on with me tonight?

Before either of us could answer, an older man in

a three-piece suit with a purple pocket square and a cowboy hat approached us, saying, "Ford, Mia, I'd like you to meet my daughter, Felicity Reynolds."

Shit.

I'd been too preoccupied with Ford to put the pieces together. I knew Trent from different events, but Felicity hadn't been a part of the same crowd. "Felicity," I said, putting warmth in my voice and smile. "It's so lovely to meet you. I'm Mia Baird, CEO of Griffen Industries."

She shook my hand, hers feeling so small and cold within mine. "Hi." Her gaze was already back on Ford.

Trent said, "I made sure both of you were seated at the table with Felicity and me. We both wanted to get to know the happy couple a bit better."

"Great," Ford said. And I realized I could tell when he was faking a smile, because he was right now. None of the usual light was in his blue eyes. Instead, a hard, determined look took its place.

It gave me a little hope that maybe I *could* tell when he was putting on an act.

Trent turned, encouraging us to follow him. Ford slipped his hand through mine and gave me a look I could instantly read.

This was bad. Very bad.

26

FORD

TRENT AND FELICITY had the worst possible timing.

Here Mia was, completely misreading my reaction to our kiss. And just when we were in the middle of an argument, they showed up—before I could even explain myself. Not only that, but I could also see the wheels turning in Trent's mind. He thought Mia and I weren't on solid ground, which gave him just another reason to poke holes at our relationship. With a sharpened pitchfork, judging by his steely gaze.

Trent led us to a table toward the front of the ballroom where a stage was set up. Typically at these dinners, there was some type of speaker who was supposed to inspire us, Coach would talk too, and then Trent always gave a speech.

I used to be amazed by Trent, impressed at what he'd done with the program since purchasing it as a self-made millionaire.

Now, I knew I'd been naïve. He may have found monetary success, but I had no doubt he'd done it on the backs of other people, judging by the way he tried to step all over me to get what he wanted. Or rather, what his daughter desired.

We arrived at the table, and I realized it was just the four of us seated there so no one would have their backs to the stage. But that also meant we had no one to act as a buffer. Trent clearly meant business.

If Mia noticed, she didn't let on. Instead, she sat in the chair I pulled out for her. "Trent, thank you so much for getting us the best seats in the house!"

He gave Mia a smile that didn't meet his eyes. He clearly saw her as competition. But one thing about Mia? She was always up for the challenge. "Have you been to something like this before?" he asked. I knew the move—it was meant to make her feel insignificant, like he wouldn't remember her if he saw her in a crowd.

She chuckled like he'd been making a joke, then slipped her hand in mine under the table. Just her touch was comforting. "I'm so glad I could sneak away for this," she said to him. "Things have been awfully busy lately."

Trent nodded. "I hear from Thomas that the company's on the rocks since Gage's departure."

So he knew Thomas—interesting.

Her jaw tightened, but she quickly masked her reaction with an amused smile. "If you want information on a trip, would you ask the bus driver or the kids chatting in the back seat?" she retorted.

Trent let out a laugh despite himself. But Felicity let out a heavy sigh, resting her chin in a bejeweled hand.

"Yes, darling?" he asked her.

She said, "Where are the drinks?"

Trent reached a hand in the air and snapped his fingers. Within seconds, a server arrived. "Can I help you, sir?" he said. He couldn't have been more than twenty.

"Awfully slow service tonight," Trent complained.

The server opened his mouth to respond, but Trent fluttered his fingers, cutting the kid off. "Drinks for the table. Sugar free for my daughter."

"Yes, sir," the server said, hustling off.

I couldn't exactly blame him. I wanted to run away too, but unfortunately, I was stuck here for the evening.

"Felicity," Mia began. "I saw your latest magazine spread. What was that like?"

Felicity seemed to brighten. "Actually, did you know there are four rounds of hair and makeup checks before you're allowed on set?"

"I didn't," Mia replied. "What do the checks entail?"

Felicity started rattling off things that didn't entirely make sense to me, but Mia nodded along. I didn't dare make eye contact with Trent, acting enraptured by Mia and Felicity's conversation.

No sooner than Felicity answered Mia's question did Mia come up with another one. "What was it like to work with that photographer? I hear they're notoriously difficult."

"Oh yes," Felicity said, launching into a tirade about demanding photographers and sharing stories of how difficult they were to work with. Trent and I hardly got a word in edgewise as Mia and Felicity carried the conversation, Mia asking questions and Felicity answering while I held Mia's hand under the table.

She had this. And with each second that passed, I was more and more amazed by her. And a little ashamed of myself too. Mia had brought out the best in someone who I'd only assumed to be Trent's entitled daughter.

The only break we got in the conversation was when the food came and the two paused for bites of their meal.

Eventually, Trent must have been fed up with it all because he waved his hand and said, "Enough. We know you love your job, Lissy. Let's hear from Mia. How did you and this one meet?" He waved his fork at me.

"Oh." Mia smiled over at me, her gaze so charming, I almost believed her. "Do you know that Gage and Ford grew up as neighbors? So before Gage retired to the board, I got to see Ford come in and out of the office or to meals, and I watched games from the suite. I remember the first time we spoke though."

"You do?" I asked, surprised.

She nodded, meeting my gaze for a moment before looking back to Trent. "See, my best friend married Gage. She and her children came to one of the football games and stayed in the suite, and Ford was kind enough to come say hi after the game. Her oldest son was so intrigued by the life of a professional athlete and must have asked Ford a million questions." She squeezed my hand. "Ford could have blown him off, signed an autograph or two and left the suite. After all, he'd just spent hours out on the field. He must have been so tired.

Instead, he talked with Levi for at least an hour. Not trying to impress anyone or gain anything. Just because he's a *good* guy. I remember having a little bit of a crush on him then, but I figured nothing would ever happen. It's hard to believe we're together now."

It was the most she'd spoken all night, and hearing her say it warmed my heart. "I remember that day too," I admitted.

Everyone looked at me, but Mia sounded genuinely surprised when she said, "You do?"

The vulnerability in her question had my chest squeezing. "I remember this cute girl in the suite wearing a black dress and pearl earrings and thinking she'd look awfully good in purple."

Even Felicity softened at that comment. "That's adorable."

Color rose on Mia's cheeks, and she shook her head at me. "I guess it was meant to be... So what about you, Felicity? Anyone special in your life?"

The question was brilliant, and she slipped it into the conversation so effortlessly.

Felicity looked despondent for a moment, saying, "Not yet." She glanced my way for half a second before looking down.

Mia reached across the table, covering Felicity's hand with her own. "I'm sure you'll find just the right person. But until then, girlfriends are the best to have. We should go get drinks sometime."

"Yeah…" Felicity seemed hesitant at first but then brightened. "Yeah, I'd like that."

"Great." Mia smiled.

The echo of the microphone sounded, and I looked to the stage to see Coach preparing to speak.

I let out a sigh of relief. It felt like we'd won so far.

But I knew there was a lot Mia and I still had to discuss once we were done with the night.

27

MIA

I OPERATED WELL WITH A MISSION. With a plan. A purpose.

But now that the evening was over and Ford and I were alone in the car, the privacy window rolled up, separating us from Zeke, I had no idea what to do. Especially with the way our conversation ended earlier with Trent's interruption.

We looked at each other for a moment as the car drove away from the convention center, so much hanging between us.

Ford's hands were linked in his lap. He looked down at them, saying, "Thank you for that." He met my gaze. What little light was in the back of the limo caught in his eyes, washing out the blue to make them look gray. "You were incredible, Mia, truly."

My smile lasted half a second before faltering. "I'm glad it helped." An ache weighed heavy on my chest, because I knew I'd crushed it in there. I could see Felicity softening, Trent getting frustrated when he couldn't pick apart my relationship with Ford. My fake boyfriend's relief at our charade coming across as sincere.

And throughout the conversation, he'd held my hand under the table. His touch was a blessing and a curse, supportive but making me wonder if he resented the connection at the same time.

I sat back in my seat, rubbing my temples. Faking a relationship with Ford was so much more complicated, more difficult, than I thought it would be. I was nearly forty, and I thought I'd worked through so many of my insecurities, but being with Ford brought them back, despite the kind words he sent my way.

"About earlier..." he began.

I closed my eyes, not ready for what was to come next. Thinking the worst was easier than having my worries confirmed.

"Look at me," he said gently.

I blinked my eyes open to see him coming across the limo, sitting next to me. Then he reached up, cupping my face to hold my gaze in place. The touch made my heart ache more because I wanted so badly for it to be real.

How had I gone from hopeful he was asking me out to wishing I'd never agreed to this farce in the first place? My eyes stung as I looked at him.

"Mia, my job is about control," he said, stroking his thumb over my cheek. "My control over my body and mind is what helps me succeed at this level."

Where was he going with this?

"But when I kissed you..." He trailed off.

"What?" I breathed.

He drew his hand from my face to my shoulder, twisted a strand of my hair around his fingertips. When he met my gaze again, he looked tortured. "When I kissed you, I lost control."

The air around us held a charge, and my breathing shallowed.

His voice was hoarse. "I can't lose control, Mia."

"Not even once?" My voice came out a whisper.

I could see his eyes on my lips, and all I wanted was a do-over. A chance to kiss him without holding back, without an audience, without worrying that he was doing it out of obligation or any reason other than he wanted to kiss me back.

"If I start with you, I won't be able to stop," he said. "And my contract with the Diamonds, my home, my charity is on the line. It wouldn't be fair to give such a small sliver of myself to you, knowing you deserve the world."

Something rebellious rose up inside me. "Isn't that my choice?"

His brow creased slightly.

"I have a career, goals, as well. I wouldn't want you to put the team second, because I'd never accept you asking me to set my career aside after all the work I've put in to build it."

He wet his lips. "Mia..." he warned. "My self-control has had about all it can take."

I leaned closer to him. So close, a tilt of my head would bring our lips together.

"Please," he whispered. But it didn't matter what he was asking for because he answered his plea by drawing me to his hard body and kissing me like I'd never been kissed before.

Desperately.

Hungrily.

Like no amount of my touch would ever be enough.

Breathless, I broke apart from his embrace, staring at him.

"Shit, Mia, I'm sorry, I—"

But before he could finish his sentence, let me know what he was sorry for, I kissed him back, taking exactly what I wanted from him, feeling his strong hands grip my hips bringing me closer to him.

I straddled his lap in the back of the limo,

grinding against him while he kissed my neck, my exposed collarbone. His erection strained against his pants, tempting and taunting in equal measure.

"Fuck," he moaned.

And I knew what he meant. I wanted more of him. *All* of him. "Give in," I breathed.

In response, he guided me down, laying me on my back on the long limo seat, and began unbuttoning my pants. I lifted my hips, wanting to see how he would feel when he lost control. He ripped off my pants, pulling them down until he brought his mouth to my clit, eating me out like a man possessed.

I gripped at his hair, writhing on the seat beneath him.

"Ford," I moaned.

He responded with a growl of his own that had me pushing close to the edge.

"Ford!"

He lapped at me harder, inserting a finger, then two, inside me, filling me up and then curling the pads of his fingers toward himself.

The unexpectedness of it urged on my orgasm, and I cried out as my walls crashed around his fingers. He didn't give up, licking and sucking until every last wave had pulsed through my body and left me liquid under his touch.

My breath came out as tired pants as I lifted

myself up to stare at him. He tugged his polo free to clean his face, then looked at me with heat in his eyes.

Only then did I realize the limo had stopped moving.

Wordlessly, he handed me my thong, my pants. But I put on the pants without my underwear. I handed the lacy material back to him.

He stared at them in awe as I went to the door of the limo. I stepped outside before saying, "To remind you how good it feels to lose control."

28

FORD

I PACKED my bag for an out-of-town game and opened the drawer on my nightstand, seeing Mia's lingerie inside.

We hadn't spoken in the week since the team dinner. I think we both needed to think about what this meant. But I'd also thought of her every night while I fucked myself, her underwear in my hand. Her taste was so fresh on my memory it was like she was a ghost, haunting me every waking second.

And this sexual tension building up inside me? I'd never played harder, lifted heavier, or ran faster just to burn off some of the energy coiled within me, begging for yet another taste of her.

I wanted more. But how could I ask for it without breaking our arrangement?

I was allowed to lose control for the night.

But the thing about self-control was once you gave it up, it was impossible to get back.

Especially when it came to a woman like Mia.

I couldn't stop thinking about the way her thick thighs felt pressed up against my ears. Her soft whimpers that led to a loud cry as she came around my fingers.

For an entire week, I vacillated between kicking myself for giving in and wishing I could call her over and add gasoline to this fire we started.

I put her underwear in my suitcase, knowing I couldn't leave them at home. I'd want her while I was away just as badly as I needed her here. At least what little piece of her I could have.

With my bag packed, I went out to the garage, threw my bags in the bed of my truck, and took off toward the private airport the team used for out-of-town games. Within an hour or so, I'd parked and a golf cart had come to pick me up. It brought me and a few teammates to the terminal so we could go through security and board the plane waiting for us on the tarmac.

I climbed the boarding stairs behind a few other guys on the team and found Milo sitting next to an open seat, Krew in the row ahead of him.

"Hey," I said, sliding past Milo to get the window

seat. I reached ahead and clapped Krew's shoulder. He was already in game mode, listening to something on massive over-the-ear headphones, a neck pillow resting on his shoulders.

He smiled up at me, then was back in the zone, eyes closed, head bobbing to his music.

"Ready for the game?" Milo asked me.

I nodded. "You?"

He nodded too. We'd watched hours of game film of the Brentwood Badgers over the last week. We knew they were especially strong on defense, and Milo and I had done dozens of drills with the other linemen to make sure we were ready for the pressure.

"Your family coming?" he asked.

I shook my head. "I know Mama Kent will be there though, waving that sign," I teased.

His mom attended every game, wearing his jersey and waving a sign that said THAT'S MY BOY #54. She'd raised him as a single mom working multiple jobs, and now that he'd gone pro, he'd paid off her house and made sure she wouldn't have to work so hard another day in her life.

"I'm gonna tell her you were pokin' fun, and then she won't bring any cookies for you after the game."

"I take it back," I said with a chuckle. "It's cool how she's there for you."

He nodded, settling back in his seat as more of

our teammates boarded around us. "Mia's not coming?"

I shook my head.

"Why the hell not?"

"She's got work to do," I said simply, reaching into my bag for a set of headphones.

"Don't they make computers with internet these days? Mobile phones too?" He shrugged. "I bet she could work just as well for a couple days from a fancy hotel in California as she could in Dallas."

The words brought an unexpected spark of hope to my chest... It was a terrible idea that would just blur the lines between us more.

And yet...

I'd never gone to a website and booked a plane ticket faster.

29

MIA

I WAS IN THE OFFICE, working on a report to share in my next meeting with one of Griffen Industries' biggest investors and sipping on a sparkling water with lime when Ford's message came through.

Relieved for the distraction from one of the more tedious parts of my work, I picked up my phone and stared in shock at the first message.

It was a screenshot of a boarding pass... for a first-class flight to Brentwood, California.

Then another message appeared on the screen.

Ford: Come to my game?

I bit my lip, rereading the message just to make sure I wasn't dreaming. And once reality set in, it took all I had not to do a happy dance. (If only Vanover wouldn't have been able to see me and ask far too many astute questions.)

After not hearing from Ford all week, I wondered if our tryst in the back of the limo had simply been a one-time thing while simultaneously and sincerely hoping it was just the beginning.

I wanted something real with him. And maybe this was the sign he wanted something too.

I looked at my calendar, seeing I didn't have travel or an event this weekend. I did have some work to do, but between hotel Wi-Fi and my hot spot, I should have no problem getting it done. Just as I was about to tell him yes, I'd come, more text bubbles appeared on the screen.

Ford: It would be great exposure for us.

My heart instantly sank, and I felt ridiculous for getting my hopes up at all. But then he sent another text.

Ford: Please?

What was this man doing to me? My heart was on a roller coaster that no sane person would ride.

What did Ford want?

How should I respond?

I had so many conflicting ideas racing through my mind. And if I'd learned one thing from business, it was to bring in advisors you could trust.

In this realm? It was my friend Farrah. And that meant... I had to tell her the truth.

I switched to a new message thread.

Mia: Do you have time to swing by the office today?

I hoped she would reply—with raising kids, her mind was scattered in so many directions, sometimes she would see a message and think she'd responded to it without actually doing so. How she raised her children as a full-time mom while taking on interior design clients from time to time, I had no idea.

But luckily, she messaged me back this time.

Farrah: Mind if Tara tags along?
Mia: Can you make sure she has headphones? Might be some rated R topics.
Farrah: OMG YES.
Farrah: OMW.

I smiled at her enthusiasm and set my phone down to call Vanover on the speaker. "Hey, block off my schedule for the next hour and a half, please?"

"Done," he replied.

Since I'd have to set some time aside for Farrah, I buckled down and focused on the report.

I was pacing in front of the floor-to-ceiling windows in my office, practicing my presentation, when a knock sounded on the glass wall behind me. Turning, I spotted my best friend holding her toddler in one arm and a sparkly unicorn backpack in the other.

My smile was instant. I waved them in and said, "Vanover, can you bring us a couple glasses of white wine and a juice box for Tara?"

"Absolutely." He grinned, smiling at the little girl who peeked up at him from behind her mom's shoulder.

After he left, Farrah got her daughter set up on a blanket on the floor, with a tablet playing her favorite cartoon. She'd just gotten the headphones—with an iridescent unicorn horn protruding from the head-band—secured on her daughter's head when Vanover returned with our drinks.

Once he was done passing them out, he went back to his desk, and Farrah and I went to the meeting table, sitting in the chairs. Farrah wore leggings and an oversized T-shirt, and I was a little jealous of her comfy clothing, since I was wearing slacks and a blouse with an underwire bra. Even though it was a Saturday, Thomas or another exec was liable to swing by.

"This must be juicy," Farrah said, sipping happily on her wine.

I tugged at the collar on my blouse, not sure how to broach this with Farrah. "So I want your advice, but first I have to tell you about something. Promise you won't hate me."

"I could never hate you. But I *could* be pissed at you." She gave me a teasing smile. "What's going on?"

I swirled my wine in the glass, watching tiny bubbles form and spin in a cyclone. "So... I might not have been completely honest about my... relationship with Ford."

Her eyebrows drew together. "What do you mean?"

I cringed, knowing how it would sound. "I might be fake dating him to get the board to like me more by association." I peeked up at her to see her setting down her glass.

"First of all, Gage told me what's going on with Thomas, and it's bullshit. They should trust you for the work you do, not stupid office politics."

"I know."

"And second..." She stalled, studying me with a mix of hurt and concern. "Why didn't you tell me?"

I covered my face with my hands, sitting back in the chair. "I was embarrassed." I uncovered my face to take a drink of wine. I needed it.

"Why would you be embarrassed?"

Heaving a sigh, I answered, "I made such a huge deal about our first date, thinking he liked me back, but while I was there, he asked me to be his fake girlfriend so he could get out of dating the Diamonds' owner's daughter."

Farrah's face scrunched with confusion. "Wait, couldn't he just say no to her?"

"Not without having his contract cancelled the next year."

"So fake dating you was preferable to real dating her?"

I nodded.

"And you agreed because?"

"Because of the board," I explained. "Tallie thought it could be a good way for me to win some internal support."

She shook her head and downed another swig of wine.

"And you can't say anything because I signed an NDA," I said. I knew she wouldn't tell a soul.

"Mommy!" Tara said too loudly, looking up at us. "Can I change it to another show?"

"That one is fine," Farrah said.

"But, Mommm——" she whined.

"Watch this one first, okay? Then we'll talk."

Tara grumbled but put her headphones back on, leaving me to talk with her mom.

Farrah turned her gaze back on me. "So why the urgent meeting? Guilty conscience?"

I shook my head. "I needed my life and love advisor."

Farrah laughed. "The divorced mom with two baby daddies?"

That made me laugh too. "*No*, the woman who's living happily ever after with her billionaire boss and a beautiful, blended family."

Her smile warmed and she tucked her foot closer to her bottom, holding on to her knee. "So what's the question?"

Flattening both my palms on the table, I said, "Well, after the team dinner last week"—I checked to make sure Tara was still watching TV, and when I was sure she was, I whispered—"we kinda hooked up in the limo on the way to my place."

Farrah's jaw dropped open, and her voice rose an octave. "You had sex with him?!"

I shook my head, made a V with my fingers, and waggled my tongue in between them.

She nearly spit out her wine with laughter, and I giggled.

"I was not expecting that gesture from you. Sounds like it was... well-received?" she asked.

"Extremely." My thighs were already clenching at the memory, wishing we could do that, and more, all over again.

"So it started fake and turned real," she said. "What's the issue?"

"It started fake, and the lines have blurred. And then, get this." I downed the rest of my wine, opened my phone to the messages from him, and passed it to her.

Her eyes tracked left to right like pinballs as she read the words, her lips slowly settling into a smile. "Mia, this is great! He likes you!"

My eyebrows drew together. "Did you miss the part where he said it would be great for this stupid show we're putting on?"

Farrah rolled her eyes. "He's really doing some mental gymnastics to keep his heart from getting involved. Did he say he's been through a breakup or something?"

"I think he's afraid of dying young, because of his mom. He feels like the team and his charity have to come first."

Farrah shook her head. "I get that. But you're not exactly a needy girlfriend. I couldn't picture you begrudging him putting work first."

I nodded. "That's what I told him."

"And?"

I held up the V again and waggled my tongue.

This time, wine dribbled down her chin when she laughed. "Damn you, Mia." She picked up the hem of her shirt to wipe her chin.

I giggled, loving that I could be my real self around her.

With a smile, she said, "So what are you doing here? That flight leaves in a few hours."

"It's a bad idea, to go for a man who isn't emotionally available."

"It might be." She shrugged. "But it could be a good idea to spend a weekend with a man good at..." She made the gesture.

I snorted out a laugh. But she had a good point. Ford may have lost control with me.

But I'd done the same with him.

And if it was all going to end in flames, I'd bring the s'mores.

I pressed the intercom on the desk linking me to Vanover. "Hey, Van?"

"Yes, Wino. I mean, boss?"

I rolled my eyes at Farrah and smiled. "Have my stylist pack a weekend bag for me. I'm going to Brentwood."

"Yes!" he cried.

I gave him a confused look through the window. Then it dawned on me. "You were listening in, weren't you?"

"Just doing my job." There was a smile in his voice. "Your car—and bag—will be ready in an hour."

30

FORD

I WENT to the hotel gym to get in a light lifting session and distract myself from the thoughts going through my mind. Mia hadn't replied, and I didn't want to think about what that meant.

This was one of the reasons I'd been hesitant about relationships. I should have been focusing on the game right now, maybe getting in some extra film review, and instead I was like a high school kid on prom night, wondering why my date had stood me up.

I started with a warmup, then went to get in some reps on the bench press. Between each set, I got off the bench, adding extra plates. My arms were feeling a good burn when I went to the rack where my towel hung, wiping off my sweaty hands.

The door to the gym opened, and I looked up, fully expecting to see another guy from the team.

Instead, there was Mia, wearing the jersey I gave her and a flirty black skirt.

My mouth went dry.

She was here.

She was wearing my number.

Thousands of people owned and wore my jersey, but none of them looked as good in it as she did.

"Mia," I managed. "How did you get past the team's security?"

She smiled shyly at me as she stepped farther into the gym, letting the door shut behind her. "I have my ways."

I grinned at her, despite wishing I was less sweaty and up in my room. Flowers and chocolate-covered strawberries waited for her there. "Let's head upstairs," I said, all my earlier angst forgotten.

"You can finish your workout," she said. "I know your work is important."

"Just when I thought you couldn't get any hotter," I replied. I went to her, fisting the jersey at her hips and drawing her closer to me.

She looked up at me, long, dark lashes framing blue eyes, her lips tinted the perfect shade of pink.

"I could skip the gym and lift you in the room," I hummed, leaning down to kiss her lips.

She smiled against my kiss, saying, "I doubt you could lift me."

Indignation flared as I pulled away from her. "Want to bet?" My pride was roaring to life, demanding to be defended.

She scoffed. "You're that confident?"

"Your weight is my warmup," I countered.

"Then prove it," she challenged, her gaze flicking from my lips to my eyes.

God, the way my cock responded to her. But I had work to do first. I went back to the bench, counting out the plates on each side of the barbell. "Two twenty-five."

"Higher," she countered.

I went to the rack, getting two twenty-five-pound plates and adding them on.

"It's a start," she said, arms folded over her gorgeous chest.

A start... I'd show her.

I went back to the bench, lying down, and took the bar into my hands, bringing the weight to my chest and then back up several times. "Easy."

She clapped her hands slowly. "Okay, you showed me. We can go to the—"

But I was already adding more weight to the bar. She might have been with guys who couldn't handle her before, but I was determined to show her I was more than up to the challenge.

I brought the weight down to my chest, muscles working off memory, and then lifted it back up.

When I sat up and looked at her, she was biting her bottom lip.

This was turning her on.

Good.

I went back to the bar, adding weight until I knew I had to be well over her size. Then I laid down, doing my best to make it look easy. When I finished, the weight clanged back into the rack and I went to sit up, but she said, "Wait."

"What?" I asked, hand on the bar above me.

That's when I saw her swing her leg over the bench so she was straddling me, riding me. My hands went to her hips, under her skirt, and I realized she wasn't wearing any underwear.

Holy fucking shit.

I gripped the meat of her hip and grinded her against me. Fuck, she felt good.

Was this really happening? Her, in my jersey, on top?

Yes.

I bucked my hips under her, showing her my growing erection. No amount of masturbating with her panties had anything on this view.

She held on to the bar, grinding on me, tossing her head back so long blond hair fell down her back. It was just long enough for me to reach up and grab it, tugging gently until she moaned.

"Let's take this upstairs," I replied.

"Security's outside the door," she hummed, bending down to kiss my jaw, my neck.

Fuck, it would be hard to wait. "I don't have any condoms."

"We don't need them," she replied, trailing kisses over my collarbone. "I was just tested last month."

I cringed because there was no good way to say this. When you were a man in my position, you had to be careful. Very careful. I'd heard of women doing crazy shit with my teammates—getting condoms out of the trash can, taking fake pills to act like they were on birth control, all numbers of things to have a pro football player's baby. "I'm clean too, but I'd feel safer if we used one." I ran my hands over the luscious curve of her ass.

"I had that taken care of years ago," she said simply, sliding down my legs to lift my shirt and kiss my hard stomach.

If it were any other woman, I would have insisted on going up to the room to get protection, but I realized with Mia... I trusted her.

The realization caught me so off guard, I didn't

quite know what to do or how to react to the information. But the blood flowing to my cock kept me from thinking too hard about anything other than her.

As she kissed my chest, I reached for her, pulling her up to kiss me. Then I reached under her skirt again, finding her already wet for me. "Fuck," I hissed, sliding up to her clit and adding pressure with my thumb.

She let out a moan, bucking her hips against me. "Ford," she gasped.

"Lift up," I ordered, and she quickly complied.

My shorts were down in a matter of seconds, thinking of nothing but how I wanted to fill her up, feel her stretch around me. Feel her shake and quiver on my cock.

Her gaze was hooded as she looked at my length, and she licked her pillowy lips.

"Are you ready for me?" I asked.

Her voice rang clear. "*Yes.*"

31

MIA

HE GRIPPED MY HIPS, and I lowered myself, slowly, onto his cock.

Each inch stretched and filled me in the best possible way, and he growled ferally as I settled myself to the hilt, letting my thighs rest on his legs.

I froze on top of him, knowing he wanted to move, to thrust, but I let my weight hold us still, and he stared up at me, a crazed look in his eyes.

"Fuck, Mia."

I wiggled my hips for him, feeling him shift inside me.

He hissed.

I grinned.

I loved seeing him like this, so out of control

when I knew control was exactly what he craved every hour of every day.

But this man had shown I was his weak spot, and damn if that didn't turn me on. Damn if it didn't make me want to take charge and show him exactly how good it could feel to just let go.

"Mia, please," he begged.

"I like it when you beg for me," I hummed.

"Then you'll love it when I come for you," he countered.

"Is that so?" I bit my lip, ran my fingers through my wavy hair.

He squirmed under me. "Lift up, and hold on to that bar. You're gonna fucking need it."

The promise sent a wave of pleasure through me, just a hint of what was to come. I eagerly complied.

"That's my girl," he said.

My girl.

Something about those words hit me in a way I hadn't expected. Had me aching to fulfill his every wish.

As soon as the pressure was lifted, he grabbed my waist and used it as leverage to fuck me from underneath. I tossed my head back, catching a glimpse of us in the floor-to-ceiling mirror. I'd been so focused on him, I hadn't even noticed the view of *us*.

I stared at his muscles clenching as he pumped

into me, the way my curves rippled at impact, how his eyes were on me and me only, taking in every inch of me.

I'd never felt hotter.

That is until he grunted out, "I'm going to fill you with my cum."

My eyelids shuttered closed, and I nodded. "Give it to me. Every fucking drop."

I lowered myself onto him, meeting him thrust for thrust, grinding against him until he cried out, hands digging into the flesh at my waist.

And I fell apart with him.

Our orgasms racked through us until all that was left was us, panting, sweaty, sated.

Something in his gaze told me this was different, what had happened between us. And my heart squeezed because I wasn't brave enough to hope for something more. Doubts flooded me just as surely as bliss had seconds before.

I lifted myself off him, knowing we must be making a mess of the bench—of each other. He quickly got up, pulling up his shorts and getting a clean towel for me to clean myself up. I didn't make eye contact while I tossed the towel in the basket marked dirty. But soon, his arms were around me, circling me from behind, and he kissed the top of my head.

"Let's go up to the room."

I only nodded, not trusting myself to speak.

He laced his fingers through mine, and we walked to the door of the gym. The team's security guard stepped out of the way for us. Ford nodded a thank you, and if the guard noticed my flush or messy hair, he didn't let it show on his face.

The two of us went to the elevator, hand in hand. And I wondered if Ford knew what the simple contact did to my heart.

Anyone could fuck. Get a release that humans were biologically programmed to desire for the sake of our species.

Holding hands was only for people you cared for... who you loved.

We reached the door, and he held the key up to the reader until a light flicked green. I wasn't sure what I'd expected to find when we got back to the hotel room, but it wasn't the single king-sized bed that waited for us.

And it definitely wasn't the dozen red roses sitting on the table. Or the platter of chocolate-covered strawberries displayed next to the bouquet.

"Ford..." I breathed, looking from the display to him.

When he'd texted me, he'd said this trip was to put on a show for everyone.

But there were no cameras waiting here.

He'd done this for me and me alone.

"Do you like them?" he asked, the trepidation clear in his voice.

I turned and answered him by kissing his lips. "They're beautiful," I murmured, then squeezed him, my cheek to his chest as I took them in. The lines of our arrangement had gone from fuzzy to nonexistent. I knew Ford wasn't ready to give me a relationship, but this felt an awful lot like one.

All his muscles seemed to melt with my approval. He kissed the top of my head, then said, "I need to shower off... Care to join?"

I grinned at the thought of seeing his exquisite body again, having it all to myself. "Absolutely."

AN HOUR (and a few orgasms) later, we were sitting in the bed, wearing matching robes and eating chocolate-covered strawberries. It felt so *fun*. Something I hadn't experienced a lot of in the last few years.

I loved my work, but it wasn't the same as kicking back and truly enjoying someone else's company.

Ford finished a strawberry and set the stem on the plate in front of us. "Can I ask you about something?"

I wiped a chocolate crumb from the corner of my mouth. "Yes, you can definitely eat chocolate strawberries off my naked body."

He chuckled and said, "I'll keep that in mind. No, it's about... what you said earlier."

I sent him a questioning look.

"About birth control being 'taken care of.'" He fisted his hands in his robe pockets. "I trust you. I just wasn't sure what that means."

"Oh..." I set down a half-eaten strawberry, wiping my fingers on a napkin. I'd had this conversation with boyfriends before, and it had always been contentious. But I didn't know what we were, so I wasn't quite sure how to approach this or how he would react. So I decided to go with the facts, plain and simple. "I had a tubal ligation done several years ago. I couldn't get pregnant even if I wanted to."

I watched his profile as he took in the news, his contemplative blue eyes downcast as he processed it. Finally, he said, "You don't want children?"

I shook my head. "No, I don't."

I waited for the questions, for the judgement. The memory of this conversation with Christian flashed in my mind. It had been the end for us. And Ford was young, not yet thirty... Would this be the thing that kept us from more?

"I don't want children either," he admitted, his voice almost a whisper.

I studied him, trying to make sure I'd heard him correctly.

Then he let out a soft chuckle. "It seems heretical to say when you grew up in a family with five kids."

I smiled. "How did you decide?"

He shifted his weight, crossing his legs and resting back against the headboard with his hands in his lap. "My mom died of cancer when I was young. I never wanted to have children and risk putting them through something like that when I know it could run in my family."

Something in his voice had me reaching for his hand. I laced my fingers through his.

He smiled over at me, lifted my hand to his lips, and kissed my knuckles. The gesture spread warmth through my chest.

"I should have a vasectomy," he said.

"Why haven't you?"

His cheeks tinged pink. "It sounds stupid."

"What?" I prompted.

"I'm afraid of needles."

That made me laugh. "You can handle two-hundred-pound guys rushing at you in a game famous for giving its players head injuries, and a little needle scares you?"

"Hey!" he laughed bashfully. "I told you it was stupid."

I had to laugh with him. But when our chuckles died down, he said, "What about you? Was it a hard decision?"

I bit my lip. "I know what I want, and I'm not the kind to settle... I think it's harder knowing what people think about childless, career-oriented women. They call us selfish. Say we're missing out on life's biggest calling. And there's a part of me that knows I'll never fully relate to people like my best friend because I won't experience motherhood like her. And I've had men call off relationships because of it."

"You have?" he said.

I nodded. "I was engaged... about six years ago. He broke it off when I got the procedure done. I didn't want him to try and convince me of something I knew I didn't want."

His gaze was downcast. "What a loser."

My lips quirked as I nodded. Because at one point, Christian had been the love of my life. But a piece of me was relieved it hadn't worked out because I got to share this paradise of a moment with Ford, someone who seemed to understand me better than most people did.

Then he confessed, "I think I worry most about

being alone when I'm older. Sitting in the nursing home with no one to visit me."

"You're rich," I countered. "You can pay people to visit you."

The laugh that fell through his lips was so warm it touched my heart. "Guess I never thought of it that way."

I smiled. "I already know all the shit I'm going to spend money on when I'm in the nursing home." I held up my fingers, counting off. "Diamond-encrusted wheelchair. Swarovski crystal walking cane. Personal stylist to do my pretty blue hair every day. Personal chef. Man candy to deliver cocktails—"

"Man what?"

"You know, everyone who works for me will be required to have a six-pack and wear leopard print speedos, that kind of thing."

Ford laughed harder, clutching his waist. "Can I be you when I grow up?"

"I have a better idea." I winked. "You can be the man candy."

He grinned back at me. "As long as it's with you, I know it will be a good time."

Feeling light as a cloud, I snuggled next to him, resting on his shoulder. And for a moment, I just enjoyed his presence. Enjoyed him.

Because deep down, I knew this wasn't fake, and it wasn't just sex. This had to be something more.

32

FORD

ONCE WE WERE DONE BRUSHING our teeth and doing our skincare routines, we put on our pajamas and slid under the covers in the king bed. It was what I imagined growing old with someone would be like.

Both of us lay under the blankets, on our backs, and met each other's gaze, bursting out laughing.

Mia rolled to her side, propping her head up on her hand. "So it's been a long time since I've spent the night next to someone. I don't even know if I snore."

I chuckled. "I won't judge."

She smiled. "I know rest is important, especially with your job, so I really don't mind getting a different room so you can get your sleep."

"Oh, come here," I said, tucking her into me so I was spooning her from behind. I brushed her soft blond hair out of the way and said, "If I can share a room with Hayes sawing logs all night, I can sleep next to you."

Her eyes crinkled slightly as she smiled. "Okay."

"Okay." I reached back, flicking off the lamp, and curled my arm around her soft waist again. Something about lying next to her just felt right.

Until she fidgeted. And then sat up. And then blew her nose. And then lay back down. And then huffed out a sigh.

I stared at her in the dark. "What are you doing?"

"I like to listen to a sleep story," she said, an embarrassed tinge to her voice.

"Okay..." I laughed. "Are you nervous for me to hear it, bigshot CEO?"

She hit my arm. "I am!"

"I've seen you naked!" I laughed. "Sleeping with you should be a cinch."

She shook her head at me. "Promise you won't judge?"

I made an X over my chest. "Cross my heart."

"Okay." She reached for her phone on the night-stand, and soon, a soothing male voice was talking slowly about lavender fields. It was kind of nice. Comforting.

She curled next to me, and I shifted again so her hair wouldn't tickle my face.

"Can I tell you something?" I asked her softly.

"Mmm."

"My mom used to sing 'Red River Valley' to us kids every night before we fell asleep. I miss that."

"I haven't heard that song before," she said.

"I could sing it for you," I offered. My chest felt raw, and I realized I wanted her to hear it. I wanted to share a piece of my mom with someone new. Someone I think my mom would have adored.

"I'd like that," she said quietly before reaching out to pause her story.

I ran my fingers over her bare arm, mustering the courage to sing. "From this valley they say you are goin'..." I closed my eyes as I poured out the words, hot tears forming along my lashes. As I sang each line, I could feel Mia's breathing slow, deepen.

And when I hit the last note, a tear dripped down my cheek, just before I heard her soft snore.

I smiled, wiping the moisture from my face. Then I leaned forward and pressed a slow kiss to Mia's shoulder. "Goodnight, Sunflower," I whispered.

Then I fell asleep and rested better than I had in a long, long time.

I WOKE up early in the morning like I usually did. But this time, Mia lay pressed against me, like neither of us had wanted to be apart throughout the night. And even though I could have spent all day like this, listening to her soft snores, watching her body shift with each breath, today was game day, and I had work to do.

Carefully, I untangled myself from the covers and put in a room service order for breakfast before getting in the shower. While the hot water cascaded over my body, I visualized the day to come. I saw Milo defending me beautifully, throwing sharp, crisp passes to Krew, who would run them to the end zone. I pictured making good calls on the field, easily spotting the openings between players, and ultimately winning the game.

When I was done with my visualization routine, I got out of the shower, threw on a pair of shorts and a T-shirt, and put on my running shoes.

When I stepped out of the bathroom, Mia was already dressed in leggings and a tank top, braiding her hair in the mirror. "Hey," she said with a smile.

I returned the look. It was so easy to smile around her. "Hey."

She nodded toward the table where a silver room service tray sat. "Your breakfast arrived."

"Ours," I countered, going behind her and

hugging her. I loved the way we looked together in the mirror. She was just tall enough for me to rest my chin atop her head. Her arms settled lightly on mine, and she looked just as contented as I felt.

"Shall we?" she said.

I nodded, going to the table. Between the two of us, we picked through the food, eating and talking about the day to come. She asked questions about being a professional football player and how I felt before games. Then she told me she had to get some work in before the game, which was perfect because I had my meditation session.

"I just need to work out first," she said.

"Me too—what are you doing?"

"I was thinking a bike ride," she said. "It's so beautiful here, and I saw rentals in front of the hotel on my way in."

Grinning, I said, "I'm going for a quick run. Maybe we can go together?"

"That sounds like fun." She finished a bite of toast and set it down before brushing crumbs from her lips. "Should we go now? I don't want to eat too much and be uncomfortable."

"Definitely." I got up, walking with her to the door and thinking it was crazy how easy it felt to be around her.

I didn't have to worry about entertaining her or

her being bored while I went through my routine. I was actually a little excited to have someone come with me for my pregame jog. I always found it helped loosen me up, especially when traveling to an out-of-town game.

The lobby of the hotel was pretty quiet this early in the morning, so no one really talked to us as we went outside. It helped that I wore a baseball cap low, sunglasses, and nondescript clothing.

Mia quickly rented her bike and said, "I'll follow you."

"Great," I replied. I'd mapped a park nearby, Emerson Trails, so I started heading in the directions I'd memorized while she easily biked alongside me on the sidewalk.

"So, do you talk on these runs?" she asked. "Or is mum the word?"

I chuckled. "We can talk. It's meant to be an easy pace."

"Great. Did I snore last night?"

I laughed. "Like an angel."

Her gaze narrowed. "Is that a yes?"

"Did I?" I countered.

"I didn't notice if you did. That song put me out like a light. It's really pretty, by the way," she said.

"I'm glad you liked it." I felt like I was bounding on the moon rather than jogging here on planet

Earth. Especially because it was so pretty here with golden morning sunlight filtering through leafy trees. The trails were nice and wide and well-maintained, so we both had plenty of room.

We were quiet for a moment, just the gravel crunching beneath us before she said, "Do you get nervous before games?"

"Not anymore," I said. "At first, I was sick as a dog before every single one. It's part of why I worked so hard on my pregame routine."

She nodded. "I get nervous before press conferences."

I stared at her, stunned, before looking at the trail in front of me. "You do? You work a room so well."

"Yeah." She steered around a small rock on the path. "Why do you think I have Tallie in my back pocket all the time?"

"Because she's brilliant?" I offered.

"Well, that too." She chuckled. Then she looked around the tree-lined trail. "It's so pretty out here."

"It has nothing on the farm," I said.

"Really?" she asked.

I nodded. "I'll have to show you sometime."

Her bike wobbled before she got her balance back. "You mean it?"

"Yeah. We don't have a game two weeks from

now. Maybe you could clear your schedule and come check it out."

Her smiled formed. "Yeah... I'd like that."

And I stayed on that cloud the rest of the way back to the hotel. Maybe a relationship with Mia wouldn't hold me back.

For the first time, I let myself think... maybe I could have it all.

33

MIA

I WAS SITTING in a nearby coffee shop, Halfway Café, to get some work done, when my phone started blowing up.

Farrah: Saw the news! You look hot in the pics!
Tallie: You didn't tell me you were going to California!

She sent a screenshot of a picture clearly taken from a bush outside the hotel. The headline was PREGAME RENDEZVOUS. I was riding a bike while Ford jogged down the sidewalk. He might have been low-key in a hat and sunglasses, but it was hard to mistake his strong jaw and muscular build.

I smiled at the picture. We looked pretty cute and sporty together.

Tallie: So was this trip for work or pleasure?

Grinning salaciously at the phone, I replied to Tallie.

Mia: Both.

Then I switched to a text thread for Farrah.

Mia: Thank you for the encouragement. Hooking up on a weight bench was worth the trip. ;)

I chuckled, setting my phone on focus mode so I could get some work done. I needed to review this presentation once more, sign off on a new marketing campaign for one of the company's hotels, and start prepping notes for a meeting with the governor. The legislature was working on a new bill to encourage more businesses to headquarter in the state, and he wanted my input.

Sometimes, my to-do list was overwhelming, sure, but I liked having so many plates spinning at once. It made me feel important, accomplished, like I was squeezing every drop out of this life I was given.

And doing it here in California? Hooking up with Ford Madigan? That was just the cherry on top.

I let the happiness settle in my heart and got some focused work in before checking my phone.

Farrah: So did Ford admit his feelings?

I bit my bottom lip, not sure how to reply. Because Ford had *shown* that he cared for me. He'd shared so much with me the night before about his view on life, football, family. But never expressed aloud his desire for what we had to be real.

Instead of replying to Farrah's text, I switched to a text thread with Ford.

Mia: Hey, in case we don't get a chance to say goodbye after the game, I wanted to say thanks for this. And good luck tonight.

I didn't fully expect him to reply, because I knew he had things going on today, but within a couple minutes, a text came through.

Ford: I got you a front-row seat so I can find you after. You can't leave town without saying goodbye.

Smiling to myself, I switched back to the message with Farrah.

Mia: We're not there yet... but getting close.

At least, I hoped.

I WAS BACK IN DALLAS, getting ready for bed, when Ford broke our unspoken rule and sent me a text message.

Ford: Did you make it home safely?

I held my phone to my chest, smiling. It was thoughtful in an old-fashioned kind of way, a guy wanting to know that you made it home okay.

Mia: I did. And you?
Ford: We fly out in the morning. I'm tucked into the hotel bed, wishing you were still in it.

My heart swelled as I nestled further underneath my covers. His words were making me just as warm as any blanket could.

Ford: What did you think of the game? No networking to distract you today.

I chuckled at his message and then tapped out my response.

Mia: I don't think I'll ever get over people making the vagina shape with their hands when Dallas scores.
Ford: They're supposed to be diamonds!
Mia: Also, you touched Milo's butt an awful lot.

Three dots appeared.

Ford: Jealous?

I laughed out loud.

Mia: Maybe a little bit.
Ford: Anything else?
Mia: I have a whole new appreciation for the uniform, if you know what I mean. ;)

I could just picture him laughing at the response. I smiled to myself, waiting for his reply.

Ford: You dirty dog.

I let out a chuckle. Even when we weren't in the same room, I was still enjoying my time with him. I hoped he felt the same way about me. But I knew better than to push him when he was just opening up to the idea of something more than a fake relationship with me.

Mia: The next couple weeks are going to be pretty busy. Especially if you still want me to come to your family farm. It's OK if you don't.

Ford: I can't wait to take you—and give you a new appreciation for Wranglers.

Mia: Looking forward to it. ;)

34

MIA

THE NEXT COUPLE WEEKS, I buried myself in work to make up for the time I'd be away over the weekend. Especially with the board meeting coming up two weeks after the trip. I had to make sure I was extra prepared for that; I wasn't giving up on the Andersen sisters. Not even close.

This would be my first vacation in *years*. It wouldn't be at a private island or an all-inclusive beach resort, but I was still excited.

Especially since Ford had begun texting me every night before bed. Telling me about his day. Asking about mine. It was quickly becoming a favorite part of my day, something I looked forward to.

He also came by the office a couple times to sign more autographs, bring me lunch, and hand-deliver flowers that instantly brightened my office and made me smile every time I saw them.

Something about the trip to California had changed things for us. He wasn't just my fake boyfriend with benefits—he was becoming a friend. Someone who understood me on a deep level like I never expected.

So when the weekend came for me to go visit Ford's family home, I was getting really excited to just be with him. I was pacing my living room, wishing ten a.m. wasn't thirty minutes away, when the bell announced someone coming up my elevator. My eyebrows drew together. Very few people had access to my apartment, and the cleaners weren't supposed to come until later in the day. Had Ford arrived early?

I walked toward the door just in time to see the elevator open and my parents come inside.

"Oh shit," I muttered.

"Language," my mom said, coming in and giving me a hug.

"I'm sorry, I forgot you were coming over today. I'm actually... getting ready to leave town." I gave my dad a hug, and when we pulled apart, he looked disappointed, which nearly gutted me. "Business trip?"

I shook my head. "I'm um... visiting a friend's hometown."

Mom gave a steely smile. "A friend's? Or Ford Madigan's?"

All of a sudden, I felt like I was fifteen years old again, with my parents asking me who I was texting and confessing it was a boy.

"Yes, it's Ford."

Dad said, "Do you think you could score us some tickets?"

"Dad, I could *buy* you tickets," I said. "You could come to my suite any time."

He shrugged. "Yeah, but they wouldn't be coming from the star quarterback."

I laughed. "Gosh, I love you guys... He's not supposed to be here for another fifteen minutes or so. Why don't I make us some coffee?" I led them toward my kitchen, and they settled in on the chairs facing the island.

I went to my coffee pot, adding the filter and then my favorite grounds imported from Costa Rica. The aroma was already making my mouth water, and it wasn't even brewing yet.

"So, what plans do you have for the weekend with Ford?" Mom asked.

My cheeks warmed slightly as I kept my back to her, adding water to the pot. "I'm not sure. He wants to show me his family's ranch. He says it's beautiful there."

I reached up into my cabinets, pulling out three mugs.

Dad said, "Mom and I drove through Cottonwood Falls once on our way to the Grand Canyon. It's been ten years now, but I remember they had this fantastic diner. What was it, Joanne? Windy's Diner?"

"No..." She paused for a minute. "Oh, Woody's! And there was this fabulous waitress, Agatha. Remember? She was so sweet with us, telling us all about the town and where we should go."

My jaw dropped. Was it the same Agatha I had met at the gala? Aggie could be short for Agatha. "What did she look like?" I asked them.

Mom said, "Kind of frizzy brown hair, curvy, brown eyes."

"I think I met her at a gala with Ford's dad," I said. "What a small world."

She smiled. "If you see her again, tell her she has a couple fans here in Dallas."

"I will," I replied over the gurgling of the coffee pot.

When the liquid filled the pot, I poured it into each of our cups and went to the fridge designed to blend into the kitchen cabinets. There wasn't much inside, but I always had fresh cream for coffee. After getting the container, I grabbed sugar from the cabinet and set it out for all of us. Somewhere in the back of my mind, I remembered being sixteen and wondering why my parents insisted on drinking the stuff.

Mom fixed her coffee while Dad took a sip of it black. "So good," he said.

I nodded, taking a sip of my own black coffee. I totally understood now.

"You know," Mom said. "This will be the first boyfriend of yours we've met in what... five years?"

"Eight," Dad said. "Since Christian."

We all grew quiet for a moment. He was the one I thought I would marry and grow old with. But I felt like a different person now than I had been all those years ago.

"Well, no need to worry about meeting Ford," I said. "I'm supposed to meet him in the garage. And you're welcome to hang out up here and finish your coffee. I can order in food for you too. I feel bad I forgot about today."

The bell rang through the apartment, and my eyebrows drew together. Was this just the day for surprises?

"Hold on," I told them, going to the elevator. Maybe the cleaning crew was coming early today.

But when the door slid open, Ford Madigan was standing there. I'd never seen him in jeans and cowboy boots before, but damn, my mouth was already watering. "Ford... what are you doing here? I was supposed to meet you down in the garage."

He came to me, sweeping me into his arms and kissing me. "I missed you too much to wait."

My stomach warmed as I kissed him, forgetting my parents were in the other room. That is, until my mom called, "Is that him?"

Ford pulled away from me, looking around the corner. "Sorry, I didn't know you had company."

"It's..." Mom and Dad walked around the corner. "Ford, these are my parents."

35

FORD

I HAD no right to be as nervous as I felt watching the couple rounding the corner to Mia's foyer. Mia's parents were older than my dad by at least ten years, but you could still see the family resemblance. Mia had her mom's build, her dad's face, and a smile that was a mix of them both.

Her dad extended his hand, saying, "Nice to meet you. I'm Hugh. This is my wife, Joanne."

I shook his hand firmly like my dad had taught me, then accepted Joanne's quick hug.

"Well," Mia said, speaking too quickly, "We'd better be going."

Her mother's face fell. "Oh, I was hoping we could have some coffee with Ford. Is that okay?"

That's when I realized her eyes were the same

shade of blue as Mia's. I couldn't say no to her. "We have time for coffee," I said warmly.

She perked right up, smiling. "Great. Mia, would you be a dear and get him a mug?"

Mia threw her hands up in defeat. "Sure. Anything else? Perhaps a hot stone massage?"

Her mom ignored the sarcasm. "Why not some glasses of water too? Need to stay hydrated."

"Okay," Mia said, walking toward the kitchen. Damn, she looked good in her travel outfit—all soft green material that clung to her curves. But I shouldn't be checking her out so much in front of her parents.

Her mom looped her arm through mine as we followed Mia. "And some of those chocolate-covered biscuits if you have them," she said.

Mia chuckled. "You know I do."

We went into Mia's kitchen. I tried not to be obvious about staring around her space and trying to get a deeper sense of who she was. But her home was minimalistic and efficient, giving little away. I could see more of her in her interactions with her parents. Right now, she wasn't a boss—she was a daughter.

As we settled in at the island, I said, "I'm impressed. I think that's the only time I've seen Mia taking orders instead of giving them."

Her dad laughed. "So you *do* know her."

"*Dad*," Mia griped as she handed me a mug of coffee. Then she whispered, "Ignore them," a playful smile on her lips.

Something about the exchange endeared me to her more. She wasn't just a strong, forceful leader. She was someone's daughter, and it was clear how much they loved her.

Joanne said, "Ford, what do you have planned for the weekend in Cottonwood Falls?"

I took a sip of coffee and answered, "I'd love to show Mia around the ranch where I grew up. We have horses and cattle. A few pigs. And then all my family lives there. I'd like for her to meet them."

Mia dropped a package of cookies on the floor. "Sorry... clumsy," she muttered.

"That sounds lovely," Joanne replied. "Does all your family work on the ranch?"

I shook my head. "It's really just enough for my dad to manage, but they help him out when they can." I told them about Fletcher's and Hayes's businesses, Knox's job as an officer, and how well Bryce had been doing in college.

Her dad said, "Your parents must be proud."

I nodded. I hoped my mom would be proud of me, but I knew my dad sure was. "You must be proud of Mia here," I countered as Mia set the cookies on the counter, a few to a plate for each of us. She kept the broken ones for herself.

"Of course we are," her dad said, giving her a warm smile. "But we always knew she'd do big things. I knew it when she was thirteen months old and handed me her diaper then laid down on the pad, like 'I'm waiting.'"

Mia covered her face, but I could still see the tips of her ears reddening.

Joanne chuckled as she dunked a cookie in her cream-colored coffee. "Mia, I'm sure between a dad and four brothers, there will be plenty of stories about Ford too."

My stomach dropped. I hadn't thought of that. *Why hadn't I thought of that?*

Like he sensed my inner turmoil, Hugh patted my shoulder. "Good luck."

Mia shook her head at us.

Her mom gave us a thoughtful look, like she was comparing Mia and me as a couple. "Are your parents supportive of the age difference?"

Mia and I glanced at each other, and I could feel her nerves as she waited for my answer. "My family's very much a 'live and let live' kind of bunch. They're happy for me if I'm happy..." I reached across the counter for Mia's hand and squeezed it. "And I am... happy."

She smiled at me. "I am too," she almost whispered.

For the next fifteen minutes or so, we held hands as we all sat at the Carrera marble island, chatting and getting to know each other. But then Joanne and Hugh excused themselves, saying they better let us get on the road. Mia and I went with them down the elevator, her bags in tow.

When we reached the ground floor, she hugged them both, long and hard. And then they surprised me by hugging me too.

"Drive safe with my girl," her mom said.

"I will," I promised.

They got into their silver sedan, and Mia and I both waved as they backed out of the parking garage and drove away. When they were gone, Mia immediately said, "I'm sorry, I really didn't mean to spring that on you. I know meeting the parents is a big deal and—"

"Whoa," I said, running my hands down her arms. She looked adorable in green, her hair pulled into a knot at the nape of her neck. "You're meeting my dad, my whole family. I think it's more than fair."

She tilted her head. "Is it though? They even asked about our age difference. And the diaper story..." She winced.

"And I like your parents. Your dad's a card. And your mom is trouble."

She tossed her head back and laughed. "True. Thank you for being so kind to them. They're going to tell all their friends how they know a famous person now."

I dropped the tailgate of my pickup and lifted the shell to put her bags inside. "Maybe we should drop by and visit them, give them more to talk about."

Her expression was unreadable as she studied me. "You'd do that?"

After I finished loading her bags in the truck bed, I went to her, kissing her forehead. "For you? Of course. If you can't tell, Mia, I kinda like you."

"I kinda like you too." She reached around my waist, holding on to me for a moment. Then she looked up at me and said, "Have I mentioned how hot you are in cowboy boots?" Her hand wound down to my backside, giving it a squeeze.

She might have meant it playfully, but after two weeks apart, I was desperate for her. It took all I had not to pick her up and take her right in the garage.

I leaned closer, whispering in her ear, "I'll wear them for you every day if that's what you want."

"Might be hard to play football in them," she breathed.

"I was thinking of other activities," I countered, nipping at her ear.

"Keep talking like that and we're not going to make it to Cottonwood Falls."

I was about to agree, wholeheartedly, when a car came into the garage. She jumped, surprised by the visitor, and I chuckled low, reaching for the truck door to open it for her.

Her cheeks were flushed with color as she got in, and I shut it for her. We were going to Cottonwood Falls. Even if we had to stop along the way to... stretch our legs.

As I started the familiar path out of Dallas, my adrenaline hummed like it always did before a game. But this time, I didn't have defenders looking to take me out or a win on the line.

I had a beautiful woman in the seat beside me and a decision to make.

We hadn't defined what we had, and I knew I couldn't stall forever. Could I give up on all my rules to have a relationship with her? A real one? I looked over at her, and when she caught me looking, she smiled.

It was as natural as breathing to extend my hand for her, to hold it as I drove with one hand on the wheel. She smiled over at me again.

"What?" I asked.

"I was just thinking about how good you'd look in a cowboy hat."

36

MIA

THERE HE WENT, holding my hand again.

The way his hand enveloped mine, all warm with rough callouses, strong, it was the best. I hadn't felt this way about a man in so long, and here Ford was, making my heart go crazy just by lacing his fingers with mine.

I tried to enjoy it, live in the moment like I rarely allowed myself to do, but my brain was going crazy, wondering where we stood. He'd met my parents and said that I was meeting his family this weekend. That had to mean something, right?

The more analytical, logical side of myself reminded me that our agreement would soon reach its expiration date. The football season was just a few months from being over, and the board would vote on the Andersen sister acquisition in just a couple weeks.

"What are you thinking about?" he asked. We were somewhere between Dallas and Cottonwood Falls, nothing but short grass prairies and gently rolling hills passing out the window. Every so often, an oil derrick broke up the prairie, beating its rhythm —a reminder that business never sleeps.

I looked away from the countryside and back to him. "It's been fun getting to know you," I said, squeezing his hand.

He smiled over at me, lifting my hand to his lips. "I'm glad it was you."

My heart did a somersault at his words. "Me too."

It was on the tip of my tongue to ask him if we were a couple, officially. The right answer could put me on the moon. The wrong answer would lead to a very awkward weekend.

So I promised myself that I would ask him on the way back home, when I had a chance to escape back to my house and not have to play nice with his family with a broken heart.

We rode in silence for a moment before I said, "What should I know about your family?"

He seemed to contemplate it. "How do you mean?"

I shifted in my seat, hooking my feet in the door pocket and asking, "Is there a word everyone hates? Or topics I should steer clear of?"

"Maybe I should warn you... I don't know."

I straightened in my seat. "Warn me about what?"

He glanced at me before looking back at the highway. "So there's this pig..."

I let out a laugh. "*What?*" That was the last thing I was expecting to hear.

"It's a thing. My brother Knox is a real prankster. And he and his friends are always releasing a pig at the *least* opportune times. In fact, it made an appearance at Knox and Larkin's wedding. I spent half an hour trying to chase that thing away."

I giggled, picturing it.

"I'm lucky it didn't make national news," he retorted. "And just so you know, Hayes will probably try to charm the panties off you. He thinks you're hot."

My eyebrows raised at that. "What? He does?"

He chuckled. "You'll know him when you see him," he said. "He's a real ladies' man. Rolling stone, that kind of thing. But he's a good guy under it all."

"Does your family know..." I began.

"That it's fake?" He looked sadly at the road ahead of us. "No, Sunflower, they don't."

We were quiet for a moment, heaviness settling between us, our linked hands connecting us through it all. I kept watching out the window, seeing horses, cows, sometimes goats or llamas in passing pastures. Then the speed limit reduced, and I saw the sign...

Welcome to Cottonwood Falls.

I smiled, knowing how much Farrah loved it here. It felt special to be visiting this town too, another way we were connected.

It wasn't a big town, so just moments later, we were turning off the blacktop, going onto a dirt road. The side mirrors showed dust billowing behind us, clouding out the bright blue sky.

I imagined Ford as a kid, riding a big yellow school bus home from school. Or a teen, driving his truck down these dirt roads. He must have been popular with the girls in high school...

"Were you the homecoming king?" I asked.

He gave me a sheepish smile.

I let out a laugh. "I knew it."

"Were you homecoming royalty?" he asked me.

"Me? I was too cool for that." I laughed. I wasn't interested in vanity titles, even as a teen. "I was student body president, though."

"Of course you were." He chuckled.

I grinned over at·him.

He slowed the truck and pointed ahead at a sign

hanging over a turnoff. The metal letters said GRIFFEN FARMS. "That's the way to Gage's family's farm. They have cattle, but they grow some crops as well."

A little farther ahead there was another turnoff. This sign said MADIGAN RANCH.

I smiled up at it, knowing how special this place was to Ford. It wasn't lost on me that he was taking me to his home, letting me meet his family. Regardless of our title or status as a couple, he was showing me that I was special to him. That meant a lot.

He steered us under the sign, and then we started on a dirt road that led up a hill. On either side of the road, I saw black cattle grazing in the pasture, and I realized why he said it was the most beautiful place on earth.

You could see for miles, nothing interrupting your view.

It wasn't a mountain range or miles of sandy white beach but...

"This is home," he said.

We had crested the hill, and a home came into view. A white farmhouse with clapboard sides and dark blue trim and...

Hundreds of yellow sunflowers.

37

FORD

I WATCHED Mia taking in my childhood home. The barn, the corral with horses fenced in. I could see some of my nieces out there already, riding the horses bareback around the enclosure.

I smiled at the view, my heart feeling so full.

The only thing that made it better was seeing the admiration reflected in Mia's eyes.

"It's stunning," she agreed. "And the sunflowers..."

"They were my mom's favorite flowers," I confided, feeling bare in front of her. "She planted them all around the house, even though Dad called them ditch weeds at first."

She chuckled softly. "Sounds like Farrah—she loves dandelions."

I nodded. "Dad came around eventually. And now that she's... gone, we all make sure there are sunflowers planted. It's like a reminder that she's always with us." I swallowed down the emotion, and Mia squeezed my hand like she understood.

We rode the rest of the way to the house, and I parked in the gravel driveway alongside the fence. When we got out, it felt like magic, with a warm breeze flowing around us, the fresh air filling my lungs and energizing me like city air never did.

With a bang, the screen door opened, and my niece Leah came toddling out in her swimsuit, curls wild around her head. "FuhFuh!" she yelled.

I grinned at her, going through the front gate to scoop her up and hug her to me. It didn't matter that her swimsuit was soaked and dripping through my shirt. Just that I was home.

Her mom, Liv, was just a few steps behind her, her pregnant belly showing a little more than last time I'd seen her.

"Hey, Ford," she said. "Mia, I'm Liv."

Mia followed us into the front yard and said hi, and then Liv called over her shoulder. "FLETCH! Help with the bags!" Within a few seconds, he came out and grabbed the bags.

"At your service," he mumbled to his wife.

She held her hands out at her side. "Sorry, my

husband-slash-doctor says I can't lift more than twenty pounds."

Fletcher rolled his eyes at me, then looked to Mia and said, "Mia, welcome to the mess. I'm the husband-slash-doctor. But you can call me Fletcher."

She laughed. "Nice to meet you."

"Miss Leah and I will give you the grand tour," I said to Mia, leading her down the sidewalk to the house.

I opened the door for us and held it open for Mia to walk inside. Thankfully, most everyone was either on the back patio or at the barn, so it was just us while Liv and Fletch trailed behind.

"This is the living room," I explained.

She looked at the room with its wooden floors, simple leather couches, and the fireplace we never used with photos on the mantle.

Then I showed her the bedrooms—there were four of them, which meant sharing rooms was common throughout the years.

"Fletch always got a bedroom to himself because he was the oldest." I rolled my eyes. "Lame."

Mia laughed. "Maybe being an only child wasn't so bad."

I smiled at her, then said, "Let's head to the back-yard. Dad's probably grilling for you. Had to show off some of his Madigan beef."

Leah squirmed in my arms, so I set her down. She waved her little chubby fingers like we should follow her. And she marched ahead of us, her little ruffled butt swinging as she walked.

Mia held my arm, whispering, "She is so stinking cute."

"I know," I agreed. "So much sass. Like her mama."

"Liv, right? Farrah adores her."

"She's the best," I agreed, then lowered my voice so only Mia could hear. "She was exactly what Fletcher needed to get back on his feet after the divorce."

Leah led us dutifully to the back sliding door and pointed at it for me to open. When I pulled it aside, the chaos really began. Dad was out there grilling, the sound of sizzling meat adding to the cacophony of food cooking, children laughing, and cattle mooing in the distance. The younger kids were running through the sprinkler and splashing on a long Slip 'N Slide.

My sister-in-law Larkin sat on the porch swing, sipping a sweating glass of iced tea. Hayes was at the patio table, arguing with Bryce about why trade school was better than four-year-college, and Dad's dog, Gracie, was huddled at his feet like a furry trip hazard.

But all conversation stopped when they realized who was here as they turned to stare at Mia like she was an exotic animal in a zoo exhibit.

Leah was over it and ran toward the sprinkler.

Dad was the first to break the silence. He set his tongs down, shut the grill, and then stumbled over the dang dog as he walked toward Mia. He grinned and said, "Welcome to our home!"

The next couple hours were a rush of activities. The little girls wanted to know who Mia was and had a million questions for her about her shoes and fancy sunglasses. My sisters-in-law poked fun at me like I was just another little brother bringing home a new girl. And Dad watched it all with a smile on his face, happy his kids were all together.

And Mia? She fit into it all. Talking, laughing, listening, getting to know the people who meant the most to me.

We stayed up talking late into the night, until the littlest ones in the family were yawning and falling asleep in their parents' arms, inaudibly declaring it bedtime.

Soon enough, it was just Bryce, Hayes, Dad, Mia, and me sitting around a small fire in the backyard.

Even though she wore designer clothes and had her hair perfectly done, Mia looked right at home, a beer in her right hand, feet propped up on the fire ring, with the fire's glow making her look golden.

I'd never seen anyone more beautiful.

She caught me looking and smiled at me. "I think I'm going to head inside and get ready for bed, if that's okay."

"Of course." I made to stand up and walk her inside, but she shook her head. "It's okay. You stay out here and chat." Then she looked at Hayes, saying, "Don't stare too hard as I walk away." And then she winked.

I didn't think I'd ever seen Hayes blush before, but he got pretty dang close as the rest of us cracked up at her comment.

We were still laughing and making fun of him as we heard the back sliding door open, and Mia went inside. But as our laughter fell silent, Dad said, "Okay, we've gotta talk."

38

FORD

EVERYONE around the fire sobered because we all recognized Dad's come-to-Jesus voice. All eyes were on him as he said, "What's going on with you two?"

Then all focus turned to me. "What do you mean?" I hedged.

Dad scoffed. "You've had your eyes on her all night long, brought her home to introduce her to your family, and yet, you've never once introduced her as your girlfriend, the love of your life, the one... You've only ever called her Mia. Something's off with you two, but I can't tell what, so you're gonna need to fill me in."

As they watched me to see my reaction, I realized I'd been riding the fence, and it was high time to choose a side. "If I tell you something, promise you won't tell anyone else?"

Each of them nodded.

And I knew it was time to tell them the truth. Even if it hurt to do. Even if I knew they'd be disappointed in me for lying. "I started dating Mia to keep my spot on the team," I said.

Hayes said, "What the fuck?" at the same time Bryce said, "That doesn't make any sense!" Dad's surprised and disappointed features spoke even louder. Finally, Dad held his hands up, silencing everyone. "Why in the hell would you do a harebrained thing like that?"

He always did have a way of cutting through the bullshit. I took a steadying breath and looked into the fire as I explained the situation. "My contract is up for renewal this year, and Trent threatened to sell me to another team if I didn't date his daughter."

Hayes said, "You turned down a supermodel?" He reached over and hit my arm. "You dumbass."

I rolled my eyes at him. "There's more to a woman than her looks. She's got to have it all to be worth spending your time with. And I'd rather fake something with Mia than try something real with a woman I don't care for."

Hayes said, "There's just one problem with that, brother."

I raised my eyebrows at him.

He took off his hat and threw it at me. "You went and caught feelings, dumbass!"

Retrieving his hat from the ground where it landed, I threw it back at him and he launched it back at me. Bryce's eyes pinballed between us, seemingly amused.

"Boys," Dad admonished. It reminded me of when we were kids, but he sounded a lot more tired now than he used to. He rubbed his temples and leaned forward. "Ford, I need to speak with you. Privately."

"Oooh," Bryce said.

But Dad replied, "Go inside." Then he looked at Hayes. "Go home, don't care who the home belongs to."

Hayes smirked. "Aye, aye."

We both rolled our eyes at him as he walked away and Bryce went inside. A heaviness settled around us, because I knew when we had one of these private talks, I might not like what he had to say.

As soon as Hayes's truck fired up and disappeared up the road, Dad faced me with a disappointed look in his eyes that nearly gutted me.

"Ford, you know how long your mother and I were together before she passed?"

I shook my head. "Fifteen years?" My oldest brother had been fourteen when she died.

"Sixteen," Dad said. "But you know how long I was in love with her before we ever got together?"

Again, I shook my head.

"Four years." He wrung his weathered hands, looking down at the wedding ring still on his finger. "But she was just a friend, and I wanted to sow my wild oats instead of settling down with the woman I knew deep down was the one." His voice broke with emotion. "I fucked around for four years. *Four years* I could have had with her, Ford. We could have had another baby. She could have watched them grow, walked them down the aisle. Hell, maybe even seen a grandbaby if they got started young enough." He shook his head, gazing into the fire. "And after everything I've learned and been through, I'll be damned if I watch my son make the same mistake. And a woman like Mia, a strong woman with a successful career, a heart of gold, she's not waiting around, waiting for a guy to make up his mind. Not even for a professional football player like you."

I looked into the fire, letting his words sink in. Flames licked at logs like his words consumed my heart. "This isn't what I planned," I uttered, my voice barely rising over the crackling logs.

Dad met my gaze with a corner of his lips lifted.

"You can make all the plans you want, but if you hold on to them too tightly, you might miss out on something even better."

We were silent for a moment, and then Dad said, "Understand, son?"

I nodded, knowing what I needed to do. But I was *scared*—an emotion only Mia brought out in me.

Dad patted my knee and said, "I'm a little tired. Mind putting the fire out?"

"I'll get it," I said, rising to grab the hose. He was a few steps away when I called out, "Hey, Dad?"

He turned. "Yeah?"

"What about Agatha?"

His expression sobered. "What about her?"

I tilted my head. "I think you know. How long are you going to wait?"

A sad smile formed on his lips. "Goodnight, son."

"Goodnight."

39

MIA

THE FARMHOUSE only had two bathrooms—one en suite for the main bedroom and one shared between the other three bedrooms. So when I finished showering, I wrapped myself in two towels so I'd be completely covered and tiptoed across the hallway, hoping that Ford's little brother—or worse, his dad—wouldn't see me.

Once I made it to the safety of the guest bedroom, I shut the door behind me. I barely had my silky nightgown on when the door opened again.

I turned to see Ford looking down at me, an emotion in his eyes I couldn't quite place.

But instead of putting words to it, he lowered his mouth to mine and kissed me, taking his time. I could smell campfire smoke on his skin, blending with his cologne. That, mixed with the way he touched me, was more intoxicating than any drink.

My wet hair cascaded down my back, seeping through my pajamas as he walked me back to the bed and laid me down in front of him. But instead of continuing to kiss me, he stepped back, studying my body with hooded eyes. He scrubbed his hand over his mouth.

"What is it?" I asked him.

His answer was to swipe his shirt over his head and lie over me in the bed, kissing me like no amount would ever be enough. Despite the urgency of his kiss, he took his time, slowly sliding his hand up my nightgown and swiping his thumb over my clit, building me up until I fell apart under his touch.

His kiss quieted my moans as I shuddered underneath him, riding wave after wave of exquisite pleasure.

But even though I was sated, he continued kissing me, teasing my nipples with his lips through my nightgown, kissing his way down my stomach, and then lifting my nightgown and bringing his mouth to my heat.

He licked and kneaded, sucked and teased, slipped his fingers in and curled them toward himself until I was rising and falling again, lost in an ocean of pure pleasure.

Only then did he allow me to unbutton his jeans, feel the length of his hard cock, moisture leaking from the tip. I wanted to please him, so I told him to stand at the edge of the bed, and I took his cock in my mouth, wrapping my lips around the shaft and swirling my tongue around the head.

He brushed my hair aside, watching me. "You know how to make me feel good, don't you, baby?" he murmured.

I hummed against his cock in answer. He bit his lip, playing with my hair while I tried to make him feel half as good as he made me. But before I could push him closer to the edge, he pulled back and flipped me over so he could eat me out from behind, my face plastered to the soft bed. I could hardly breathe through what he was doing to me. Couldn't do anything but clench onto the already tangled sheets and ride out another wave.

"Ford," I gasped, rolling to my back and tugging on his arms to bring him closer to me. "What has gotten into you?" My breaths were still shallow, trying to catch up.

He didn't answer, an intense, fearful look in his eyes.

"Ford." I held his face in my hands. "What is it?"

His breath came out stunted, and he squeezed his eyes shut. "If I say it, we can't go back."

"Say what?"

He shook his head. "I can't... I..." He lay down beside me, covering his face with his hands.

And some part of me understood. Ford was an athlete. He didn't talk with words but with actions. And I knew that was the language he needed to hear from me.

So I crawled atop his body, straddling him and lowering my raw center over his cock. I eased on top of him, inch by inch, until he was buried inside me. Tears leaked from his eyes, and I didn't know what they meant. But I knew I couldn't get enough of him, knew that I didn't want this to end.

So I lifted and lowered myself on top of him, silently begging him to say what he was holding back. He held on to my hips, watching me, eyes deep, dark blue in the fully lit room.

"Mia," he breathed. My name on his lips was a drug. I wanted more.

I picked up pace, adjusting so I could ride him longer without my muscles giving up.

"*Mia*," he repeated.

"Say it," I commanded, nearing the edge myself. I braced my heart for *the end*, knowing we'd gone as far as we could together. He'd never wanted a real relationship. Not when I showed up to his house professionally styled for a simple first date. Not when

I convinced him to let loose in the limo. And seeing me with all his real-life relationships probably brought that point home. Clearly, I wasn't a small-town girl from Cottonwood Falls. Wasn't what he ever really wanted.

So I braced myself for pain. For heartbreak.

But there was no way I could prepare myself for the words that tumbled from his lips.

"Mia, I love you."

My mouth fell open, chest heaving from the effort of being on top. "You..." I knelt in place, feeling him inside me, feeling his words swirling around my brain, trying to find purchase, understanding.

"I love you," he said.

Moisture stung my eyes as I realized what he was saying. He... "You love me?" I whispered.

"I do," he said, shifting his hips underneath me to lift me, to press farther into me when we were already as close as two people could get.

"Ford, I love you, too," I admitted.

He looked up at me in wonder.

I nodded. "I love you," I repeated, the words feeling like magic on my lips.

Energized, he rolled me over, getting in missionary. "Wrap your legs around me," he ordered.

I held on with my legs, my fingers clinging to his shoulders as he pumped into me.

"Say it again," he commanded.

I smiled, holding his face. "I love you, Ford Madigan."

The words had him releasing all of himself, coming inside me as I held on to him with all my strength.

And I realized, all these years, *this* is what I'd been missing without even knowing it.

Love.

It was the one thing money couldn't buy.

But he'd given it to me anyway.

And as he lay next to me in bed, chest heaving, a small, satisfied smile on his lips, I realized I was terrified. Because now that I knew what I had, life would never be the same without it.

40

FORD

THE FIRST THING I noticed when I woke up was Mia, naked in my arms.

I slowly blinked my eyes open, remembering everything from the night before.

Mia loved me.

My lips spread into a smile.

Dad was right—this wasn't part of my plan; it was better.

I kissed her shoulder, and she slowly shifted in my arms.

"Good morning, Sunflower," I hummed.

She rolled over to face me, bleary-eyed but looking content. "Good morning."

I leaned in for a kiss, but she covered her mouth. "Morning breath."

"Like that could scare me away." I kissed the back of her hand, and then she removed it, kissing me back. When we broke apart, I said, "I didn't ask you last night, but I'm not sure how this works. Do I ask you to be my girlfriend?"

She laughed, her blue eyes crinkling in the corners. "You really are out of practice."

I rolled my eyes at her.

"We can just say we are... if that's what you want."

"We are," I said quickly.

Her giggle made my heart feel light. I'd never felt like this before—hadn't expected to even consider love and romance until I was finished with my football career, or at least signed on with the Diamonds until retirement. But here I was.

I got out of bed and started pulling on my clothes for the day. "Take your time getting up," I told her. "I'm going to head out for a run around town. Are you good here with Dad and Bryce?"

She nodded, curling the blankets up around her chest. "Do you think they'll mind if I do a little work?"

I pulled on my socks and shoes as I answered her. "I'm sure they won't. They know you're a BFD."

"BFD?" she asked.

My lips spread to a grin. "Big fuckin' deal."

She laughed again, and swear, I wanted to hear that sound for the rest of my life. But it was too soon to be saying things like that. So instead, I kissed her long and hard, giving her something to remember while I was gone.

Pushing me away, she said, "Keep this up and all your cardio will be happening in this room."

I smirked. "Wouldn't mind that."

Rolling her eyes at me, she said, "You're far too disciplined for that. Go on." She shooed me with a flutter of her fingers.

It was harder than I wanted to admit to leave her in that room, looking so damn scrumptious with the sheets wrapped around her. But I peeled myself away, walking over creaking wooden floors to the kitchen, where Dad stood over the stove in shorts and a T-shirt, cooking.

I used to think it was so strange, seeing him dressed so casually when he only ever wore jeans and a button-down during the day. Like seeing Clark Kent in sweatpants and contact lenses.

"Morning," I said.

He turned to me, returning the greeting, and I noticed he had glasses on.

"When did you get those?" I asked him. At his confused look, I said, "The glasses."

"Oh, these." He waved the spatula in the general

direction of his face. "Eye doctor says I'm getting old."

I shook my head at him. "Sixty is old now?"

"Thirty was old when you were a kid."

"Fair," I replied. I remembered thinking he was so ancient as a kid—but he had only been my age back then.

"Going for a run?" he asked.

I nodded.

"Take some bacon with you." Before I could protest, he dumped a few pieces into a wad of paper towels and handed them to me. "Toss 'em when you get far enough away if you need to, but it makes me feel better to know my kids are fed."

A wave of appreciation for my dad washed over me. He'd raised us five all on his own and still hadn't stopped worrying about any of us. "Thanks, Dad." I stepped closer and gave him a hug. "It's good to be home."

He smiled at me, then whispered, "You talk with Mia last night?"

Heat colored my cheeks and found the tips of my ears. But I was already grinning like a pig in mud. "Yeah. It's official."

Dad grinned, clapping my shoulder. "Proud of you, son."

Those four words meant more to me than anything. "Thanks."

He smiled. "Better get going—before that bacon gets cold."

"Okay," I said, heading toward the door. I ate the bacon as I walked down the sidewalk and went to my truck. It was a little fattier than what was on my plan, but if full-fat bacon didn't say celebration, I didn't know what did.

I hopped in my truck—the keys were still in it—and drove away from the farm. In ten minutes or so, my destination came into view.

Cottonwood Falls Cemetery.

41

MIA

EVEN THOUGH I'D showered the night before, I took another shower to wash off all the nocturnal activities. And as I got ready for the day in the small bathroom, I imagined Ford as a kid, getting ready for school in here, fighting for sink space with his four brothers. There was still a toothpaste holder glued to the wall with five spaces in it.

When I finished brushing my teeth and blow-drying my hair, I applied makeup and left the bathroom, heading to the kitchen, where I could hear the hum of conversation. I wasn't sure how long Ford would be gone for his run, just that he wasn't back yet.

His dad and younger brother sat at the table,

talking over plates half full of bacon and eggs and cups of coffee.

When they noticed me, Gray hopped up and sent me a smile, reminding me of my own dad on a weekend morning. "Let me get you a plate for breakfast," he said. "What would you like?"

"You don't need to," I said. "I can serve myself."

"Nonsense," he replied. "You're our guest. So, I made breakfast potatoes—from the garden—eggs from my son Fletcher's house, and bacon from some of our pigs. Didn't gather it all this morning, of course." He chuckled. "But it's all farm to table."

I grinned at him. "Really? That's such a treat. I'll have it all, thank you."

Gray exchanged a glance with Bryce, who wore a look of approval. "Not picky," Gray said. "I like that."

Why did that make me feel so proud of myself?

I went to sit at the table across from Bryce. He looked so much like Fletcher. All dark hair and dark glittery brown eyes. Their mom had the darker features —I could tell from the photos of her around the house.

"So tell me about college," I said to Bryce. "It feels like forever since I was there."

He chuckled. "Nothing much has changed, I'm sure." He glanced at his dad, then gave me a sly wink. "All studying and hard work. No parties happening at all."

Gray chuckled. "Exactly."

I grinned at their exchange. "What are you studying?"

"Computer science," Bryce said. "I'll graduate next year."

"If you're looking for a job, we're always hiring in the IT department."

"Really? Wow, I'd love to apply when I get a little closer to graduation."

"You can get my contact info from Ford," I replied with a smile. If Bryce was anything like the rest of his family or the other people I knew from Cottonwood Falls, he was sure to be hardworking and down to earth. We needed all we could get of that at Griffen Industries.

"Great," Bryce said as Gray handed me a plate full of food and a mug of steaming coffee.

"Need cream?" he asked.

"Like I need air," I teased.

He went to the fridge. "It's just the supermarket brand. Nothing special."

I chuckled, taking the cream. "Thank you."

I took a bite of the eggs, covered in cheese and salsa, and my mouth watered. This was really good. Better than the food I paid a small fortune to have

prepared for me. "You said this is food you produce?"
I asked.

Gray nodded.

"It's *so* good. Do you take orders?"

He grinned. "I mean, I'm a little far from
Dallas."

"Right." I chuckled. "Can I put in an order for...
the ingredients?"

"Sure thing, but right now, I want to get to know
you."

I felt a little embarrassed for trying to talk business with my boyfriend's dad, but that was my life. It
was all business, and I was good at it too. Meeting a
boyfriend's family? That, I didn't have as much practice with.

Bryce said, "I'm going to my room to get some
homework done." Then he scrambled to clear his
plates and left. His quick exit left me more than a
little on edge as I sat at the table with my food.

"Do you have an interrogation lamp?" I asked
Gray.

He chuckled heartily. "It's nothing like that."

"Good," I said, relieved. Then I doctored my
drink and took a sip.

"You're the first girl—woman—Ford's brought
home is all," Gray said.

Wow... I knew Ford said he was out of practice, but I guess I hadn't realized that I was the first ever.

Gray studied me a moment. "I knew he'd need a woman who understood his job..."

I lowered my cup, meeting his gaze. "Why do I feel like there's a 'but' coming?"

He shrugged. "What about a woman who understands *life*? I know all about your title. I want to know about *you*. And your priorities."

I leveled my hands on the oak table. "Not many people ask me about myself," I admitted.

His smile was gentle. "You'll find the Madigans are a rare breed."

I had to laugh. "That's true. Well..." I began by telling him how I grew up in a modest home next door to my best friend, Farrah, who I was still close with today. I talked about being raised by older parents and how I had to work my way through college and then grad school. I told him how much I enjoyed working with Gage and admired his work ethic. And I told him about trying to acquire the Andersen sisters' business and why it meant so much to me. "For me, Gray, it's not work or life. Work *is* my life. It's where I can create meaningful change, not just get a paycheck."

He smiled at me. "I like you, Mia."

I grinned, utterly relieved. "Thank God, because

it would be awkward to buy bacon from you if you didn't."

He tossed his head back, laughing. "Gosh, Ford needs you."

I smiled back at him. And I was honest as I said, "I need Ford. I needed someone who wouldn't want to dim my light to make his look brighter."

Gray looked totally content as he picked up our plates and walked them to the sink. I swore I heard him say, "Maya would have loved you."

42

FORD

I DIDN'T GO SEE my mom's grave right away. I
knew it would be hard to see her name etched in
marble when she should have been here with us. She
would have been in her fifties now, still young.

So I stalled, taking advantage of the early
morning chill, and went for a long run around the
dirt roads surrounding the cemetery. This was how I
used to train in high school—land in the country was
divided up by "sections," a mile on each side. I could
run around a section once to get four miles in, twice
for eight, and so on. Sometimes, I'd count telephone
poles to track my distance, knowing there were about
a hundred yards between each one. Sixteen to a mile.

Today, as I ran, there was a mix of nostalgia,

anxiety, and love all taking turns filling my head and heart while I ran.

I missed my mom.

Mia loved me.

What if I messed everything up?

I'd come so far since running country roads in high school.

What if it all went away?

Mia loved me.

And I loved her.

By the time I ran the section a couple times, I was exhausted, spent physically and emotionally. I slowed to an easy jog toward the familiar spot where we'd laid my mom to rest all those years ago. I'd been barely old enough to know what was happening as each person was given a chance to toss dirt on the casket, saying goodbye.

As soon as I got home the day of her funeral, I changed out of my suit and ran. I ran as far and as fast as I could, realizing I could make myself tired enough so the ache in my muscles won the battle over the ache in my heart.

That day was still sharp in my memory as I reached our family plot where my mom's grave was mixed with other family members'. Grandparents. An aunt and uncle. But her white marble headstone, vases on either side filled with silk sunflowers, stood out.

I finally came next to her gravesite, eyes tracing the familiar words permanently etched in marble.

Maya Madigan
Beloved wife and mother
"Lead with love."

The years showed the shortness of her life. Thirty-eight years old. Mia's age exactly.

My heart clenched at the thought, nearly bringing me to my knees.

I focused my gaze instead on the trinkets surrounding my mom's grave, trying to ground myself in the moment. There was a turtle statue, a ceramic football player I'd gotten for her when I made the Diamonds as a first-round pick, and other small items my siblings and nieces and nephew left for her.

One day I wanted to leave a memento from a winning Super Bowl here.

But for now, I sat on the buffalo grass slightly to the side, extending my legs to stretch as I sat with the memory of her. "Hey, Mom," I said softly.

I knew deep down she wasn't here, but I swore I felt her presence somehow. My smile trembled for a moment, because I realized this was another one of those milestones she wouldn't be here for. She'd never get to meet Mia. See us together.

Just like she hadn't been there for my first professional football game, to see me play in the Super Bowl.

"I miss you," I whispered.

Of course she didn't answer.

Hadn't answered since I was ten years old. But that didn't keep me from hoping.

I looked around at the empty cemetery. Beyond the limestone and chain fence, all you could see were wheat fields and blue skies. No one was here but me.

Emboldened by privacy and needing to bring Mom along on this part of my life, I told her all about Mia. How strong she was, how successful and beautiful and kind and determined. I explained how Mia made me feel—invincible but somehow weak at the same time. Challenged to be the best version of myself, just to keep up with her.

I finished by saying, "You'd love her." I touched the rough top of her headstone with my fingertips and waited for a moment. "I'll see you later, hopefully to tell you we won the Super Bowl."

As I walked away, I imagined the sun shining down on my shoulders was Mom's way of saying she was with me, that she approved, and maybe, just maybe, she was proud of me too.

WHEN I GOT BACK to the house, I found Mia and Bryce sitting at the kitchen table, both working at their computers. When they heard me come in, they swiveled their heads toward me.

I smiled at them—Mia already seemed right at home sitting on worn wooden chairs that had been there as long as I could remember. She pulled out her earbuds and said, "That was a long run. How are you still standing?"

I went to her, kissing her temple. "Just did eight miles, then I had a few errands to run... Want to get changed into jeans? I have a surprise for you."

She gave me a curious smile that lit her soft blue eyes. "Sure," she said, getting up. As she walked to the bedroom, I called, "Wear boots."

Once she was gone, Bryce lowered his head-phones to hang around his neck and pretended to crack a whip.

I rolled my eyes at him. "One day, you'll understand."

"I hope not," he retorted. Then he folded his arms across his chest, looking up at me skeptically. "So what were these errands you had to run?"

"It's a surprise. For Mia. Not for you, *college boy*," I

teased, using the nickname Hayes had especially or him.

He shook his head exasperatedly, looking so much like Fletcher it was crazy. "If I hear from Hayes one more time that I should have gone to trade school..."

I leaned up against the wall. "You know how it is. Everyone thinks their way is the right one."

Bryce tilted his head. "You're right. I've been thinking he should have a business degree to run that shop."

"Nah," I replied. "Running that shop's an education all its own."

"There you go, sounding like Hayes again," Bryce grumbled.

I smiled at my little brother. "Time gives the best perspective."

"Okay, fortune cookie."

Mia's boots clacked on the floor as she came into the kitchen, and damn, did she look good in denim and leather. Paired with a flowy white blouse, she looked like country heaven. I took her under my arm, kissing her temple.

"Help," Bryce said, making prayer hands. "He's giving me life advice."

Mia looked up at me, smiling. "Is it good at least?"

"Yes," I answered at the same time Bryce said, "No."

She chuckled, shoulders shaking under my arm. "So, what's this surprise?" she asked me.

"It's outside, waiting for you. Let's go."

43

MIA

VERY RARELY DID anyone surprise me. Even more rarely was the surprise pleasant.

So I couldn't stop smiling the whole way outside as Ford led me down the gravel drive toward the barn. I knew whatever he had waiting for me would be amazing.

When we reached the big red building and I saw two saddled horses waiting in the corral, I stared at him in shock. In fact, I couldn't speak. I pointed at the horses and then at us. "Really?"

His easy grin caught all the light coming down from the clear blue sky. And he looked so damn handsome, his family home surrounded by bright yellow sunflowers silhouetting him. "We're going for a horseback ride, then a picnic by the creek," he said.

My mouth was hanging so far open I couldn't form words. Horseback riding? That was something I watched in romantic movies or read in novels—not something that happened to this city girl in real life. It was too good to be true. Especially considering I spent my years from eight to ten years old obsessively reading horse novels and collecting figurines. "Really?"

He nodded, opening the gate to the corral. I was glad he told me to bring boots as we stepped over the mixture of dried manure and dirt, making our way toward the horses. They were gorgeous, their short sleek coats catching the light. One was the typical chestnut color you'd expect of a horse, but another had the most interesting coat, white flecked with bits of copper and onyx. That one had a white mane and tail that nearly glistened in the sunlight.

As we drew closer, I watched with awe as the animals swished their tails to shoo an errant fly or nipped at their chests. Every so often, they shifted, making their hooves clop in the ground.

Ford pointed at the chestnut one, saying, "This is Acres," and then to the white speckled one. "And this is Blister."

"Blister?" I said. "He's such a pretty horse though."

Ford chuckled, stepping closer to pat Blister's

muscled shoulder. "Apparently, Dad got blisters from the saddle because it took so long to break him to ride."

As I looked up at the creatures, I said, "Are you sure they can hold my weight?" I didn't want to hurt them.

"These are strong horses," he answered. "Built for work. And if they can carry me, they can carry you."

I stared up at them in awe, and then back to the man who gifted me something money couldn't really buy. "Can I pet him?" When I glanced at Ford, I noticed the midday sun sharpened and highlighted just how attractive he was.

I was so distracted by his looks, I was surprised when he covered my hand with his and brought it to the horse's side. His palm was warm as he guided my hand over Blister's soft coat, powerful muscles twitching underneath.

I smiled up at him. "This is like every girl's child-hood fantasy."

"You were a horse girl?" he teased.

I smiled. "Who wasn't?"

"Well then, riding one should be a treat."

My heart thumped with fear. I'd dreamed of riding horses since I was a kid, but... they were taller than I imagined. Powerful in a beautiful but scary way. "I don't even know how to get up there."

"I'll get you a bucket," he said. "Easy."

He disappeared into the barn, leaving me to stand by Blister. I noticed long, thick eyelashes over dark glassy eyes. "You won't buck me off, will you?" I whispered.

The animal didn't answer before Ford came back with a bright orange five-gallon bucket. Then he turned it over and set it next to the roan horse. "Climb up and put your foot in the stirrup."

I looked at him doubtfully.

"I'll help you up if you need it."

I gave him another skeptical look, but then remembered our tryst in the weight room. He could handle me. The thought turned me on when I should have been focusing. "Okay, okay," I finally said. "Hold on to me."

He put his large hands on my waist, and I liked the feel of his support as I stepped onto the bucket, took hold of the saddle, put my foot in the wooden stirrup, and used all my strength to hoist myself on. The saddle cupped to my ass, and honestly, I felt kind of hot up here.

Judging by the way Ford grinned up at me, a slight heat to his gaze, he agreed. "That wasn't so bad, right?"

I shrugged a shoulder, acting like it was no big deal. (It totally was.)

Then he took the reins connected to my horse, untying them from the post. "First, I'll walk you around so you can get used to the feel of riding," he explained. "Then you can try on your own. Sound good?"

I nodded. But my heart still lurched as he began leading my horse through the corral. I grabbed nervously onto the saddle horn. Blister's jaunty gait would definitely take some getting used to.

"Use your core muscles to hold yourself upright, and you can press into the stirrups to absorb some of the movement."

I nodded, focusing on the task at hand. I'd gotten my MBA. Surely, I could get this down too.

After a few laps around the corral, I was starting to get the hang of things. Ford kept adding skills until soon I was holding the reins and guiding Blister to trot in circles on my own.

There was something so freeing, so powerful, about sitting atop a horse and gazing down at the world around me. Feeling the wind blow back my hair. Feeling my muscles work in tandem with the animal.

"That's my girl!" Ford whooped from the opposite side of the corral. "I think we're ready!"

I grinned. "Yee haw!"

His laugh made my heart feel light. As I led Blister toward him, he easily untied and swung up onto Acres like he'd been doing it all his life. Probably because he had. "You made that look so easy!" I called. "You didn't even need a bucket."

The horse pranced underneath him as he settled in. He calmed it down, talking and guiding it in circles.

"Are you sure it's okay?" I asked him. I wasn't sure I could handle a horse like that.

"Yeah, this is Dad's new horse. Still a little high-strung."

"Okay," I said uncertainly. He was the expert, and I realized... I trusted him. I just couldn't bear the thought of him getting hurt, especially during football season. "So where are we going?" I asked.

"Follow me."

We rode through the gate of the corral, then he led the way into another pasture. When we reached the top of the next hill, we had an incredible view.

He pointed out a white farmhouse maybe a mile away. There was another red barn and dozens of cattle in a different pen along with farming equipment. "That's the Griffens' place," he said. "And their feed yard where they fatten the steers for meat."

He pointed toward a stand of trees in the valley

forming a triangle with the two houses, a stream winding through it. "This is the creek where we'd always meet up with the Griffens and play."

I smiled over at him. "It sounds like a great childhood."

"It was." A misty look crossed his features before he nudged his horse's side, continuing the ride toward the trees.

I followed him, studying his strong form perched atop Acres. I wondered if riding had been an escape for him and his brothers when they were younger. I could picture it—getting atop a horse and just running from all your problems.

But then again, maybe that's what football had been for him. A way to run. To avoid the pain of losing his mom, of seeing her suffer and coping with the aftermath.

My heart swelled for the younger version of him as I walked behind him. The world knew him as Ford Madigan, star quarterback. But now I was seeing there was so much more to him the world would never get to see. I was lucky he had let me in.

We reached the stand of trees, prairie giving way to shade grass and a minefield of fallen branches. Under a shady cottonwood tree, Ford slowed his horse and hopped down. "This is it." He tied the reins to a thick tree branch before coming to help me down. It was a little easier than getting on. But as I stepped back, my muscles had to adjust to solid land again. "I feel like I have sea legs," I said, shaking out my extremities.

He laughed. "Why do you think the cowboys in the old westerns always walked so funny?"

"True," I chuckled. I did the exaggerated cowboy walk, arms awkwardly to the side, imagining spurs jangling at the back of my ankles. "How's this?"

He came to me, kissing me slowly. He was smiling when he pulled away and said, "I love you." He linked his fingers with mine. "Come on, I have something to show you."

44

FORD

ONCE WE GOT close to the last part of my surprise, I covered Mia's eyes. I wanted to see her reaction.

After guiding her to our destination next to the riverbank, I pulled my hands away, revealing a red gingham picnic blanket, a basket full of fresh food, and a chilled bottle of champagne.

Here in the shade with a slow breeze blowing through the leaves and the sound of the water slowly flowing by, it was pure bliss.

She covered her mouth with her hands. "Ford, this is so gorgeous. You put this all together for me?"

"I had a little help," I admitted, going to the blanket, shucking my boots, and sitting cross-legged. When she joined me, I began pouring her a glass of champagne. Once hers was full, I poured my own.

Then I held it up for a toast. "Mia, I love you, but I know actions speak louder than words. I have every intention of showing you just what I mean when I say that."

She smiled softly at me, clinked her glass to mine. "I love you, Ford Madigan."

We took a sip before I opened the basket to show her an assortment of vegetables, fruits, meats, and cheeses. I offered her a plate, and she picked several options, nibbling on some soft cheese first. "So good," she hummed. "I swear everything tastes better in Cottonwood Falls."

"This is from the dairy," I told her. "Liv used to work there."

"Of course it's local." She chuckled and wiped a crumb from the corner of her mouth. "I'm definitely having my personal shopper pay visits here."

I smiled and admitted that I did the same with my chef. He sourced much of my protein and dairy from Cottonwood Falls, and even my fruits and vegetables in the summertime. "Once you eat home-grown food, the stuff you get at the supermarket just isn't the same."

She nodded. "There's a lot that's different here." Her gaze held mine for a moment, and she parted her lips like she was about to say something but closed them again.

"What?" I asked.

"I just want to know... what changed? You were so against dating before."

I lifted a corner of my mouth, admitting, "I met you."

Her cheeks blushed as she looked down at the blanket and back to me.

"It's not just a line," I promised, intertwining my fingers with hers. "You're like no woman I've ever met before. You have your own life, your own goals, and you showed me that I could have both." I squeezed her hand. "I could have love and football and an impact with my charity. No one ever showed me what was possible like you did, just by being yourself."

Her smile was liquid warmth as she leaned closer, kissing me softly. When she sat back, her gaze was on our surroundings. "Do a lot of people come out here?"

"No, it's just us." I paused. "Although we do throw Maya's birthday parties out here each year. She likes to go tubing with everyone she loves."

"My kind of girl," Mia commented.

"Mine too." I always had a soft spot for my oldest niece. Maybe just because I knew her first.

Mia stood up, facing the river.

"Where are you going?" I asked.

Instead of answering, she lifted her shirt over her head, revealing a lacy bra with her full chest nearly spilling over. Then she unbuttoned her jeans and slid them down her legs. Soon, she had ditched the thong and bra as well, dropping them into a pile on the picnic blanket.

With most of my blood running to my hardening cock, it was all I could do to sit there and stare.

"Care to join me for a swim?" she said with a flirty smile.

Somewhere in the back of my mind, I thought, *I probably shouldn't.* Slippery mud probably wasn't a good idea. But how many times had I come out here as a kid without getting hurt?

I couldn't miss out on this moment with Mia. Especially not when it had always been fine before.

My lips slowly formed a wolfish grin. "Try and stop me."

My shirt was off in a second flat, but I had to watch in awe as she walked her naked body toward the stream, her ass rippling with each step, reminding me of when I was slamming into her the night before.

She waded into the cool water until it rose above her waist, just her tits skimming the water's surface. Then she lowered herself under and rose up again, water rippling down her face, her chest, her darkened blond hair.

Her lips parted as she took a breath and shook out her mane. And fuck, it took all I had to wait to join her until I had my boots and jeans off.

Then I went to the water with her, sliding in the stream. Mud and rocks squished under my feet, and cool water swirled around me.

It was one of those moments that made me glad to be alive.

And it got even better when I took her in my arms, kissing her desperately.

She met my passion with her own, wrapping her legs around my waist and letting me hold her up as her fingers tugged at my hair. Her hard nipples pressed against my chest, contrasting all her soft curves. I dug my fingers into her thighs, loving how pliable she was under my touch, how I could feel her heat growing and building where her center pressed against my lower abs.

Breathlessly, she pulled away from me, heat glazing her blue eyes, water still beaded on her face, her shoulders.

I glanced from her eyes to her dark pink lips. "You're so sexy," I breathed.

She smiled, leaning in and kissing the tip of my

nose. "Says the man with a twelve pack of abs and 'football's brightest smile.'"

I brushed her hair behind her ear. "Quoting magazine headlines at me?"

"Well, if *Trending Magazine* says so, then it must be true."

I rubbed the tip of my nose against hers. "They must have caught me when I was smiling at you." I reached one of my hands up from her hip, slowly lowering her so her feet touched the bottom, then cupped her cheek in my hands. She really was so beautiful.

"Can I tell you something?" she asked me, leaning into my touch.

I nodded.

She covered my hands on her cheeks with both of hers. "I know everyone thinks I'm this strong, savvy woman, and I am. I have to be. But I feel like I can be soft with you."

My heart swelled, because that's exactly what I wanted to be—her landing place, her rock. "You can, Sunflower."

She tipped her chin up, kissing my lips, softer, slower.

And I soaked in every drop of her kiss, of this moment, just us together with the water slowly moving past us, a lazy wind rustling the trees and grass.

It might not be a flashy room or hundreds of roses or a display of fireworks flashing through the sky, but this was everything I wanted. Because I wasn't *falling* into love, tossing and turning through the sky toward some unsure landing.

I was suddenly surrounded by love, encapsulated in a soft, supported bliss I'd never experienced before.

I'd never stop fighting to be the man who deserved Mia's love.

45

MIA

I WOKE up knowing I loved Ford.

But somehow, seeing the way he looked at me, feeling how much he loved me, making love to him in the stream as the water rushed by... I loved him even more than I did before.

After making love, we splashed and played around for a little while, and when my hands started to prune, I said, "I'm going to lie out on the blanket and dry off."

"I'm going to swim around a bit," he replied.

I watched for a moment as he lay back in the stream, floating with just his face and chest breaking the surface. He looked so much younger here, at peace. When we made this agreement, I didn't quite understand why it was so important to him to stay in Dallas when he had enough money to fly back any time he wanted and could play football anywhere. But I was starting to understand. It wasn't just about living close to home and being near people he loved; it was about being anchored to this place where he could be fully himself.

With a small smile, I walked out of the stream. The sandy soil crunched under my feet as I walked to the picnic blanket and lay back on the gingham. Grass and twigs broke up the texture under my skin as I looked up at the canopy of cottonwood trees with small patches of bright blue sky peeking through.

Between the water covering me and the breeze, goosebumps formed on my skin, tiny peaks and valleys. Shivering slightly, I went to get my clothes, sliding them over slightly damp skin.

It was great being out here in the middle of nowhere, unconcerned with the world around us. Soon, I'd have to get back to reality, checking my phone, responding to emails and such. But for now... I was at peace.

I finished buttoning my pants, moisture from my hair dripping down my back. I wrung it out and took in Ford swimming down the stream and back, arm muscles powerfully slicing through the water, feet casting splashes behind him.

When he got closer to parallel with me, he stood, shaking water from his short hair and wiping moisture from his face. He cast me a sultry smile before walking from the water, droplets cascading down his hard stomach, falling to his semi-hard cock.

I licked my lips, ideas racing through my mind of the next thing that could occupy our time.

His foot must have landed unsteadily, because he stumbled slightly. I thought it was no big deal, until he let out a cry, water splashing around him as he fell to his hands and knees.

My heart lurched, and I yelled, "Ford! Are you okay?"

I fully expected him to jump up and say he'd lost his footing on some mud. But he stayed on his knees, crawling out of the water. I raced to him and saw blood dripping down the side of his foot, mixing with mud caked there.

"What happened?" I asked, trying to tell how bad it was.

He moved to sitting, studying the gash on the side of his foot—it had to be at least three inches long, and it was gaping open. My stomach sank as I knelt beside him. "Ford, you need stitches."

His expression was stony, not revealing a thing. "I

need you to get my clothes." His voice was so emotionless it scared me.

I got up, running to the picnic basket to get a bottle of water and his clothes. Then I hurried back. "Let me rinse it out before you put your clothes on."

He nodded stiffly, not offering any more words before I emptied the water over his wound. He hissed sharply as more blood rushed out of the gash. The mud had hidden some of the damage— it was worse than I had feared. Ignoring the guilt and worry threatening to take over, I got to work, helping him dress in his pants before wrapping his shirt tightly around the wound and tying it together.

"My phone," he said.

I felt faint as I walked to get his phone from the blanket where he left it. Forcing myself to take deep breaths, I carried it back to him. With a few shaky taps on the screen, he held it to his ear.

He squeezed his eyes shut. "Dad, I need you to come pick up Mia and me... We're still at the creek... I think I stepped on some barbwire or glass or something." His voice broke. "It's pretty bad."

At the emotion finally showing in his words, my heart ached for him. I sniffed back my tears, hurriedly packing things away into the picnic basket. And at the roar of a truck engine, Ford stood up. He had on one of his cowboy boots, the other in his hand.

"Let me help you," I said. "Put your arm around me."

He didn't say a word, choosing to hop toward his dad, who was already out of the pickup and rushing toward us. Instead of asking, Gray just grabbed Ford's hand, drawing it up and around his shoulder. Gray's arm was tight around his son's waist as he led him toward the pickup.

My heart clenched, and I felt so awkward and alone as I gathered up the picnic blanket and basket and rushed after them, picking my way through the grass and branches until I reached the truck. It was only a single cab, and Ford sat on the passenger side. "You can sit in the middle," Gray said to me. "Go in on my side. I'm getting the horses."

Gray ran off, and with Ford's gaze hard on the dash, I asked him, "Do I need to ride a horse back?"

I could see the color draining from his face as he sat back, his eyes pressed shut. "No."

I wasn't sure how that was possible, because there were only two people capable of riding a horse and one of us had to drive. Not to mention that I didn't trust myself to drive where there wasn't a road.

But Gray returned, leading both the horses with their leather reins in one hand. I slid into the middle seat, and he got in, holding on to the reins through the open truck window. Blister and Acres ran alongside the truck as he drove the mile or so back to the house. It was painfully slow, especially sitting between two silent men. The countryside didn't feel so pretty and peaceful anymore.

It felt stressful. Remote. Too far from help. "Is there a hospital in Cottonwood Falls?" I asked.

Before Ford could answer, Gray said, "Fletcher's on his way."

Of course. Ford's brother was a doctor. He'd know what to do.

I held on to that little piece of hope, even though I could see blood soaking through the shirt wrapped around Ford's foot.

I didn't know much about football, but I knew you couldn't play on an injury like that.

What if Ford's dream of winning the Super Bowl was over, all because I suggested playing around in the creek?

And if I was thinking that, I knew he had to be as well.

Suddenly, "love" felt so flimsy, like vapor wisping through my fingertips, impossible to grasp, to hold on to.

Gray pressed on the brakes by the barn, saying, "Mia, drive Ford up to the house. Get him situated in the dining room for Fletcher. I'll put up the horses."

I nodded, scooting over as he got out and began leading the horses to the barn. At least now I had a purpose instead of sitting stiffly, silently, next to Ford.

He was on the right side, eyes closed, fists clenched in his lap. All the bouncing and jerking of the pickup over rough ground had to be painful for him, on top of all the emotional turmoil.

How had it been only hours ago that I was learning to ride? Living the high of newfound love?

It all seemed so distant now. I'd never felt lower as I put the truck into gear and started up the driveway. Ford still hadn't said a word to me. Not that I blamed him. He looked like he was going to be as sick as I felt.

I drove the rest of the way to the house and got out of the truck. I wanted to help him get inside, but he got out of the pickup on his own. He made it just a few hops before he swayed.

"Come on," I said, going to him and forcing him to accept my help, just like his dad had done. Another reminder that I didn't know Ford all that well yet. Maybe I'd never get the chance.

Begrudgingly, he held on and hopped beside me until we got inside. I helped him to the table like Gray had asked, and he sat down in one of the worn wooden chairs. I tried to imagine what Fletcher might need, going to the kitchen and searching through cabinets and drawers until I found a pile of rags and a bowl to fill with cold water from the sink.

I dipped a rag in the water and handed it to Ford, who looked paler than ever, a little green too. "Put this on your forehead. It should help with the nausea."

He didn't move, eyes trained on the ground.

"Take it," I said, my voice coming out harshly.

He looked at me, and I knew, deep down, I'd remember that look for the rest of my life. His eyes were dark blue, bottomless pools. No hope, no light. It was all... gone.

But at least he did as I asked, sitting back and resting the rag over his forehead. My phone began to vibrate in my belt bag, but I ignored it, worried about Ford.

"Is there anything else I can get you?" I asked. "Maybe I can find some ibuprofen or Tylenol."

The front door opened, and we both shifted our gaze to see who'd arrived. I'd expected to see Gray, but instead, Fletcher was swooping purposefully inside, wearing shorts and a T-shirt, not scrubs or a lab coat like I'd expected of a doctor. He carried a black leather bag with him.

"What happened?" he asked as he reached us.

Without waiting for an answer, he knelt before his brother, slowly unwinding the shirt covering his wound.

Ford's voice was weak as he said, "I stepped on something at the creek. Barbwire, maybe some glass. I don't know."

"So you'll need a tetanus shot just in case," Fletcher said. His expression was grim as he studied the wound. "Stitches also. Do you have a contact for your team's doctor?"

Ford nodded, adjusting his hip to get his phone out of his pocket. He searched through the contacts and said, "Sent it to you."

While Fletcher scanned his phone for the message, my own device started ringing again, and Ford addressed me for the first time. "Go get it."

I shook my head. "They can wait."

But he stared me down, voice coming out clipped. "Answer your phone, Mia."

Fletcher quietly excused himself to call the team doctor, but Ford didn't act like he'd heard, focusing on me with those empty eyes.

"But, Ford, I—I want to be here for you."

"Handle your business," he gritted out. "I don't need or want you here."

Wow. I knew he was having a hard time, but that was uncalled for. "Ford..." I began, but he cut me off.

"This was supposed to be fake!" His voice rose, slicing through me. "It wasn't supposed to be real. I wasn't supposed to be hurt while playing around with *you* against my better judgement. I shouldn't have put you over my work, just like you shouldn't be putting me first now. So go, Mia. This was a mistake. Just go."

46

MIA

FORD'S WORDS to me were like a door slammed in my face.

A message received loud and clear.

Our love was a *game*. A distraction from more important things.

My eyes were stinging as I left the kitchen to open my bag and answer my phone. I could hear Fletcher speaking quietly to Ford, but couldn't process it with the ache in my heart. Nor with the surprise at seeing Vanover's name on my screen.

He knew not to contact me unless there was an emergency. Part of me was relieved to have something else to think about other than Ford regretting everything between us.

"Hello?" I said. I got into the room where we

stayed, the bed already made, and sat down on its soft surface.

"Mia, have you checked your email?"

"No, I've been..." Worried. Scared. Rejected? "Busy," I finished lamely.

"I've been trying to call you, but it went right to voicemail."

"I must not have had a signal." I shifted the phone to my other ear. "Vanover, what's going on?"

"The Andersen Avenue vote was moved to tomorrow morning, first thing. I sent the calendar change two hours ago, but you haven't replied. You need to start preparing."

My eyebrows drew together as I paced the small room. Suddenly, it felt more confining than cozy. "I didn't approve that. We weren't supposed to meet for another *two weeks.*"

"Unfortunately, Thomas cleared it with the board," Vanover said. "I could reach out to every-one's assistants to reschedule but—"

"That would make us look unprepared and hurt their confidence in me as a leader." I rubbed at my temple with my free hand. "Thank you for letting me know." Now I needed to figure out how to get back home to prepare. But Ford's injury...

"Zeke should be arriving at the Madigan Ranch soon to collect you," Vanover said. "I figured you would need all the time you could get and Ford might want to stay."

Just the sound of his name broke my heart. "You're a lifesaver, Vanover," I finally said. "Thank you."

"That's what I'm here for," he replied. "I'll be in the office when you get here and have food and drinks ready at your desk."

"See you soon," I replied, hanging up my phone. Part of me wanted to stay here with Ford, to help. But he'd sent his message—through silence and through his stern words. I was to take care of my business.

I roughly shoved my phone back in my fanny pack and began returning my things to my suitcase.

I was midway through zipping it up when I heard the doorbell. I went to the window, seeing the sleek black car, dust blurring the black paint. Then, I heard Bryce's voice. "I didn't know the doorbell still worked."

My stomach dropped, knowing what this would look like to Ford, to his family.

Like I was running away.

I left my packed bags on the bed, going out to the living room to see my driver talking with Gray and Bryce.

The men turned to look at me, and I saw disappointment in Gray's features. Surprise in Bryce's.

"Mia, can I help with your bags?" Zeke offered.

I nodded. "I'll bring them out to you." Turning, I went to get my luggage, feeling the men's eyes on my back. From the other room, I heard Ford calling, "Who's here?"

Gray hesitated before answering, "It's Mia's driver."

My heart stuttered as I raced to get my bags and bring them back to the living room. I thanked Zeke, who quietly took them out the front door. But once it closed behind him, I was alone with Gray and Bryce.

"I need to talk with Ford," I said, brushing by them to the kitchen.

Ford looked hurt, and Fletcher looked like he wished he could fade into the pebbled wallpaper.

Ford was the first to speak. "Did you call the car before or after I got hurt?"

"It's not..." I began to defend myself. But midsentence, I realized it didn't really matter. He'd hardly spoken a word to me since he got injured, cast me aside when all I wanted was to help. I lifted my chin. "I have work matters to attend to in Dallas."

He pressed his lips together, nodding slowly. "I wanted you to leave anyway. Just go."

I heard Bryce suck in a breath. He and Gray must have followed me around the corner.

And even with Ford's family watching, I wanted to yell and tell him that he already dismissed me. But there was no use arguing or defending myself. *I* knew the truth.

So I turned away from Ford and spoke to his dad, fighting to keep my voice from trembling. "Gray, thank you so much for your hospitality. It meant a lot to be welcomed so warmly by you and your family."

His gaze was troubled as he dipped his head in acknowledgement.

Then I nodded to Fletcher and Bryce, avoiding eye contact with Ford, and turned to leave this family. This home.

I'd felt so comfortable here just hours before. And now?

The way Ford had treated me tore at my chest, at the fragile petals of love blooming between us. I knew he was going through a tragedy, but I also knew my worth. How someone treated you at their lowest said more than how they treated you at their best. And even if it hurt like hell to hold a boundary with my heart, I also knew I deserved better.

I was halfway down the sidewalk to the car when the front door banged open.

Even knowing Ford was hurt, I couldn't help but

hope it was him chasing after me. Instead, I saw Bryce coming down the sidewalk. "Mia, wait up," he called.

I paused on the sidewalk, disappointment mingling with worry at what he was going to say, what he must think of me.

He cast my driver a nervous look before facing me. Then he lowered his voice and said, "Don't let Ford hurt your feelings. He's just upset. He'll cool down."

"I know," I said. What more was there to say?

Bryce patted my arm gently. "He cares about you. He's just not good at showing it yet."

My heart was shattering at each of his words, breaking, because Bryce wanted so badly for his brother to be happy, but I knew I needed more from a partner. I lifted a corner of my lips. "If I had a little brother, you're the one I'd want."

He smiled slightly. "You make me sound like a little kid."

I chuckled. "No, you're a good man," I told him. "You'll apply for an internship one day, right?"

"I will."

I nodded. "I'll tell them to look out for you."

"Even then, they won't see me coming." He grinned and turned to walk away.

But I said, "Bryce?" I bit my bottom lip nervously.

He turned back to me. "Yeah?"

"Take care of him, okay? I can't imagine what it would be like if... if he couldn't..." I couldn't bring myself finish the sentence.

"I know," he said quietly.

There was nothing left to say, so I got in the car. My driver pulled away, leaving Madigan Ranch, Cottonwood Falls, and the love of my life in the rearview mirror.

47

FORD

THE SCREEN DOOR shut behind Mia, and we all flinched at the sound echoing through the house. Then it was so quiet, the sound of my racing heart was almost as loud as the things my brothers and dad *weren't* saying.

That is until Bryce gritted his teeth. "Are you going after her?"

I gripped the sides of my chair tightly, shifting my weight. "No. I wouldn't even if I could."

Bryce gaped at me then turned to my dad and Fletcher. "Aren't you going to say something?"

Fletcher didn't quite meet his gaze. Dad's frown deepened.

Bryce let out a huff, then left the three of us in

the dining room, going after Mia. I heard him call out her name.

My heart begged me to go after her with him, but to be honest, the biggest emotion I was feeling was *shame*. Followed by abandonment. Worry. Devastation... all the above. I wasn't good enough for her. Not then, and definitely not now.

Dad had the decency to stay silent, leaving me to my cyclonic inner thoughts, but Fletcher asked, "Do you want to talk about it?"

I shook my head.

All this time, I'd been admiring Mia for being a strong woman. She was fiercely committed to her goals, and the only time she'd strayed was during this crisis. Me on the other hand?

I'd been weak.

I'd become the kind of man who lost track of my priorities just to impress her. If she weren't here, I never would have gotten on a horse, much less gone to the stream and messed around like that. Even once a year, when my niece had her tubing party, I wore protective water shoes at least.

Love had made me careless. Malleable. Subject to whims instead of my goals.

I was a better man on my own, without the self-indulgence of romance.

Mia deserved better. My team deserved better.

My family, the kids I served in Texas... we all deserved better than what I'd done.

Fletcher's phone rang, making all of us jump. He glanced at it, saying, "The team doctor." He brought the phone to his ear. After a moment, he explained the situation with some medical terms I understood and some I didn't. Then he listened for a while.

"What's he saying?" I hissed.

Fletcher held up a finger, and when I pressed him again, he went to the other room altogether.

I slouched down in my chair, covering my face with my hands. This felt worse than losing the Super Bowl, because back then, at least one team had been happy. One team had been celebrating. People even told me how amazing it was to come in second place. Plus, there had been hope that we'd win the next time.

But no one was happy now. I could see it etched into everyone's faces. Especially Mia's. None of us knew how bad this was, what it would mean.

The door opened, and my heart jumped, wondering if she had come back.

Again, *weak*.

Then sneakers sounded on the wood floor, and Bryce came into the kitchen, a crease etched into his brow.

I opened my mouth to speak, but then Dad beat me to it. "She okay?"

Bryce answered with a somber shrug.

More footsteps sounded as Fletcher came back into the room. "The team doctor wants to stitch you up at the facility. Guess he's worried I'll do a botch job." There was some disgruntled muttering about his medical degree and residency. Then he let out a sigh. "I can drive you there, keep an eye on it."

"No, stay with your wife and kids," I said.

Fletcher started to argue, but Dad jumped in. "I'll drive you. Bryce, follow in my truck so I have a ride back."

Bryce nodded, looking so much like Fletcher, arms crossed and everything. "'Slong as I don't have to ride with Ford."

Fletcher huffed out a sigh. "Fine. I can see I'm not needed here. Let me bandage you up at least."

Within a few minutes, he had my wound wrapped for the trip. Then my brothers helped me out to my truck, the late afternoon sun glancing off the windshield.

Acting like I was an invalid, they helped me into the pickup. I swatted Fletcher's hand away when he tried to buckle me.

"Hey, I have kids—it's a habit," he said.

My smile lasted all of half a second.

Fletcher said, "Have the doctor call and update me, please. And if you need anything, let me know. I'll be in Dallas within two hours. Liv will be okay with the girls."

I nodded, grateful for him.

Even Bryce wished me good luck before shutting the door and walking to Dad's pickup.

That was the thing about family.

They loved you, even when you didn't deserve it.

After a couple minutes, Dad had my bags in the truck bed and was sitting in the driver's seat. He started the truck and pulled out the driveway, leaving home in the rearview.

Dad said, "I'll need you to give me directions when we get a little closer."

"Okay." I leaned my chair back, staring at the gray headliner. Even with my eyes open, my mind kept seeing the look on Mia's face when I told her I didn't want her here.

But she'd been so quick to pack her bags and leave. Had her driver been on standby this whole time, ready to whisk her away? Had she been planning for this to end badly, one way or another?

The question ricocheted through my mind as we drove down the highway, and the only reprieve I got was when Dad said, "You've been moping long enough."

Which wasn't really a reprieve at all, because now the attack was coming from my dad.

I stared over at him, convinced I hadn't heard him right. "Moping? I'm a professional football player with an injury. It's not something you just get over."

"*Moping*. And I don't care what name you wear on the front of your jersey; you have Madigan on your back. That means something."

Frustrated, I pushed the lever to raise my seat and stared over at Dad, suburbs blurring out the window behind him. "Tell me, how *should* I be reacting?"

"Well first of all, you should be calling Mia and apologizing for pushing her away."

I gritted my teeth together.

"Second, you should apologize to Bryce for snapping at him."

Could he hear my molars grinding?

"And third of all, you don't give up hope until you have all the information."

"Dad, I'm just a few months away from the end of the season, and I've already been dealing with turf toe. It's not looking good."

He gave me a wry smile. "Miracles don't require facts."

I looked out my window, annoyed by his optimism.

"You're thinking something," he said. "Go ahead."

I made myself look at him as I said it. "How can you believe in miracles when we needed one with Mom and she didn't get one? It's all chance."

Dad was quiet for a moment, and all I could hear was the rush of wind outside the vehicle and some overplayed country song on the radio. I already wished I could take back the question.

I could feel myself being shitty. Earlier to Mia, now to my dad. It was like this angry snake had replaced my tongue, lashing out every time I opened my mouth. I didn't know how to stop it. Which only made me feel worse. Weaker than before.

There was more patience in his voice than I deserved as he said, "Do you know how many people live their lives in marriages they hate? Resenting the person who lies in bed next to them?" He pressed his lips together, and when he spoke, his voice shook with emotion. "I loved your mom every day of her life, and I *know* she loved me too until her very last breath. If you ask me, that's a miracle."

My throat felt tight. "You're right, Dad. I'm glad you got a miracle. I'm just not sure I'll get mine."

48

MIA

I SAT AT MY DESK, poring over my presentation. I was supposed to have two more weeks to work on this. To come up with an angle proving that acquiring Andersen Avenue was the best choice for Griffen Industries.

But I didn't have two weeks. I had one night.

And even one night wasn't all that helpful because I kept checking my damn phone for a message from Ford.

I wanted to know if he was okay—if he'd heal or be out for the rest of the season.

Even though I'd taken a quick shower in the company gym, I could practically smell the silt of the stream, feel the coarse tangle of my hair slowly drying from its submersion in the murky water.

But even with all effects of the water washed away, Ford's rejection lingered in my heart, pumping and spreading throughout my body, permeating every bit of me until reality hit me with each pulse.

Ford.

Is.

Gone.

It's.

Over.

He.

Wanted.

Me.

To.

Leave.

And yet, some invisible vice wouldn't let my worries go until I knew he was okay.

Not that my concerns mattered. The meeting would take place tomorrow morning regardless of all this turmoil. I wouldn't be excused from presenting because of a fractured heart.

That was part of my job. There were benefits, immense benefits, but there were also costs. Like having to focus on work when all I wanted to do was rush to Ford and shake him while simultaneously being at his side and wishing he was okay.

I let out a frustrated groan and stared at my computer. I didn't have time for this.

To be stressing and worried in an adult relation-ship when all it would take was a simple text from him letting me know he was okay. I'd hoped he would reach out to me when he was ready, but I was starting to wonder... would he ever be ready?

As if he could hear my mind spinning, Vanover came into my office, carrying a takeout box and a Styrofoam cup with a lid. "Eat this," he said. "And then you should go home and get some rest before tomorrow morning."

I took the food and glanced toward the windows in my office. The sky was dark, tinted orange from all the glittering city lights. It was nearing midnight. "I have to get this ready. I'll be here all night."

"I figured you'd say that, so I got you this. Two shots of espresso." He passed me the cup.

I took it from him, saying, "You're a lifesaver, Vanover."

He smiled. "That's what I'm here for." He started to go toward the door.

"Van, you should go home," I said softly.

He turned back, opened his mouth to argue, but I shook my head. "When this is all over, I'm going to be spent. I'll need you to make sure I get to my place and get some sleep."

He gave me an understanding smile and said, "Good luck."

"I won't need it. I have coffee and vengeance on my side."

With a chuckle, he left the office.

And now I was alone in this big building.

In this big life I had created for myself.

A stab of loneliness sliced at me.

There was something comforting about having Ford as a boyfriend, someone who understood me on a deep level. And now... I couldn't bring myself to even think the word "over."

So I opened the takeout box, seeing my favorite food inside. Chicken fried chicken with mashed potatoes and green beans.

My eyes stung, and a shaky smile formed on my lips.

I wasn't alone. Vanover didn't need to do this— he could have gotten my usual dinner order, but he'd really had my back today. Somehow, he knew I'd needed to finish this. And I would still be pushing it close.

Fueled by his support, I ate my food while I continued going over my reports, finalizing the presentation before finalizing a script for my pitch. I would practice it several times before anyone came into the office. And my stylist would be here in the morning to make sure I was presentable.

Page by page, word by word, I got into the zone.

This was where I felt most at home, solving a problem, pushing up against impossible odds. Thomas might not have known it, but he'd done me a favor.

Tell me I can't do something, and I'd make damn sure to prove you wrong. Even if I had to do it with a broken heart.

49

FORD

I COULDN'T BRING myself to go home.

Not after the news I got from the doctor.

So I said goodbye to my dad, assuring him I'd take a taxi home, and stayed at the facility. Walked to the turf I knew so well.

My crutches creaked and crackled as I made my way onto the field. A cool fall breeze nipped at me as I walked farther over the spongy surface. Only the moon lit my path as I went farther, farther, to the fifty-yard line.

In the dark, empty stadium, I could see sixty thousand purple seats stretching up to the sky. The benches on each side of the field. Stark white lines marking our path forward. Yellow goalposts forever waiting for a game-changing kick.

Ironically, I felt small standing here all alone. Without my team. Without a competitor to defeat.

It was just me.

And I had no one to go home to.

That had never bothered me so much before. But now?

Even though Mia hadn't ever stayed in my bed, I couldn't bear the thought of returning home and sleeping without a goodnight text.

Without hearing "I love you" one more time.

I'd blown it, in so many ways. And soon, the entire team would get the message.

The doctor told me I needed to stay off my foot for the next week, and then we would check how it was healing. But with the location of my injury, he expected me to be off my foot another week after that, at least. We couldn't determine how severe the nerve damage would be until the wound closed.

A strong gust blew past, raising goosebumps on my skin.

With a shiver, I readjusted my grip on the crutches' handles, turning to take in more of the field, the tunnel that led to the locker room.

Cameras typically surrounded me on the way in. Soon, they'd be surrounding me for entirely different reasons.

This would cause a headache for the team's publicist and Coach Hinkle.

Would our second-string quarterback be ready?

Would it tank our chances at making it to the Super Bowl?

I closed my eyes at the thought, but then black turned orange as a flashlight beam panned over me. I opened my eyes again to see one of the security guards studying me, a person on either side of him.

Milo still wore his buffalo plaid pajama pants with a white T-shirt. His blond hair kept in check under a cap. Krew was more ready, in sweats.

Whatever strength I had left shattered as they came toward me. My hands shook on the crutches, making it impossible to move.

They stopped a couple feet away from me, concern glittering in their dark eyes.

"I'm... sorry." My voice cracked.

It felt like the rest of me was cracking too. But Milo stepped forward, wrapping me in a bear hug that held the pieces together. Krew patted my arm too.

None of us knew what my injury meant for the team.

But at least I knew I wouldn't have to find out alone.

MY PHONE WENT dead sometime the day before, and when I woke up the next morning, I had no urge to charge it and see what messages waited for me. I did want to talk to Mia, but what would I say?

Sorry I'm not the man you deserve?

Sorry I thought I was ready for a relationship, but turns out I lost myself in my love for you?

All of it fell flat in my mind, so I knew it would never be enough said out loud.

But I knew Coach would want to talk more than we had yesterday, so I plugged my phone in anyway.

With a heaviness in my chest, I got up, went to the bathroom and brushed my teeth and washed my face like I did every day. I had to hop on one leg so I didn't put pressure on the stitches and bust them. As I was wiping my face dry, I heard my phone ringing in the other room.

My heart leapt a little, hoping it was Mia. But instead, I saw my dad's name on the phone.

I swiped it, answering, and said, "Hey, Dad."

"I just wanted to see how you were doing, son." I could hear the wind in the background, like he was outside working and had thought of me.

"It was a rough night," I confessed, my voice

breaking. I sat down on my bed, feeling useless and weak. "Krew and Milo brought me home."

"I'm glad," Dad said. "Have you heard from Mia?"

Just her name wrenched my heart. "No. I haven't."

"Have you reached out to her?"

He knew me too well. I rubbed my brow with my thumb and pointer finger. "No."

In the background, I heard a cow *moo*. The sound made me wonder what life would be like if I had stayed on the farm, worked the land, been a helper to Dad. It would have been a nice life. But deep down, I knew it wouldn't feel like enough. Maybe that was the cross I would have to bear in my life—always coming up short. In football, in romance.

Shaking my head, I remembered what my dad had said. Madigans didn't act like this.

"Everything good with you?" I asked him.

He heaved a long breath. "You know, when you have kids, it feels like a piece of your heart goes where they do. Grandkids too. And right now, a piece of my heart is hurting. So am I good? Not one hundred percent. But I'm here for you, kid, and I know it will get better."

My lips twitched up. "I'm not sure how."

"You know, son, you have an entire charity that

works to get people mental health support. Maybe it's time you took your own advice."

I closed my eyes, hanging my head. Dad was right. My thoughts were a jumble, and I knew I had no chance at figuring out this tangle on my own. Of becoming the man Mia deserved without a little help.

50

MIA

"AND THAT IS why I believe acquiring Andersen Avenue is not only a smart financial decision but one that will improve public perception of Griffen Industries for years to come," I finished, changing to the next slide. "Any questions?"

The table lined with men and women in suits looked back at me, soaking in the information. Gage sat at one corner, and I could see it in his eyes—he was proud of me. But Thomas? He looked *pissed*.

He'd presented a run-of-the-mill e-commerce business with decent returns and no soul.

Me? I'd *killed* that presentation, even with little warning on the time change and no sleep the night before. All I needed was the chance to bring it home with some solid questions and answers.

Tallie raised her hand first, asking the question we'd prepared as soon as she got to the office. "Have you considered the additional PR resources that will be required to receive the goodwill you're hoping this will bring?"

I nodded. "First off, I'd like to say, it's not a *hope* of gaining goodwill. Texans have a strong history of looking out for each other, and by partnering with a philanthropic business like Andersen Avenue, we will be signaling with concrete action that we are an organization committed to those values. Secondly, you'll find the cost for additional PR and marketing staff has been included in the budget presented on page seventeen of your handouts."

Several papers rustled, and Tallie gave me a subtle smile.

Shantel, our head of HR, asked the next question. "What training will be required of the Andersen Avenue team on Griffen Industries' corporate culture?"

"Great question," I said. "During the transition, there will be an orientation process just like with other businesses we have acquired in the past."

Then Thomas spoke up. "And you will be overseeing this transition?"

"Of course," I replied, straightening my shoulders like I was a soldier going into battle. It was an odd question, but if I knew him, he had an angle in asking it.

"Are you sure you have the capacity to take on such a large venture, especially with such a high-profile relationship that has you traveling the country for... games?"

The room fell silent. It was a slight, and everyone knew it.

But it was also a gift. Without realizing it, Thomas had given me my chance to address everyone's unspoken doubts without looking desperate or pleading.

I looked at him with a placid smile. "I'm curious if you'd have asked that question of your male counterparts?"

Step one—point out that his issues with me were foundationally flawed. Done.

Thomas cleared his throat. "My male counterparts aren't CEOs of a billion-dollar company taking on a time-intensive project that won't pay off for over a year."

Step two...

"As you mentioned, I'm CEO, and it's important to be aware of the numbers, via the CFO." I gave a pointed look at Thomas. "Can you let me know how our numbers have tracked in the last quarter, since I began seeing my 'high-profile' partner?"

He mumbled something.

"What was that?"

"Up 4.3 percent."

"Thank you," I said. Then I turned to the CMO. "Nick, can you share the search volume of 'Griffen Industries' the last quarter?"

The CMO shuffled through a manila folder, then pulled out a paper. He adjusted his spectacles and said, "Search volume has increased six hundred and fifty percent over the previous quarter." He shuffled through more papers and pulled out a new one. "Our social media mentions have also increased by fifteen hundred percent, and sentiment is ninety-two percent positive."

"Thanks, Nick," I said, pacing over the carpeted boardroom floor at the head of the table. Then I spoke to our head project manager. "I thought this question might come up, and I believe in transparency, so, Penny, can you share my on-time completed task percentage, as well as the percentage of tasks that had due dates moved back?"

Penny nodded, reaching for her clipboard. "Eighty-five percent on-time task completion, which is seven percent higher than the company average, and twelve percent of tasks had due dates moved to a future date, two percent lower than company average."

"Thank you, Penny."

She nodded, making her brassy bangs wobble.

Thomas began to speak, but I held up a finger. "I'm not done."

His face turned a light shade of red.

But his fire just fueled my own.

I was *done* playing games with my life to earn respect that should have been there all along. Tallie may be brilliant, but so was I. And my team had just shown indisputable data to prove that fact.

So I gave what might be the most important speech of my career. "Before I was CEO, I worked under Gage Griffen, the founder of this company. For years, I spent *well over* sixty hours a week with him, getting the best education of my life.

"I learned how someone of his caliber thinks, acts, and makes decisions. And one thing I learned is that if people are doubting your vision, that's when you need to push harder. Because you have a vision not many people can see, which means you are seeing an *opportunity*.

"I have a vision for Andersen Avenue that can improve the community around us *and* Griffen Industries' bottom line. The question for all of you, as leaders within this company, is: Are you going to let go of an incredible opportunity because it's different than what we've seen before, because it's wearing a dress instead of a suit?"

Shantel said, "I move we put this to a vote."

Nick said, "I'll second that."

My heart ran wild, but I steadied myself by placing my hands flat on the conference room table.

This was the moment of truth.

51

FORD

OVER THE NEXT SEVERAL DAYS, I kept typing and deleting messages to her, not sure what to say. She never reached out. Never texted or called. And even without words, I'd gotten her message loud and clear: The next step was mine to make.

At least, I thought it was, until I got an email from Tallie on Saturday afternoon detailing everything I was supposed to do for our fake relationship. She also left a note at the bottom of the email that had my jaw dropping.

ANDERSEN AVENUE HAS BEEN SUCCESSFULLY ACQUIRED, SO *moving forward, there will be no need for you to make additional office visits. We will adjust future outings accordingly.*

I SAT BACK on my couch, staring at the screen, feeling the finality of that message.

Mia had done it. She'd convinced the board and reached her goal. Pride roared through my chest, beating out my own selfish disappointment. No matter what was going on with us, she kept succeeding. Just another testament to the woman she was.

I opened my phone to call her and tell her congratulations, but just before I hit send, I realized I couldn't. We'd yet to discuss what had happened. So I opened our text thread, my heart aching at the last messages we sent each other.

She was saying how excited she was to meet my family.

I couldn't handle texting her again, breaking this time capsule of when things were good for us.

So I put my phone down, knowing I'd see her tomorrow at the game and still having no idea what I would say.

I KNEW I'd need to sit out this week's game, but that knowledge hadn't lessened the blow of pacing on the sidelines all four hours of the game. I had never been more upset or disgusted with myself in my years as a professional football player.

It was worse than losing the Super Bowl.

Especially glancing back to the Griffen Industries' box and knowing Mia was at the game. I couldn't see her—she never drew close to the window—but I could feel her presence just as surely as I could feel the itch of my healing skin.

It seemed like the game dragged for five days instead of hours. The only consolation of the day was a win on the scoreboard, even if it was narrow. How I was still standing, I didn't know. I just barely made it back to the locker-room hallway where I always met my family after games. This time, my heart felt as heavy as my situation as I approached them. They were all here, from my dad to my brothers, sisters-in-law, and nieces and nephew.

When I got close enough, Dad gave me a hug, then Emily came up to me. "Did I stand on the sidelines good enough for you?" I half-heartedly teased.

She hugged me in response.

I had to swallow down the lump in my throat to keep from crying as my niece held me in her arms. A hug was exactly what I needed.

I was blinking back tears as I thanked everyone for coming and gave them big hugs goodbye.

But as they made their way out of the building, I realized there would be no more stalling.

It was time to see Mia.

I slowly made my way on crutches to the Griffen Industries' suite. Each step felt like a mile when I knew she was at the end.

I wanted to see her, but at the same time, I knew it would be a painful reminder of what I lost.

Was I strong enough?

Only walking inside would be my answer. I took a deep breath, standing outside the door. Mia's voice was warm as she said goodbye to someone I didn't recognize. With them out the door, I stepped inside the suite to find her alone, looking over the football field while two workers cleaned up the space, removing drinks and snacks.

I closed the door behind me, and the sound drew her attention.

Our gazes collided, caught, before her eyes tracked down to my foot, kept in a black boot just as an extra precaution.

But instead of speaking to me, she addressed the suite attendants. "May we have a moment?"

Within seconds, the people working the room were gone. It was just the two of us.

"How long are you out for?" she asked.

My heart ached. So many things between us, so much to say. And this is what we were left with. "I'm hoping my doctor will clear me to practice next week," I managed. "We'll see."

"Oh." An awkward silence as she picked up a few stray beer cans and carried them to the trash can. Just another little way she was incredible. I wanted to tell her that. But I was frozen, leaning on my crutches.

How had I gone from telling her that I loved her to not knowing how to even stand around her? I regripped the crutches, wishing I could just hold on to her, apologize for everything that I'd done. That it would be enough.

"You acquired the Andersen sisters?" I said, if only to stay in her presence a little bit longer.

She nodded. "That's why I left early. Thomas changed the meeting date, and I had to present to the board on Monday morning... We're finalizing paperwork tomorrow."

More silence. A distance between us that hadn't been there just days ago. "That's great, Mia. I'm proud of you." I meant it.

She nodded.

There was another stretch of silence that hurt just as much as any words she could have slung my way. Especially because she kept picking up. I wondered if she was only doing so because she was uncomfortable around me. She couldn't stand still.

"Mia," I said.

She finally stalled on her path.

"Come here?" I asked. I wanted nothing more than to apologize and move past all the stupid stuff I'd said when I was hurting.

She eyed me for a moment, her expression belying her pain. I could see it in the set of her shoulders, the fine lines under her eyes, the pinch of her lips. She was hurting, just like me.

It didn't make me feel any better.

When she came closer, it took all I had not to reach out to her, to hold her. No matter how much I wanted to, I knew I'd lost that right.

So I poured my emotions into my words, hoping a miracle would help me get everything out just right. "Look, Mia, I'm sorry. I'm sorry for snapping at you, and I'm sorry for the silence from my end," I said. "I had to get my head wrapped around everything that happened, and the more days that passed, the harder it seemed to reach out. I kept typing out messages, then deleting them because none of them felt right."

Her eyes were on the ground, her lips tugging down.

God, I missed her. I wanted to kiss away her

frown. But I also knew I put it there. I couldn't be what she deserved. "Tell me what you're thinking."

"I think we both know this is over," she said. "A real relationship was a bad idea."

I couldn't quite meet her gaze. I was too ashamed. But the thought of losing her altogether... "I won't see you again?"

She looked up at me like I had gone insane. "Ford, I agreed to fake date you until your contract was renewed or until Felicity got a boyfriend." She took a measured breath. "I will stick to what I promised you and nothing more. You showed me the kind of man you are when things go wrong, and I am not going to sign up for more of that."

"Mia, I..." I couldn't find more words. "I'm sorry" just wasn't good enough.

She shook her head. "I deserve better than what you gave me, and I'm not settling for less."

I was about to respond, but she dipped her head to me and said, "Tallie will reach out to you for our next public appearance. Goodbye, Ford."

52

MIA

I HELD my head high and kept my expression even as I walked away from Ford. As I walked away from the man I truly loved with all my heart.

Because underneath it all... I loved myself more.

I loved myself more than to allow myself to be someone's doormat, a first choice when things were going well but an inconvenience when things were going badly. I loved myself too much to accept anything less than the best.

Even if it meant I had to be alone.

I held it together until I got into the back seat of the car and Zeke took me away from the stadium. I closed the privacy screen between us. And there, alone in the back seat, I let myself cry. I took off the blazer that had once been a sign that I was his and tossed it onto the seat beside me. Now it was just a reminder that this was all for show.

When the car stopped, I sniffed back tears and braced myself to go home alone.

But when I entered my condo, I saw my best friend waiting for me. She got up from the couch and came to hug me, and I let myself fall apart in her arms.

"I didn't know you were going to be here," I said.

She brushed my tears away from my cheeks with her thumbs and said, "Ford thought you might need a friend."

His name, his thoughtfulness, her presence... it brought me to tears again. I held on to her, saying, "I think you might be my soul mate. Maybe I'm not meant to be with a man."

She giggled as she brushed back my hair. "Don't tell Gage that."

I stepped away from her, taking some deep breaths and wiping at my eyes. "I've been through heartbreak before, but I don't want to do it again." My heart felt so heavy in my chest, knowing what was to come. Sleepless nights. Checking my phone to see if he'd messaged me, only to find nothing new. Watching him at games and knowing I would never have him again. Not in the way I wanted.

Farrah said, "I know. It's going to be hard, but

we'll get through this together." She squeezed my hand. "I have frosting and wine on the coffee table, and there's ice cream in the freezer. What would you like?"

"All of it," I said.

"You start a movie," she said. "Your pick."

"Something gory," I replied. Something to show some of the emotional bloodshed I felt inside.

She chuckled at my half-hearted joke. "Is there anything else?"

I smiled, for half a second, grateful that even if I'd lost Ford, I still had my best friend. I made myself a promise never to lie to her again—she deserved nothing less than my full honesty.

For the next couple hours, we watched a movie I can hardly remember and ate far too much sugar. I didn't check my phone until she stepped into the other room to tell her kids goodnight. And when I did, I saw new messages from Ford on the screen.

Ford: I really am sorry. Please forgive me.
Ford: I do love you.
Ford: I know you deserve better.

I replied with two words.

Mia: I do.

But just because you forgive someone, and just because you love someone, doesn't mean they still need to have access to hurt you again.

I WOKE up with my alarm the next morning, both Farrah and I lying in my massive bed.

"Ughhh," she groaned. "It's so early."

I silenced my alarm and said, "Stay and sleep in. You deserve it."

She mumbled a thanks, and within seconds, she was softly snoring again.

If my chest didn't ache and my eyes didn't sting from so many tears, I might have chuckled. Instead, I got up from the bed and went to my dresser, putting on my yoga clothes. Then I went downstairs, where my driver was already waiting to take me to my private hot yoga class.

An hour later, exhausted and sweating like a glass of lemonade in summertime, I came back to my condo. Farrah was still sleeping as I got ready for the day.

I knew I should have been on top of the world; officially acquiring Andersen Avenue was a major accomplishment. There would be press conferences throughout the week and dozens of interviews to talk about the acquisition. But I couldn't get away from the sinking feeling in my heart like it might not be enough. Like I wanted more out of my life than only business.

When I arrived at my office, Vanover was waiting with a cup of coffee. I took it from him and stopped in my tracks. There was a fresh flower delivery at my desk.

"Have these removed," I told Vanover.

He studied me for a moment, hesitating, then smoothed his dark wavy hair. "Well, the thing is..." Then he picked an invisible piece of lint from his lapel.

"What?" I asked.

"I would love to, Mia, but it would signal something to the rest of the company. You've had these flowers in here since you and Ford got together. And if it gets out, then he'll be—"

I let out a sigh. "Fine, but order me another bouquet to go with it. Something green."

"I will," he said. He studied me for a moment, seeing far too much, and before he could make any astute observations, I asserted, "I'm fine."

He raised his eyebrows.

"I'm fine," I reassured him. Even though I wasn't. But I would be. I hoped.

I turned and went to my desk, hearing Vanover mutter, "Oh shit."

I turned back to him to see what on earth he was talking about.

Several people were coming out of the elevators with more sunflower and lavender arrangements, and something that looked suspiciously like a box of chocolates.

Vanover said, "I think this is a double delivery. A fresh bouquet was sent earlier this morning."

The lead delivery person stepped forward and said, "Ford Madigan told us to send this."

I swore under my breath. I needed to get back to work. "Put the flowers on the reception desk," I said.

The other delivery people carrying the flowers did as I asked, but the man with the box of chocolates and a card in a white envelope came to me. "These are for you."

I had half a mind to throw the card in the trash, but the same curiosity that killed the cat had me opening the flap and reading the card inside.

Congratulations on the acquisition. I'm so proud of you. You amaze me every day. -Ford Madigan

My eyes stung with moisture, and I blinked it

back quickly, handing the card and the chocolates to Vanover.

"What would you like to do with these?" he murmured.

"You can have them," I said softly, trying to keep it together. Trying to remind myself I said goodbye to Ford for a reason.

I went back to my office to prepare for the meeting with the Andersen sisters. We had less than half an hour before they would be here, along with press to record them signing the agreement.

The flowers seemed to stare at me until I went to the conference room to meet them, a dozen photographers watching by.

I signed for the company, and then while Leticia was signing, asked Andrina, "How does it feel?"

She smiled back at me and said, "It's amazing to see what women can do when they get their hands on more money."

I grinned at her, feeling truly happy for the first time today. The three of us women had done an incredible thing, and so many people were going to benefit from it.

I couldn't let whatever was going on with Ford overshadow this.

So when I posed for the photos, my smile was real.

53

FORD

I STARED AT MY DAD, who was in my entryway, lacing up his tennis shoes to go for a run with me. Well, he'd be biking while I ran. Just a reminder of that day Mia and I shared in California that had me hoping for the beginning of something beautiful.

"You know you can go home, right?" I asked him. He'd decided to stay with me after the game to keep an eye on me.

He finished lacing up his shoes and stood up, stretching out his hips a bit. "If one of my kids needs me, I'm here."

"I understood that when you insisted on coming to my doctor's appointment, but now?" I shook my head at him. "Do you really think you can keep up with me?"

He rolled his eyes at me. "Your doctor said you're ready for an easy run, not a race."

"Fair," I replied, but now I was reconsidering it. It had been over a week of only training arms and abs. My foot wasn't a hundred percent, but at least the wound was completely closed, pink skin knit together in a hard, jagged scar. My doctor said as long as I eased back into training, I might be able to reach full capacity within a few weeks.

He held open the heavy front door for us, and I began an easy jog around my property. I enjoyed running in the grass, beating a trail into the earth. Today was cold enough I had to wear a headband to keep my ears from aching. My dad wore a sweatsuit he probably bought in the eighties.

But he pedaled beside me, easily keeping up. "How's the foot feel?" he asked.

It was hard to explain. My skin felt tight, like it was tugging at itself, which made each step feel awkward and uncomfortable. I settled on saying, "It's okay."

"Good," he replied. "What are your plans for the day?"

"We have a team meeting, game tape review, practice. Then a check-in meeting with the charity board." My feet were beginning to fall into a rhythm. Three steps to a breath in, three steps to a breath out.

I missed this.

But Dad reminded me of something else I missed. "What about Mia? Any plans with her?"

I gave him a look before focusing back on the trail of brown and yellow grass, trees missing most of their leaves. "No."

"Why not?"

I had to remind myself to loosen my shoulders for an easier gait. "I sent her flowers and chocolate to celebrate her acquisition... The delivery people told me she gave it to her assistant."

Dad was far too amused by that.

"Keep laughing and you're going to fall off your bike," I huffed, rounding a corner at the fence.

He was still smiling as he biked beside me. "You thought some flowers were going to win her back?"

Now I was a little embarrassed, my foot completely forgotten. "I thought it would help," I admitted.

"She's a rich, successful woman who's been supporting herself for years. If she wanted flowers or chocolates, she could buy them herself. You need to give her what she really wants. Something money can't buy."

"What I really need is a time machine," I said. My muscles were starting to burn. We must have been a mile and a half in.

Dad was breathing easily as he said, "Do you want to be with her?"

That had me stopping in my tracks. He was a few yards ahead of me when he stopped his bike and got off to talk to me. I had my hands laced behind my head to catch my breath, stretch my chest. After a few deep breaths, I said, "It's not that easy."

He tilted his head. "What does that mean?"

It was embarrassing to talk to Dad about what I'd done, especially since he'd been putting up the horses and hadn't witnessed it. I'm sure Fletcher told him, but snapping at Mia because I was upset wasn't my finest moment. Neither was losing myself in a relationship.

"I'd do anything to make her happy," I said, my throat getting tight.

Dad reached out and touched my arm. "Of course you would."

"That's the problem!" I said, pacing because I was frustrated. "I'd break all my rules for her. Lose myself just to see her smile. But that's not the man she deserves, Dad. She deserves a man who is wholly himself and brings the best of himself to the table. And she won't settle for a man who pushes her away when things get hard."

He was quiet for a moment, thoughtful. "So then you have two choices."

I looked up at him, waiting.

"You can become the man you think she deserves, or you can stay who you are and let her go. And for the record, there's nothing wrong with that," he said. "You are an incredible man, Ford. You're kind to your family, you're a leader for your teammates, you're changing lives with your charity when plenty of men in your position would be spending every dime on themselves. You are good exactly as you are. The question is, are you interested in getting better, maybe for Mia, but ultimately, for you?"

I gripped my shirt, holding on to it at my waist. I was sweating just enough that a cold breeze made me shiver. "We better get going," I said.

He nodded, getting back on his bike. And we worked our way around the property, the question spinning through my mind.

Evolution was in my DNA as an athlete. I'd always strive to be more. But when it came to Mia, I had to wonder... Was it already too late?

When we got home, Dad and I both went to our own rooms to wash up. But instead of getting in the shower right away, I pulled out my phone to get a different perspective.

It seemed like everyone in my life was coupling up, in the throes of love. I needed to talk to the one person who was completely okay being on his own.

And within a few rings, he picked up.

"What's up?" Hayes said, the clanging of car repair sounds going on in the background.

"Never thought I'd say this, but I need your advice."

Hayes laughed heartily. "This calls for some office time. Hold on."

I waited on the line while the background sounds faded until they went totally silent with the shut of a door.

"I'm sitting at my boss desk. Hit me."

I rolled my eyes, picturing Hayes sitting back, boots on his desk, spinning that lip ring of his. And I almost felt embarrassed asking this question, but hell... desperate times called for desperate measures.

"You're single," I said.

He waited. "Did you call to tell me that?"

I ground my teeth together. "And you plan to be single for the rest of your life, right?"

"I mean, define single."

"Hayes," I chided.

He huffed. "I'm not getting married or shacking up if that's what you mean."

"It is," I replied. I took another breath. "How? Why?" Part of me thought it would be so much *easier* if I could just be satisfied being alone.

"Cause I'm a fuckin' wimp," he replied. It was the last thing I expected to come out of his mouth.

"What?"

"Think about it," Hayes replied. "Hot sex any night with any woman. My own place with no one griping at me to clean it up, or worse yet, making the thing a mess. I can change my schedule anytime I want without disappointing anyone. No one's asking me to sell my motorcycle. It's great. *Or* I could pick one woman, and yeah, I might love her, but then you have to deal with all the changing moods, changing hormones, sickness, money issues, another whole side of a family, more opinions about my business, my life... and God forbid I fall for someone and something happens like what happened with Mom. You saw what that did to Dad. So, for me, it's an easy choice. Why the fuck would I want to go through all that when I'm happy as I am?"

I took in his words, thinking Hayes might be the unsung genius of us all. My life *was* easier before Mia was in it.

But then Hayes asked, "Are you happier with or without her?"

54

MIA

FOR THE LAST COUPLE WEEKS, Ford had been busy with out-of-town Diamonds games, and I was busy with travel for work. But rumors were starting to swirl that we'd broken up, so it was time for another public appearance.

He would be attending the gala to celebrate the Andersen Avenue acquisition. There would be press there, along with Dallas's elite social crowd, including Trent Reynolds.

In my career, I'd attended hundreds of events like this. But I was so nervous for tonight, I thought I could crawl out of my skin and under a rock like a hermit crab. Like a woman who was about to see her ex-not-so-fake boyfriend.

My stylist and hair and makeup artists made sure

I looked fabulous, but I still felt uncomfortable, wondering what he would think of me. How we would act around each other after everything we'd been through.

When I couldn't fidget any longer or ask for a new piece of jewelry or different pair of shoes, I went to the elevator to meet Ford in the parking garage.

My heart squeezed tighter at the bell ringing with each floor.

And when I got to the bottom, the fractured pieces of my heart scattered like raindrops at Ford Madigan's feet.

Like all the times before, he stood at the back of the limo, legs crossed, resting on the car body. He had on a plum suit that perfectly complimented my lilac gown. And his smile, a mix of hesitation and warmth.

"You look... incredible," he managed.

Another fractured drop of my heart hit the floor as I spun for him. A dance that no longer felt new and exciting but was a painful reminder of all we could have been together.

When I stalled, our eyes met, and I swore I saw moisture in his before he blinked it back and held the door open for me.

I slipped into the back of the limo, settling across from the door. Once he got in and closed the door behind him, we were alone in the car, only soft music breaking the silence.

"It's good to see you," he said eventually.

I looked away from the dark city passing by outside the tinted window. "Is it?" Because I was hurting, unsure how I'd make it through the night.

"It is, Mia. I..." He paused, scrubbed a hand over his mouth. "I hate this."

That caught my attention. I took him in, wondering what was coming next. Torn between hoping he'd call off the charade so I could finally lick my wounds and fearing the same end, meaning I'd never get to see or spend time with him again.

Realizing I was waiting for him to explain, he crossed the limo and sat beside me, taking my hands in his. I had to close my eyes against the pain searing through my chest. I missed him, his touch, so much I dreamed about it.

Everything in my life was going right. But I'd never been more miserable.

"I miss you," he said. Another stab of pain. Because I missed him too.

I missed our goodnight texts. I missed the way he held me. How he made me feel like my success wasn't intimidating but something to be admired.

"Do you miss me?" he finally asked.

My throat felt tight as I nodded. I didn't trust myself to speak without falling apart.

His features seemed to lift with hope. "I know I messed up, Mia, but I do love you. Can I have another chance? I'll do anything."

I glanced down at my hands resting in my lap. There were three rings on my left hand. One on my right. Thousands of dollars on just my fingers. But I would trade all of it to go back to that day and beg Ford to behave differently. I took a slow, steadying breath. "Ford, I love you. With all my heart." My voice broke, and tears threatened to fall. "But it isn't as simple as a grand gesture and another chance. You showed me that when your back is against the wall, you'll push me out of your life and avoid me."

His gaze lowered. He clearly felt ashamed, and part of me wanted to rescue him from that feeling. But the wiser part of me knew better.

"The only way we could ever have another chance is if you showed me, somehow, that you had truly changed. That you'd grown to a point where you wouldn't hurt me and push me away when things get hard. Because I wasn't just with you to be with a famous quarterback—I love *you*. All of your fame could be gone tomorrow, and I'd still be here."

His lips quivered as he looked up at me, eyes red from unshed tears. "I'm—"

The limo slowed and stopped. Within seconds there was a knock on the door before Zeke opened it up. We both cleared our expressions, put on brave faces, as we stepped out of the limo. Appearing as the perfect couple I thought we were.

Cameras flashed around the red carpet into the hotel ballroom, and Ford kept ahold of my hand until we got to the photo staging area. A press backdrop was behind us, alternating the Griffen Industries and Andersen Avenue logos.

We posed together for photos. And for a moment, he pressed his lips to my temple and whispered, "I'll do whatever it takes. I promise."

55

FORD

IT TOOK me a long time to realize I had no idea how to prove to Mia that I was changing. Anyone could go to therapy once a week, but actually doing the work, making lasting changes, that was harder to prove.

I'd asked my dad and my brothers who actually had successful relationships for advice, but I needed to ask someone who knew Mia better than anyone else. So I called Gage Griffen and asked if I could come over and speak to him and his wife.

Farrah was Mia's best friend. And Gage worked more hours with Mia than anyone on the planet— aside from Vanover. He was my backup plan, followed by Tallie.

And even though Gage was my friend, I was still

nervous as I parked my truck in front of his unassuming suburban house. The only thing that stood out about it was the bright yellow front door.

I knocked on it a few times and instantly heard the clatter of life behind the door. Children yelling, two of them arguing over who would answer. A pan falling to the floor. It made me smile, reminding me so much of my own home growing up.

The door swung open, revealing their daughter Cora wearing matching pajamas. She must have been eight or nine. "Hi, Ford!"

"Hi, Princess," I said with a smile.

She blushed. "No one calls me that anymore."

Gage came up behind her, holding a toddler in his arms. "She's growing up too fast. Come in."

"Good to see you," I said as I followed him into the house—I must have been there a handful of times, but it looked different each time with fresh art and pictures crowding the walls.

"The kids are watching a movie," he said. "Come out to the patio with us."

I followed him, seeing Cora go sit by her brother, Andrew, on the couch. Then they called Tara over, and she toddled to sit between them, hogging the popcorn bowl. They had an incredible family.

When we got to the back porch, Farrah was already out there, curled under a blanket on the patio couch in front of the gas fire pit. Gage asked me if I wanted a beer or if she needed a refill, but I shook my head, going to sit in a chair across from Farrah.

He sat next to his wife, pulling her legs over his lap in a familiar way that had me missing Mia like crazy.

Farrah said, "If you weren't a football player, I'd tackle you."

Okay, she was pissed at me too.

Gage tilted his head at her. "You said you'd play nice."

She shrugged, drawing the blanket to her chin. It would have been chilly out here if not for the warmth coming from the fire. I leaned a little closer to get more of its heat. "Look, I know I fucked up. And I want to make it right, but Mia needs to see that I've changed. I just don't know how to show her if she's not going to give me another chance."

Gage pressed his lips together, nodding thoughtfully. Farrah tilted her head as she studied me like she was trying to tell if I was full of shit. I couldn't blame her.

Finally, Gage asked, "Well, what are you doing to make it better?"

I listed off the things I was doing in therapy to change my attachment style. My therapist said it was common for someone who lost a parent young to avoid people when they were upset, but she was hopeful I would get better with time and practice. I *knew* I could.

Gage said, "The thing about CEOs is that they operate on data. Mia will need to see something concrete—reports of some kind—to show that you're making the improvements."

Farrah nodded. "But reports are so not sexy. And I'm sure she wouldn't want your therapist writing her letters keeping track of you."

But then a lightbulb went off in my mind. "What if I wrote her letters?"

Farrah gave me a small smile. "He's not as dumb as I thought he was."

Gage gave her an admonishing look. "Farrah!"

"What!" she protested. "He broke my best friend's heart..." Then she looked over at me. "But I'm glad you're working to fix it. I know she loves you, Ford."

The confirmation from Farrah was like a hug from a friend when you're on the verge of tears already. I swallowed down the lump in my throat. "I'm not sure if that's enough," I said.

Farrah lifted her lips to the side. "Love isn't enough... Gage and I have been together for years now, and if we just counted on the *feeling* of love to carry us through, we'd never make it. A relationship, a marriage, requires thoughtfulness, forgiveness, patience, self-control, growth, and more. But if your love leads you to action, I know you'll make it through."

WITH FARRAH'S words echoing in my mind, I went home and wrote the first letter to Mia. I wasn't sure how long it would take, but I wouldn't give up. Because Farrah was right; love wasn't an emotion.

It was my dad coming to stay with me just because he thought I didn't want to be alone.

It was Krew and Milo coming to the field at midnight to drive me home.

It was Vanover making sure Mia ate on her busy days at the office.

And now, it would be me, writing to Mia to show her I wasn't running. Not anymore.

NOVEMBER

Dear Mia,

Two weeks ago was the best day of my life.

I woke up in the morning next to an incredible woman. The way the sunlight came in through the window made her hair look golden. And then she opened her pretty blue eyes and placed them on me.

She gave me a kiss that made me feel like it was actually possible to float on a cloud. After I said goodbye to her, I went to the cemetery where they laid my mom to rest, and I told her all about this incredible woman who had every piece of my heart.

HELLO QUARTERBACK

I feel like Mom would have been happy for me too if she were here.

And when I came back home, I saw her sitting at the table with my little brother, both of them working on their computers, like two little peas in a pod. I fell in love more in that moment, seeing her with my family. Knowing our lives were braiding together, getting stronger with each strand.
Then she rode a horse, trusting me enough to try something new. I loved how she could be vulnerable, be a beginner, with me. We rode across the pasture together... It was better than any trip I've made to Paris or London or Rome.

And the way she smiled at the picnic... I'll remember that smile for the rest of my life.

Almost as well as I'll remember her shucking her clothes and walking into the water while I watched slack-jawed, wondering how I got so damn lucky.

I never thought I'd make love in the river, but she proved me wrong, in the best possible way.

But I never thought I'd get injured either, and it was like my whole world crumbled in front of me. I wasn't sure what the future held for my football career, and I definitely wasn't sure I was good enough anymore for this incredible woman.

I've built my life to be worthy based on what I could give to others. A good teammate, a philanthropist, a good brother, son... But I couldn't give you all of me, wasn't brave enough to let in someone new to see my life falling apart of my own doing.

I'll regret that for a long time. Maybe forever.

But I'm learning in therapy that I was wired to run away when things get hard. And I'm working to develop the capability to stick around no matter what.

I know it's hard for me to show proof of something so nebulous, so I'm going to write you letters. I'm going to show you what I'm learning, how I'm growing, and share all the pieces of me with you that I was holding back before.

I'm yours, Mia. And I hope, one day, you'll be mine.

Love,
Ford

Dear Mia,

Fall is my favorite season. When I can go out for a morning run and feel the air as crisp instead of hot and heavy. I especially like seeing all the leaves changing colors on my property.

It's like God made a painting just for me, and every day, when I step outside, it changes just a little bit.

I don't remember exactly when I first started liking fall, but I think it had something to do with my mom. She would make these art arrangements out of leaves with us boys and Mod Podge them to canvases. Then she'd hang them around the house instead of going out and buying fall decor. She thought it was silly to buy up a bunch of junk just to store it or throw it away and buy new the next year when there was so much beauty to have all around.

My brothers and their kids came over today to make leaf art on canvases. We had so much fun, but my cleaning crew probably hates the amount of glue little Leah got everywhere. (She runs way too fast for a toddler.) They left some of the art for me to hang on my walls.

I'm sure they could sell for millions, but I think I'll keep them for myself.

Love,
Ford

Dear Mia,

Today was a harder day in therapy. We talked about my mom's passing and how I got into sports afterward. It was my coping mechanism. But my therapist said I should come up with alternate options as well. She wants me to try painting this week since I had so much fun with the leaves. We'll see how it goes.

Love,
Ford

Dear Mia,

It was so much fun to go out to dinner with you last night, even if it was just to get Trent off my back. I had never been to that restaurant before, but your chef friend made an incredible meal. One thing I really like about you is how, wherever you go, you're like a magnet. People are drawn to you, and I think it's because of how you make them feel. You make people feel like anything is possible. At least I know that's true for me.

Love,
Ford

Dear Mia,

I remember when I was a kid, we would always watch football on Thanksgiving. After my mom passed, ladies from around town would bring us different Thanksgiving dishes, and my brothers, Dad, and I would all sit around the coffee table, eating the casseroles and turkeys and cranberry sauce that came out of a can while we watched football. I remember wishing that I could be on the screen someday. It's wild that I am now.

I missed seeing you at the game, but I hope you had a really good time with your parents. Did they like the turkey I sent? I hope so.

Love,
Ford

Dear Mia,

I am so proud of you. Opening your own mentorship program for young women and girls who are usually kept on the sidelines is completely amazing. It was fun to watch you shine at the opening banquet and to see how excited your first group was to participate.

I got to talk with one of your cohort members, and she said that before you accepted her application, she had been ready to give up on her business. You already changed at least one life by doing this, and that's all that really matters, right?

Love,
Ford

DECEMBER

Dear Mia,

It's hard to believe that it's December. It feels like yesterday it was summertime, and we were outside at the gala for Ford's Friends. I think the changing of the weather is just another reminder of all that's changed between us.

And a lot that's changed with me too. Hayes went too far with a joke, but instead of burying it inside or ignoring him to keep the peace, I told him he hurt my feelings. He apologized right away. I know it seems like something little, but I broke a pattern today. I'm proud of myself. I hope you are too.

Love,
Ford

Dear Mia,

What is it about this time of year and charity events? I feel like we've been to half a dozen fundraisers and Christmas parties, but they've been so busy that I've hardly gotten to speak with you alone.

You haven't mentioned the letters I've sent you yet, and that's OK. These letters aren't really to spark conversation, just to document all that's changing in my life.

And a way to stay connected with you. I miss our goodnight texts like you wouldn't believe. I swear, sometimes when I close my eyes at night, I see you. And when I open my eyes in the morning, I'm disappointed because you're not there.

It's getting really hard to be around you and feel like I'm never going to have another chance. But I promised you I wouldn't give up, and I meant it. But I'll stop if you tell me to. Whatever you want, Mia, that's what I want to give to you.

Love,
Ford

Dear Mia,

Christmas is coming up, and you might not know this about

me, but I love shopping for Christmas gifts. I used to hate it because I never had enough money to give when I was younger. Dad could never get us a lot since he had five boys to take care of on his own. The essentials were about all we ever got. Which was fine. But now that I have some extra cash, I love making Christmas as big and ridiculous as possible.

I pay decorators to come to my house and make it a Christmas wonderland. And not just the living room, the bedrooms too. There's Christmas bedding, Christmas shower curtains, Christmas toilet cozies—you name it, I have it. (Mom would have been so annoyed by the excess—haha—but it's one of the rare times I let myself splurge.)

We all open gifts on Christmas morning. I always get my dad a brand-new pair of boots because if I didn't, he would wear the same ones until they fell apart. Hayes gets something for whatever restoration project he's working on. This year, it's a part for a '55 Camaro. Fletcher is a little bit harder to shop for, but Liv has been helpful to give me some tips each year. Bryce gets some new gadget for his dorm to impress his roommates. And my nieces and nephew get the new and best of whatever they're liking at the moment. It's so much fun to see them open their presents. I think it's one of the highlights of my year.

It also feels like a transition time between the regular season and the playoffs. I can feel the pressure starting to build. The

Super Bowl is getting closer, and my team is counting on me to show up. To be there for them. I'm feeling the stress too. Trent hasn't threatened me since we've been going to all these public events, but I still wonder if I'll be up for a trade at the end of this season. I don't know. I just hope it goes well. I can't imagine living anywhere but Dallas. Anywhere but close to you.

Love,
Ford

Dear Mia,

I know it was all for show, and it lasted all of a second, but getting to kiss you on New Year's was already the best part of my year.

I hadn't realized just how much I missed kissing you, holding you, until the moment was over. You looked at me, and I swear there was something in your eyes. Something you weren't saying.

If you have anything to say to me, say it. Don't hold back with me.

Love,
Ford

JANUARY

Dear Mia,

We made it to the Super Bowl! I get two tickets. One is for Dad, and one is yours, if you'd like it. I'll send it to Vanover.

Love,
Ford

Dear Mia,

I've made a lot of progress in therapy, but right now, I'm struggling.

It's the 20th anniversary of my mom's passing. Twenty years without her.

Something about this anniversary just feels different.
I'm sorry I had to miss your event, but I'm leaving for Cotton-
wood Falls. My brothers and dad and I are holding a special
ceremony, just family, at my mom's gravesite to remember her.

It will be hard. But I'm showing up for the hard stuff. No
excuses this year.

If you're a praying person, I could really use a prayer
right now.

Love,
Ford

56

FORD

THE NEXT DAY, I got my first letter back from Mia.
   It said,

I'm praying for you.
Love, Mia

   The biggest arrangement of flowers at the ceremony was from her. I wasn't sure how, but they were fresh sunflowers and lavender.
   And after the ceremony was over, my sister-in-law, Liv, passed me a note.

I'm in Liv and Fletcher's guest house if you need me.
Love, Mia

I looked up from the note to Liv, dressed in yellow, my mom's favorite color. My heart lifted with scary hope, like finding out you could fly, only to discover how far you were off the ground.

"Is it true?" I whispered.

She nodded.

Everyone was going their separate ways, but I didn't walk. I ran to my truck. I couldn't go fast enough as I drove down dirt roads to my brother's house. It was a white beacon against the blue sky and yellowed winter grass.

I tripped over my feet, going to the guest house and hoping, praying, that Mia was really there.

I opened the door and saw her, waiting for me on the couch.

My eyes drank her in, searching for any hint that this wasn't real. That she wasn't really here. That my heart had run crazy with my mind.

But her blue eyes connected with mine, and she breathed, "Ford."

She stood, and I crossed the room, taking her in my arms, holding her, crying. Letting out the pain of knowing I'd lived without my mom for twenty years. Knowing I'd been without Mia, the love of my life, for months. It had been torture to show up for dates, seeing her hold her distance when all I wanted was to truly be with her.

She soothed me, patting my back and murmuring words of comfort. And when the height of my emotions passed, she brought me to the bed and lay with me while I let the rest of it out. "I missed you," I finally managed, my voice as raw as my heart.

I was surprised to see she was crying too when she took my face in her hands and said, "I've missed you so much. Your letters... I looked forward to them every day, Ford. You have no idea how much it meant to me to see you growing and to have you let me in for something like this—thank you for letting me be here for you."

"Always," I breathed, bringing her to my lips. "Mia, it's you and me."

"It's you and me," she promised. "I'm not letting go."

I held her tight. "I'm going to mess up," I said into her shoulder. "I'm not perfect. But I promise I won't push you away like that again."

She squeezed me back, speaking into my shoulder. "I don't want someone perfect. I want you, Ford. And you've shown me the kind of man you are. The man who makes mistakes and does what he can to learn and grow. I couldn't ask for a better man."

I held her close, kissing her tear-stained lips.

I savored every drop, every tear, because it meant she was here, she was *real*.

"I need you closer," she whispered.

And I needed her too.

Our kisses deepened, our clothes found their way to the floor, until we were bare to each other, body and soul. And for a moment, we just took each other in. I studied her body, all its curves and divots. The way her tears had smeared mascara down her cheeks. How her chin lifted, proud, despite it all.

What I saw was beautiful... what I saw, was mine.

"I love you," I said, going to her again and pulling her close.

She eased onto my cock, sitting in my lap. Rocking against me so we could hold each other, see each other, as we made love more passionately than we ever had before.

The closer she got to coming, the more tears fell down her cheeks. And I wiped each of them away, kissing her, promising her the world she deserved, until we collapsed into a pile of love and pleasure, tears and healing.

Us.

And I knew I had been wrong all these years, thinking I needed to squeeze as many accomplishments into whatever time life decided to give me. Because being loved, being known and accepted by Mia, meant more than any numbers on a scoreboard.

She'd shown me who I was and who I could be.

And I couldn't wait to discover more of myself with her at my side.

57

MIA

I WENT into my office on Monday, a slight smile on my lips. Ford had spent last night at my place, and I'd never slept better than I did in his arms. I was happy to dive into my next project, a week-long orientation for the team at Andersen Avenue.

My life was great. I had the man of my dreams, parents who loved me, friends I could count on, and the best team.

What could go wrong?

My speaker crackled, and I heard Vanover say, "Look sharp."

Straightening, I looked through the glass wall, seeing Thomas walking toward my office, a cream envelope in his hand. Before he could knock, I waved him in and gestured at the chair across from me.

"To what do I owe the visit?" I asked. Pleasure would be taking it too far. "I have a meeting with Tallie in fifteen minutes, so I can't chat too long."

"This will be quick," Thomas said, not sitting down. He passed me the letter with my name printed on the front.

Taking the bait, I opened the envelope and pulled out the page. Flattening it on my desk, I read the words inside.

To whom it may concern:

Please consider this my official resignation. I am available and willing to work until one month from today, with emphasis placed on finding and training the next CFO. However, according to current company policies, I understand my position expires upon this notice.

Regards,
Thomas Weatherford

I LOOKED up from the page, watching him. "You're leaving?" I said, trying not to look too happy. I thought I'd be dealing with him forever.

"You're a terrible actress," he replied, disdain clear in his tone.

I stood to face him. "Look, Thomas, I know we've had our disagreements in my tenure as CEO, but I do hope you've found a better fit."

"I have," he replied, lifting his chin. "Although we may not hold much warmth for each other, I have dedicated nearly a decade to this company. Please let me know if there's anything I can do to help with this transition."

My heart warmed to him, even if only a little. "I appreciate that. I'll have Vanover call security to escort you out."

He nodded, extended his hand. "Good luck, Mia."

I dipped my head in acknowledgment and shook his hand. At this point, I realized it wasn't worth it to hold on to anger or resentment toward him. We were on different tracks in life, and it was good that we were heading in different directions.

Vanover had security in shortly, and I stood beside Van while we watched Thomas walking out.

Once the elevator doors closed, Vanover leaned over and said, "My red flag is that I think I could have changed him."

I bumped his shoulder. "My beige flag is that I think you could have."

He grinned over at me. "I'll send Tallie in when she arrives."

"Thank you," I said and went back into my office.

I imagined working with a new CFO, someone as supportive as Tallie or Vanover.

A knock sounded on the glass, and I turned to see Vanover letting Tallie inside. "Hey," I said to her, smiling warmly.

"Hi," she said. But she seemed stiff.

I looked at her hands. They seemed emptier than usual. "What? Only one folder today?"

The door closed behind her, and she nodded stiffly, passed me her folder. This was beginning to feel a lot like déjà vu.

"What is this?" I asked.

"Just read it," she said, closing her eyes.

Suddenly, my heart was sinking. I pulled open the folder, finding another letter inside. This one, hand signed.

Dear Mia Baird,

I would like to thank you so much for the opportunity to serve you directly. I have learned so much under your tutelage about being a leader with integrity and a successful woman in busi-

*ness. You have been, and will always be, an inspiration
to me.*

*However, with your permission, I would like to accept an
opportunity working directly with Andersen Avenue as their
in-house public relations professional. I understand this
position pays less than my current one, but I believe in the
mission and my ability to help the company grow over
time.*

Thank you for your consideration,
Tallie Hyde

I WAS SURPRISED to find moisture in my eyes as I
set the letter down and faced her again. She let her
feelings show in her deep brown eyes. "What do you
think?" she asked.

My heart beat painfully. "I think I don't want to
lose you. As an employee, but even more so as a
friend."

She gave me a weak smile. "You couldn't get rid
of me."

I got up and walked around the desk to stand
across from her. "Then I guess all that's left to say is...
good luck."

She sniffed, straightening her shoulders, and extended her hand.

But I pushed it away and gave her a hug. She wrapped her arms around me, squeezing me back. "Thank you so much, Mia."

"Thank *you* so much." I had to wipe my eyes when we pulled apart. "When do you start?"

"Two weeks from today, if that's okay with you."

"As long as you give me a replacement half as good as you. All of this is thanks to you, Tallie. I couldn't have acquired the Andersen sisters... or fallen in love with Ford, without you."

Her eyes widened. "You did?"

I smiled, nodding. "We made it official on Saturday."

"I thought there was something there," she said with a smile. "I'm glad it worked out."

"Me too."

We talked for a little while, but then it was time for my next meeting, this time with Vanover. I swore she passed him a note as she left the office, but I couldn't be sure.

"I hope there's less crying in this meeting," he said when he walked in, adjusting his jacket.

I rolled my eyes at him. "We'll have to see."

Then he seemed apprehensive. "Is there a reason to cry?"

I shrugged. "You tell me." I got out my phone and sent him an email I had drafted for this moment. "Check your inbox."

His eyebrows drew together as he got out his phone and tapped on the screen. And then the rest of his features pinched. "This is an offer letter for Chief People Officer. Did you need me to proof it?"

My lips were spreading into a smile. "I need you to review it and let me know if you accept."

His jaw dropped. And if I wasn't so in my feelings about the possibility of him leaving too, I might have laughed.

"Wh-why-who?" He stumbled over his words.

I leaned forward, resting my elbows on my desk. "Look, Vanover, we both know you weren't going to be my assistant forever. You have incredible talents, and you *get* people like no one else I've ever met. You're *qualified* for this position too, and there will be a training period with Shantel and me as well to prepare you for the C-Suite. It will be hard, but I know you're up for the challenge. I want you on my team for years to come. So please, take your time to review this, and when you're ready, say yes."

"Yes." He nodded quickly.

"Van! You haven't even read it yet!" I said.

"Yes." He came over to me, giving me a sideways hug. "Yes. That's all."

"You don't want to negotiate?" I asked.

"I know you're fair, Mia. You wouldn't screw me over."

I smiled. This was exactly the relationship I was hoping to have with a teammate. "You're hired. You'll train your replacement before assuming your new duties."

He wiped at his eyes. "Thank you, Mia. You have no idea how much this means."

I grinned at him. "I think I do. Gage recognized the potential in me not too long ago when I was 'just an assistant.' I wouldn't be here without him."

Vanover nodded. "Is it okay if I take lunch early? My mom will want to hear about this."

I chuckled. "Of course."

As he rushed away, I turned to the windows in my office.

Today, it was a cool day with pale yellow sunlight coming through the cloud cover. I stared over the city, feeling like I was truly on top of the world. There would always be mountains to climb, new goals to reach, but for now, I'd let myself enjoy the possibility that lay at my feet.

I felt, deep in my heart, that the best was yet to come.

58

FORD

IT HAD BEEN A YEAR, almost to the day, since I had set foot on a field for a Super Bowl game. And now, as I followed my team onto the spongy turf, a million memories flashed through my mind.

I saw the plays I did wrong last year. The plays I did well. The faces of my teammates realizing it wasn't for us. The confetti falling from the sky.

The odds of us being back for a second year in a row were slim, especially after my injury.

But I had given all of myself to this team. After having to sit out several games, I had trained harder than ever before to be the best quarterback I could possibly be and make sure I saw playing time on this field. My teammates had worked hard too, put in just as many hours to make it here.

For me, today was about more than making a comeback; it was about proving to myself that I could have everything I wanted in life—love, impact, and professional success. Over the last month with Mia, I'd learned that love wasn't an "or." It was an "and."

I loved Mia *and* I wanted to win a championship game.

I loved Mia *and* I was protecting my body from injury.

I loved Mia *and* I loved my charity.

The last month had been a dream—trading nights between my place and hers. Enjoying the time we could spend together and making the most of the time we couldn't. There were stolen kisses, late suppers, times when she slid into bed long after I had gone to sleep, but we made it work in our own way, no longer letting the past dictate our futures.

Just like I wouldn't let a loss last year convince me we'd lose today.

"Over here," Milo said. Krew was already standing with him by the bench. We were just about to begin warmup.

I walked over to them, trying not to let the enormity of it all overwhelm me. "Hey," I said to them.

Milo put an arm on Krew's back and another on mine, and we huddled our heads together. "Today is our day," Milo said. "We've got each other's backs, yeah?"

Krew nodded. "We've got this."

I looked at my friends, realizing this might be the last game I ever played with them, depending on what Trent decided to do with my contract. "I need to say something."

They both turned their gazes toward me, and I had to take a breath to keep my voice from shaking. "The last five years, playing with you two, have been the best of my life. Thank you for being my teammates, and thank you for being my friends." Despite my effort, my voice broke with emotion.

They hugged me back, the three of us together. I knew no matter what happened with my contract, we'd be friends for life, talking about the good old days playing for the Diamonds long after we hung up our gear for the last time.

"Let's do this," Krew said.

I nodded, getting my energy up.

Then I went to the bench and got a football from one of the assistants. The second-string quarterback, Krew, and I took to the side of the field, passing the ball back and forth to warm up. I'd pass the ball to Krew, he'd toss it to Josh, and then Josh would throw it back.

The sound of seventy thousand voices faded into

the background, giving way to my breath and the slap of leather falling into my hands, until it was time for the game to begin.

The national anthem was a fever dream, separating warmup from the game. A game that felt so much more like life. There would be plays made today. Good ones, bad ones, fumbles. Ones that set you back and ones that put you ahead.

But in life, I knew I couldn't lose. Not with Mia by my side.

The offense took to the field for the first play, and Milo looked over his shoulder at me. "You ready for this?"

I glanced to the crowd, to the section where I knew my dad and Mia were sitting. I saw her in my purple jersey, and I smiled. "Let's fucking go."

59

MIA

THE NEXT FOUR HOURS—WATCHING the game, not knowing how it would unfold, whether Ford would win or lose, whether he would get hurt— were pure torture.

Every time he got knocked down, my heart froze until he stood back up. Every time the other team scored a point, my stomach sank. And when the Diamonds scored a point, adrenaline pounded through my system as I rose to my feet and cheered like a woman possessed.

It was a roller coaster unlike any other game I'd attended before. The score was too close to tell who would win.

But in the last two minutes, Ford ran the ball into the end zone and scored the winning point.

Time seemed to freeze until Gray breathed beside me, "They won." Then his voice grew louder. "They won!"

It took me a second to realize it, for the words to process, but soon Gray and I were cheering and dancing with everyone in the stands while the clock ran down to zero. The crowd was louder than a thousand thunder crashes as the announcer said that the Diamonds were the official winners of the Super Bowl.

Purple and white confetti rained from the sky, and Gray grabbed my hand. "Let's go to the field. He'll want to see you."

Ford may have just played the game, but my heart was racing as I followed Gray down the steps and onto the field, running toward the man who held my heart. I jumped into his arms, and he caught me easily, holding me close as confetti continued falling all around us.

"I love you," I said into his ear. "I love you," I repeated, tears streaming down my cheeks. This was everything he'd worked so hard for. And now it was finally here.

He held me tighter before setting me on the ground in front of him. I placed my hands on his chest pads while his arms circled around my waist.

His eyes were gleaming, tearful with pride, with joy. "I missed you," he whispered.

I let out a laugh. "It's just been a day."

"Promise we won't do that again?" he asked.

I had to smile. "I'm not going anywhere, and I know you won't either."

He held me again and then lowered his lips to mine.

The world faded away while he held me, while he publicly claimed me on the most important night of his life. The happiest night of mine. And when we broke apart, I wiped away tears as his dad held and congratulated him.

Then the team's publicist grabbed Ford and said, "It's time for your speech."

60

FORD

I COULD HARDLY FEEL my legs, because it seemed like I was floating as I walked up to the stage that had been built for the winners.

The Diamonds.

Confetti was still falling from the sky, and it felt like my lips were set in a permanent grin. Then I saw Krew coming up to the stage with me. I hugged him to my side, thankful that he was more than a teammate. He was a friend, and we were getting to share this together. With any luck, Trent would renew my contract and we could come back and do it again next year with Milo too.

Coach Hinkle was the first person to speak, talking about how hard we'd worked, what an honor it was to win this game. I stared out at the field, buzzing with people in purple and white, and I easily spotted Mia and my dad.

When the press aimed a microphone at me, they asked, "What do you have to say about tonight?"

I looked right at my dad and Mia, and I said, "I got my miracle."

EPILOGUE
HAYES

SPRING BREAK MEANT my family all went to Ford's house in Dallas for a get-together. Bryce was off college for the week, and so were all my nieces and nephews.

The last several years, we'd all taken advantage of the break to spend time together. And it was fun seeing how things had changed over the years. Maya went from a little girl in diapers to a teenager, leading deviously her girl gang of cousins and sisters.

Knox and Fletcher were married. (Fletcher for the second time, but we didn't talk about that.) Ford was stupid in love with Mia, hardly taking his eyes, or his hands, off of her.

My dad even invited his friend-not-girlfriend,

Agatha, to today's activities. And Mia's parents were here as well.

Springtime was warming up, which meant we were all outside, swimming in the heated pool, playing hard games like cornhole and eating a never-ending stream of grilled meat. (Dad was trying not to act offended that Ford hired his private chef to grill, never mind the fact that it freed up time for him and Agatha to play with the grands.)

And even though it was a great time with music playing over a speaker system, there was an undercurrent of tension, worry. Ford's contract with the Diamonds was under negotiation, and we had no idea of he'd get to stay in Dallas or not.

Needing a drink to ease the tension, I walked to the outdoor drink fridge and got a beer, dodging a few water balls on the way. Just when I thought I'd missed them all, one nailed me in the back of the head.

I turned to see who had launched the missile to find my three-year-old nephew, Jackson, with a shit-eating grin.

"You're gonna get it!" I called playfully, beginning to chase him into the grass.

His peals of laughter made me smile the whole way, even with water dripping down the back of my neck.

"EVERYONE! EVERYONE!" Maya yelled.

I finally caught Jackson, lifting him over my shoulder and tickling his side. His swim trunks were just getting me even more soaked.

"EVERYONE!" Maya repeated. "OVER HERE!"

I followed the sound of her voice to see her and Emily posted up by Ford's back patio doors. "PLEASE COME INSIDE FOR A PRESENTA-TION!" Maya yelled.

All the adults gave each other confused looks as we followed them inside. When I caught up with Knox, I said, "You know what this is about?"

Knox shook his head. "Knowing those two, it's trouble."

"True," I replied.

We all went inside, settling onto Ford's couches. Everyone who had been swimming was now wrapped in thick towels.

"Hayes," Emily said, coming to get my hand. "You need to sit here." She guided me to the couch so I could sit right in front of the TV, next to Ford and Mia.

"What's going on?" I asked Emily.

She held back a smile. "You'll see."

Once we had all settled down, which was quite the accomplishment considering the amount of people in here, Maya said, "I've gathered you all for a presentation."

"Presentation?" Fletcher asked his daughter. "Thought you were done with school for the week."

"This isn't school related," she said, every bit as serious as her dad.

Then she turned on the TV, and I stared in horror at the words on the screen.

WHY HAYES SHOULD GET A GIRLFRIEND: A PRESENTATION BY MAYA AND EMILY

"Oh, hell no," I said, already getting up from the couch. But Ford held me down. Damn him and his NFL training.

"Fine," I muttered. "Let's get this over with."

Maya smiled evilly. "Great. Let's get started."

She moved to the first page of the presentation.

Exhibit One: Forever alone.

There was a group photo of our family from the reception where we celebrated the Super Bowl. Then she pushed the remote, and a circle formed around my head.

"Hayes is the only person in this photo who doesn't have a girlfriend," Maya said.

I opened my mouth to protest.

"Aside from Bryce, who needs to focus on his studies, and Grandpa, who's denying his feelings for Agatha," Maya said.

Fletcher gasped, while Agatha blushed bright red, and Dad covered his face. "Hey, I thought this was about Hayes!" he said.

Maya shrugged. "Two birds, Gramps."

He shook his head at her.

"Moving on," Maya said.

Exhibit Two: Think of the children.

There was a photo of all my nieces and nephew together in purple outfits.

"Knox got married to Larkin, and I got a really great cousin out of the deal," Maya said and gave Emily a squeeze. "Do you really want to deprive us of lifelong friendships?"

I looked over at my brother Knox to see him hugging his wife. They did look awfully happy. How, with these little hellions, I was starting to wonder.

Maya passed Emily the remote, and she clicked it.

Exhibit Three: Aren't you bored?

There was a collage of photos of my brothers and their families playing together, having movie nights, attending games.

"What do you do at night if you don't have kids or a wife to play with?" Emily asked. "That sounds awfully boring to me."

I muttered. "Trust me, I'm not bored."

Ford elbowed my side.

"What?" Emily asked.

"Nothing," I replied. "Let's wrap this up."

She handed the remote back to Maya, and Maya changed it to the next slide of their presentation.

THE SOLUTION? It said in big bold text.

"There is a solution to this," Maya said. "And in fact, we have great options for you."

Option one: Ms. Peterson

A photo of a nerdy teacher in glasses that had a pearl chain to keep them on came on the screen. It looked like it had been pulled from the yearbook somehow.

Maya had everyone's attention as she said, "The first option is my math teacher, Ms. Peterson. She's twenty-five, so a little young for you, but my dad says you don't mind."

All the adults snickered.

"She graduated summa cum laude from Baylor University, has three cats, and no boyfriend. A match made in heaven."

"Next," I said.

Maya shrugged and passed the remote to Emily. Emily brushed back her long brown hair and clicked to the next slide.

Option two: Della

Liv's best friend with dozens of freckles and red curly hair came on the screen. And Liv quickly said, "NEXT!"

"But—" Emily began.

"Not my best friend," Liv said. "Next."

I put my hand over my chest. "Now I'm a little offended."

She rolled her eyes at me.

I shook my head.

Then the next slide came up.

Option three: Ms. Brenda

"Brenda's a little old," Emily said while Fletcher laughed into his hands. "But she works for Maya's dad, so you already know her. And she seems really nice and always has candy for us, so I know she'd be a good aunt."

My face was getting redder by the second. "Please tell me that's the last option."

Emily passed the remote back to Maya. She clicked to the next slide.

NEXT STEPS.

"Now, Uncle Hayes, we know you're out of practice having girlfriends, which is why we've set up dates with each of these women for next week."

"No," I said, getting out of the chair and going to Maya. I clicked the power button on the TV. "Listen up, everyone," I said. I stared at all my family members in the room and saw Larkin holding up her phone. "You're recording this?"

She held back laugher, nodding.

"Okay, then point it here and listen loud and clear, everyone. I, Hayes Madigan, promise to never have a girlfriend, wife, or long-term situationship as long as I alone shall live. Got it?" I looked at Maya first.

"But—" she began.

"No buts," I said.

She huffed out a sigh. "Fine."

Then I looked at Emily, who nodded too. I was

about to ask them to cancel the dates when Ford's phone started ringing.

Maya pouted at him. "I thought I told everyone to silence their devices."

Ford looked at the screen. "Sorry, it's my agent."

I swear, all of our hearts froze. But Mia said, "Answer it!"

His hand shook as he lifted his cell phone and held it to his ear. "Hello?" His face was serious, a crease formed between his eyebrows as he nodded and listened. "Okay. Thanks for letting me know."

He lowered his phone to his side, and for half a heartbeat, I feared the worst. That my brother wouldn't be here anymore.

It was easy to say you didn't need serious relationships when you had a family like mine, people who were there for you no matter what. If one of them was leaving... I didn't even want to know what that would feel like.

But then that fucker's lips lifted into a grin, and he said, "Five more years in Dallas."

And as everyone broke out into cheers, I saw his lips moving as he said something just for Mia. It looked something like, "Five years with the Diamonds... and a lifetime with you."

WANT to read Haye's happily ever after? Get your copy of Hello Trouble today!

Want a little glimpse at Ford and Mia in the future? Grab your free bonus story, End Game, for free today!

Get the free bonus story today!

Get your copy of Hello Trouble today!

AUTHOR'S NOTE

There's so much that I could talk about in this author's note, because Hello Quarterback, while at first glance, is a cute contemporary romance, actually went pretty deep when you think about it! There were conversations about death and dying, the choice to be child free, sexism in the workplace, abundance mindset, family priorities, business ethics, and so much more. So when I sat down to write the author's note, as I do at the end of every story, I closed my eyes wondering what I could say about this story. And this is what I felt called to share.

There are a million different ways to enjoy a lemon. You can observe it on a tree, growing in an orchard. You can place it in an arrangement for visual appeal. You can zest the rind to add flavor to a recipe. You could cut it into wedges to add to a drink. You can slice it in half and grind the pulp out of it to get out every single last drop. Or you could pull the seeds and plant a new tree.

(I promise I'm getting somewhere with this.)

I have always thought that the only way to enjoy life, the *lemon* if you will, was to squeeze every last drop until there was no bit left. And once you were done squeezing the drops out, you should probably take the rind and make some candy out of it too so there was nothing left behind.

After all, life is short. And we're not guaranteed a certain amount of days or experiences. We're not guaranteed that our experiences will all be happy. In fact, odds are, sometimes life's going to be pretty dang sad.

But as I wrote this story, and really got into Ford's point of view, I started wondering... is there a different way to enjoy life without pulverizing every drop out of it? And does that method *actually* make the most out of life?

And I think the answer is yes, there is a different way.

There are people who climb to the top of the corporate ladder like Mia and do everything they can in the business world, while sacrificing on time at home with their families.

There are people who choose to put their careers on hold, so they can be at home with their children full time.

Others live as nomads, traveling the world to see all it has to offer.

And others yet are born and die in the same place, enjoying life right where they were planted.

It's easy to judge and make comments about other lifestyles. One person might think the homebody is wasting their potential while a "homebody" says career-oriented people should take a step back and learn to be satisfied with life.

But I believe having so many kinds of people with different perspectives helps us keep things in check.

For me, I didn't want to choose between a career and children and travel. But seeing my friends who stay home and enjoy a slow summer might inspire me to slow down and savor moments with my children. And when life gets to be a little bit bland, a friend's post about their recent vacation might inspire me to go out and explore. Seeing a mom friend go above and beyond for a class party could give me ideas on how to make day-to-day life more special for my children. And seeing an author friend reach new levels of success shows me just what's possible professionally.

While doing all of this, we are planting seeds that

will hopefully grow sweet fruit for us and those around us. But, what can grow bitter fruit is not actually deciding what we want to do with our lemon, our lives, instead letting others around us choose our paths.

When I graduated high school, I thought it would be impossible to make a career as an author. Even though I'd demonstrated over and over again my passion and talent for writing, I let public opinion of "smart" choices sway me. I gathered it was "smart" to choose a certain career path and "risky" to choose writing.

But really, the risky choice was to gamble my precious time on Earth on other people's ideas while the opportunity to write was slipping away with each passing second. The best decision I made was to give up on what looked like a "good" opportunity and chase after something better.

Einstein said time is relative, but maybe he should have said time is limited.

And then the question becomes... What will you choose to do with yours?

ACKNOWLEDGMENTS

How are we at the end of Ford's book? I remember when I first introduced him, and he was just a young football player, the famous brother of Fletcher. It seems like my little baby is all grown up. And just like with children, storytelling takes a village. So I need to thank my village for all the ways that they have contributed.

Thank you to my husband, who has stepped into the role of stay-at-home dad. As well as book hauler, emotional support animal, and so much more. Thank you for always supporting my dreams.

Thank you to my children who sacrifice time with their mom so she can write these stories. I love you always.

Thank you to Team Kelsie who has grown and changed so much since Hello Single Dad released! I'm so thankful for you and your support. I appreciate your love of my readers, and how you always work to make sure both my readers and I are taken care of.

Cameron Snow, thank you so much for allowing me to spread the word about my books at a level I never even imagined. You have truly changed the course of my business and my life.

I know they'll never read this, but thank you to the Denver Broncos for being my first professional football game. I had a lot of fun watching you beat the Packers.

Thank you to my editor, Tricia Harden. I hope at this point you know what a valuable part you are of my book creation process. I'm so happy to say that you've touched of every book in the hello series so far, and I'm excited to see what we can create in the future.

Thank you to my proofreader, Jordan Truex, who is the fastest reader I have ever met! I appreciate your work ethic, your heart for others, and also your friendship. I am so glad that books have brought us together!

Thank you to my narrators, Luke Welland and Allyson Voller. My readers adore your work, and I am so thankful that we are able to bring them more stories with your voice and talent.

Thank you to my brother, Dakota Haas, who edits these authors notes so that you can hear them in my own voice. It is so fun to be working creatively together.

Thank you to my cover designer, Najla Qamber, who's talent and eye for beauty has given this series such a beautiful spotlight on platforms like TikTok, Facebook, and Instagram. I absolutely love the cover for this book, and my readers do too!

Thank you to the moderators of Hoss's Hussies, my online readers group. You are such a kind and supportive group of women, and I am so glad to have you in the community.

Thank you to all of the readers in Hoss's Hussies who have eagerly awaited this story, been so patient with me and the writing process, and make sharing a book with the world so much fun.

Lastly, thank you so much to you, sweet reader, for picking up this story and spending time with me. Just like I mentioned in the author's note, I know time is limited, and I'm so thankful that you chose to share some of your life and your heart with me I appreciate you.

JOIN THE PARTY

Want to talk books with Kelsie and other readers? Join Hoss's Hussies today!

Join here: https://www.facebook.com/groups/hossshussies

ALSO BY KELSIE HOSS

The Hello Series

Hello Single Dad

Hello Fake Boyfriend

Hello Temptation

Hello Billionaire

Hello Doctor

Hello Heartbreaker

Hello Tease

Hello Quarterback

Hello Trouble

ABOUT THE AUTHOR

Kelsie Hoss writes sexy and heartfelt romantic comedies with plus size leads. Her favorite dessert is ice cream, her favorite food is chocolate chip pancakes, and… now she's hungry.

When she's not writing, you can find her enjoying one of the aforementioned treats, soaking up some sunshine like an emotional house plant, or loving on her three sweet boys.

Connect with Kelsie (and even grab some special merch) at kelsiehoss.com.

facebook.com/authorkelsiehoss

instagram.com/kelsiehoss